I0654113

TERRA'S ANTHEM

TETRASPHERE - BOOK 4

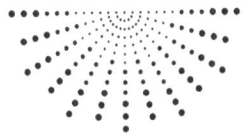

P.T.L. PERRIN

~

TERRA'S ANTHEM

~

Tetrasphere Book 4

By P.T.L. Perrin

~

Terra's Anthem – Tetrasphere Book Four

By P.T.L. Perrin

All rights reserved. No part of this book may be reproduced, scanned, or distributed in any form, including digital and electronic or mechanical, including photocopying, recording, or by any information storage and retrieval system, without the prior written consent of the Publisher, except for brief quotes for use in reviews.

This is a work of fiction. Names, characters, businesses, places, events and incidents are either the products of the author's imagination or used in a fictitious manner. Any resemblance to actual persons, living or dead, or actual events is purely coincidental.

Cover by: Ewald Sutter, Azar, Trostberg, Germany

Cover Photos: Storm: © Pixattitude | Dreamstime.com

Background: glacier-170559_1920, Pixabay

Edited by Lydia Moore and Mary Vallale

Copyright © 2018 by Patricia T.L. Perrin

Published in the United States of America

Worldwide Electronic & Digital Rights

Worldwide English Language Print Rights

Print ISBN-13: 978-1-950940-07-3

SeaQuill Press

Jupiter, FL 33458

❀ Formatted with Vellum

~

To Dad, Lt. Col. Robert W. Tracy, my hero and the veteran of two wars, whose courage and commitment taught his children to face down fear and pursue our dreams. And to Mom, Gerda E. Tracy, my first chief encourager, whose love and trust gave her children freedom to become who we are. And first and foremost, to our Creator, who welcomed them Home.

~

~

"The mountains take one look at God and melt,
melt like wax before earth's Lord.
"The heavens announce that He'll set everything right, and every
will see it happen — glorious!
Psalm 97:5-6,9 (The Message)

~

"But it is God whose power made the earth,
whose wisdom gave shape to the world,
who crafted the cosmos."
Jeremiah 10:12 (The Message)

~

1

JEWEL AMARYLLIS ADAMS

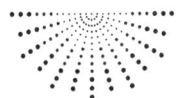

I don't know why I'm standing in the meadow. I don't remember getting out of bed, putting on my jeans and sweatshirt, lacing up my sneakers–nothing. But here I am, staring at the Dracan ship hovering in front of the trees.

My feet move of their own volition, pulled by an unseen force while tears pour down my cheeks unhindered. My gut clenches. Shaula, the Dracan who abducted and imprisoned me, stands in the light of the open portal, muscular arms crossed in front of his chest. His vile eyes gleam yellow.

My arms hang limp, and I can't move to tap on my wristband. I can't open the telepathic link to call out to my friends for help, but my connection with Pax is always open. In my head, I scream his name. *Pax!* I pray he's awake and can hear me. *Pax!*

Jewel, where are you? His love and panic change to rage at the reptilian he sees through my eyes.

Stop! He shouts it in my head, and I do. His pull is stronger than Shaula's, thank God.

Turn around, he says, and I do.

Now run!

I don't look back to check if Shaula is chasing me, but in moments his hold on me breaks. I glance back then and see the empty meadow. He's gone. For now.

Drained of energy, I sink to the ground, double over, and sob, remembering the horror of being Shaula's captive and the pain Pax went through to find and rescue me. Both have a claim on me now, but I only love Pax. It makes no difference to Shaula. He'll kill everyone I love to get to me.

Headlights signal Pax's car racing down the long driveway to my house. He's wasted no time in getting here. I push myself off the ground, meet him in the driveway and fall into his arms.

He holds me close and murmurs in my hair, "I'll kill him. If it takes my last breath, I'll free you from him. He's as good as dead."

My trembling subsides in the strength of his embrace. He kisses me deeply, pouring his love into the kiss.

Let's go inside. You're freezing.

I shake my head and answer, *I'm not cold. I'm terrified...for you.*

Together we walk to the house where I used to feel safe. No longer. Shaula can reach me anywhere.

The smell of baking muffins nauseates me, and I excuse myself to go to my room just as Sky comes out of hers. Pax's twin sister has been staying with us since we returned from the Bahamas, and I couldn't be happier. She's the sister I've always wished for.

She smiles at me, hugs her brother, and the two of them head toward the kitchen. His mental voice comforts me while I close the door behind me.

Get some rest. I'll be here when you need me.

The tears come more often, now. When we first returned from Peru, I was caught up in my new-found connection with Pax and in our birthday celebration. I didn't give Shaula a second thought. Now he's all I think of, even though our other problems are so much more pressing. If we don't solve them, the world will destroy itself, and Shaula won't matter anymore. Nothing will.

I see him in my mind's eye, with his dull scales, razor-sharp teeth, and those yellow eyes. Even the memory of the evil in them makes me shudder. He laughs as if he knows I will eventually give in to him and lose everything and everyone I love. Pax. I could lose Pax. I'd rather lose my life.

~

MY ROOM IS TOO CONFINING, and I slip outside before anyone notices. The meadow in front of our house, now innocent and empty of threat, beckons me with its spring flowers and thousands of little critters going about their business. I step carefully to avoid harming a single creature, admiring the brightness of each life-force, and drinking in the millions of colors in the grass and flowers. Amid so much life, I'm alone with my thoughts for a brief time.

"Jewel?" Sky's voice calls from the front porch. I turn and wave, knowing it's useless to ignore her. Her flaming aura flows in streaks of crimson and yellow, indistinguishable at this distance from the fire of her long red hair. I expect to hear her voice in my mind, but she runs toward me instead of activating the link. As an empath, she must know I need to keep my thoughts to myself.

"May I walk with you?" she asks.

"Of course. I could use the company. Is Pax alright?"

"He's still eating and talking with your Mom," she answers, taking small, careful steps as she walks like I'm doing. She knows I can see much more than she does and respects my love for even the smallest animals, now scurrying away from us.

She sends a pulse of calm and says, "I thought the two of you were in constant mental contact."

"We can turn it off, like the link all of us have through Dad's wristbands. I guess I'm reluctant to talk to him right now, and he probably senses it."

"Yeah. For someone with the nose of a bloodhound, he can be sensitive to moods even when he isn't close enough to detect pheromones. I think being my twin has trained him." She laughs, and the mental picture of him with a dog's nose gets me laughing, too.

She taps her wristband, opening our private link. *When we talk like this, I know your mood better. You're deeply bothered. Is it Shaula?*

An involuntary shiver creeps up my spine. *He's close. He came to the meadow this morning but left when Pax broke his power over me. He won't give up, and I'm afraid for Pax and the rest of you if I don't go with him.*

Streaks of dark red shoot through her aura. Her anger is palpable. *We didn't risk our lives to rescue you from that monster just to have you give up and go back to him. How could you even think of doing that to Pax? He'd give his life for you in a heartbeat, and you know it.*

I know. The tears spill over again, and I swipe them away, annoyed at their intrusion. Before all this, I rarely cried about anything.

"Do you think he can hear your thoughts the way Pax can?" she asks aloud. She has stopped walking, and I turn to face her.

"I've been afraid to think about it, frankly," I say. I feel the blood draining from my face. "What if he can hear my conversations with your brother? What if he can hear all of us through me? What if I'm betraying all of you?" A shudder races up my spine. "It's a mess. Not only do we have to figure out how to fix millions of artifacts before the world blows itself up, but we also have to break Shaula's grip on me before he destroys us all." I can't control the burn of tears, and my gut churns with anger. I can't control anything anymore. Could I ever?

"Let's go inside," she says with a little shiver.

Something more than my problems is bothering her. She's projecting. "What is it, Sky? What's wrong?"

"Storm is troubled, and I think I know why. We need to get over there."

2

STORM DARROCK RYDER

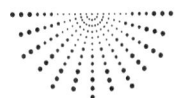

"Storm, wake up." My sister's voice sounds pale and blurred, the way an out-of-focus old photograph looks.

"Wake up! You're destroying your room!" She's right. The tossed books and toppled dresser come into focus as the nightmare's grip loosens. I force myself to sit up and take deep breaths until the bed stops shuddering. The dresser rights itself and my books and lamp float back into place. Juliana is busy clearing the mess, mumbling something about brothers under her breath.

I don't dream. At least I didn't until I had the nightmare in Peru where I lost Sky to some wicked-looking giants. She somehow shared the dream, and it happened exactly the way we saw it.

This nightmare was worse. Sitting up, I push the covers off and open the curtain, letting the sun's heat thaw the icy glaze of fear squeezing my heart. Juliana taps her wristband.

What was that about? Her voice in my head sounds more worried than annoyed.

A nightmare. Nothing more, I answer.

Like the one you had in Peru? Her question brings back memories of South America. With my luck, they'll keep replaying in my head all day.

I hope not. If this dream is predicting the future, then we're in more trouble than I thought.

Juliana gives my room one last inspection, shrugs, and heads back to her room.

When it became apparent Sky, Pax, Jewel, and I were the ones the ancient Cherokee prophecy spoke of, the four who were chosen to save the world, I thought we might pull it off. We figured out what we're supposed to do and how to do it, and we made progress. I was confident we'd finish the job and get back to finding my parents, but my hopes were shattered when we were shown the magnitude of the work ahead of us. Last night's dream made it worse.

What's going on with you? Jewel's mental voice breaks through my thoughts.

Why do you ask? I retort. How would she know, anyway? She's no empath. Sheesh. My thoughts and emotions used to be private. Now everybody gets in on the action, and I resent it.

Sky is worried about you, and Pax is worried about her. We're heading over. No arguments. Let Sequoia know.

Pax can't stand me, and for good reason. He smells my pheromones when I'm around his sister. They don't lie. It would kill me to love her and then lose her like I lost my parents, so I push my emotions behind a wall even she can't penetrate, as strong an empath as she is.

I wonder if I can slip out before they get here. Throwing on some jeans and a tee shirt, I stuff my feet in my riding boots. There's no sweeter smell than the mountains in May, and I'm eager to ride my dirt bike up to Clingman's Dome, my favorite spot to clear my head.

"Storm, come have breakfast," Sequoia calls from the kitchen.

There's no chance I'll sneak out now. Not past my aunt. Resigned, I go in, hug Sequoia, pat her belly, and take a seat at the table. Pure joy hits me, and I grin. My cousin, snug inside her mother, is awake and happy. Her gift of empathy is even stronger than Sky's. What will she be like after she's born? As she grows up? If it takes the last ounce of strength I have, I will do everything I can to try to save the world for her.

"The others are coming, Auntie. They'll be hungry."

Sequoia smiles and cracks a few more eggs into the pan. Nothing ruffles her. She and Wolf have raised me as their own since my parents disappeared eight years ago. We thought they were dead until we discovered my sixteen-year-old sister Juliana among Jewel's rescuers.

She and our parents had been caught in a time-warp in the sunken city Atlantis. They were led to believe I was dead. It's screwed up. I try not to resent my sister for the years she spent with them, but the rage festering inside won't let it stop. It doesn't help that her telekinetic ability is greater than mine.

"Murphy's coming!" Juliana sings on her way to the kitchen. Her eyes are shaped like mine, large and oval, like cat eyes, but brown with gold flecks and orange highlights. Right now, they're crinkled at the corners, which only happens when she's happy. Murphy makes her happy.

Cars pull up outside and the front door bursts open with Sky's typical enthusiasm. My pulse races when she tosses her flame-red hair and nails me with her deep blue eyes, but I pretend to ignore her and focus on my food, instead. Her annoyance is a kick in the gut. She's learning to weaponize her ability, and I'm target practice.

Pax and Jewel come in, followed by Juliana's boyfriend Murphy, and they greet Sequoia with a hug before Murphy wraps his arms around my sister.

Murphy appears entirely human right now. He's a Dracan hybrid, but it's obvious he's crazy about Juliana, and she feels the same. Inexplicably, I trust him with her. He's bound to be my brother-in-law, if we live long enough. It's a big "if."

"Before you get into one of your discussions, eat," Sequoia says, brandishing a frying pan full of eggs scrambled with peppers and onions.

"We hear and obey, Medicine Woman." Pax teases her, taking his place at the table. My uncle Wolf, fresh from a walk in the woods, joins us, thanks Creator for the food, and we dig in.

"Something is bothering you, Sky. What is it?" Sequoia asks as Juliana sends the dishes floating through the air to the sink, where

Murphy rinses them and puts them in the dishwasher. The worry Sky's projecting is affecting all of us.

"It's nothing, Sequoia." She lies. Sequoia just raises an eyebrow and she caves.

3
CAROLINA SKY FLETCHER

W olf pulls his wife to her feet and helps her settle in one of the recliners in the living room. He stands behind her and rubs her shoulders. I can almost hear her purr, until he stops and takes a seat in the other recliner. He motions for me to sit next to Storm on the couch facing their enormous stone fireplace. The others bring in kitchen chairs.

Sequoia's face is solemn while she gently rubs her tummy. The baby stirs and sends us love. I don't want to spoil the moment by talking about the stupid dream, but her gaze doesn't leave my face, and I'm compelled to talk.

Storm has made himself comfortable, feet crossed on the coffee table and arms folded behind his head in a show of indifference. The unease he's projecting is what drew me here, and he can't tuck it behind the blasted wall he's built against me. Did he have the same dream I did? Again?

I send him a jab as I open the link. *Is this what's bothering you? You had a dream, too, didn't you?*

He nods, not answering. My gut ices up. Even knowing everything worked out in Peru, I can't be sure this will, too. I take a deep breath, send up a quick prayer, and begin talking.

"I saw each of us in different places. Lightning surrounded me, striking too closely and making the most horrible crackling and booming noises, almost as loud as an artifact's call. I wasn't alone."

I swallow, trying to dislodge a sudden lump in my throat. Saying it out loud only makes it more real.

"Storm was in a huge cavern. Strange plants grew nearby, and the air seemed thinner and colder. He wasn't alone, either."

I shiver at the memory of the freezing cavern. I have the distinct impression Storm was no longer on Terra, but I don't say it aloud.

"Pax was surrounded by creatures in a dark shadowy forest." I don't mention the strange tingling on my arms as I watched Pax.

"I couldn't tell much about Jewel's environment, other than it was cold and dark. I'm sorry," I say, turning to my friend. "I wish the dream had put you in a tropical paradise." Pax reaches over and pulls Jewel onto his lap, holding her tightly.

"My blood ran cold. If we aren't together, we can't fix the world. Storm, does my dream match yours in any way?"

He stands abruptly without answering, whirls and marches to the door. I feel the fury and know it's best to let him go before he starts tossing things around. Even Sequoia doesn't call him back. His dirt bike roars to life and I send calm and love to him. Why are we both getting these dreams?

"He'll be alright," Wolf says. His brows are drawn together, and deep grooves outline his frown. "The question is, if this is prophetic, then when will it take place? Since there's no telling at this point, we must move forward as if it isn't foretelling the future. What will happen, will happen, but I have confidence it is all in Creator's plan to save Terra."

My heart grows lighter at his words.

"I know what comes next," Sequoia says. All eyes turn to her.

"We're going to Andros. All of us. Our baby insists."

~

"I CAN'T WAIT to learn to dive," Jewel says for the umpteenth time since Sequoia set things in motion. Her joy tickles my heart, lifting me above the quicksand of my dream so it can't suck me back into hopelessness.

"I wonder if we'll connect with Cruiser and Triton," she says.

I wonder, too. Triton and I shared a deep emotional bond. Will he know when we come back? Will the Proteus be there, with Dr. Julian Emery, Gabe, and Izzy?

"At least we know Tony and Meg Michaels will be there to greet us, and to get you certified," I answer.

She smiles. "And Lucaya and her son Donny. I look forward to getting to know them better."

Lucaya is the healer for the tribe of Black Seminoles in Red Bays, Andros. She and Sequoia had hit it off while we were searching for Jewel, and she'll be delivering the baby.

Tell the others, Mom's voice in my head sounds urgent. *Sequoia is going into labor. The Allarans are on the way, and Wolf has notified Tony we're coming today.*

I can't help my delighted squeal, and quickly tap the code opening the link to all six of us. *It's time! Baby's coming! I hope you're all packed. Meet us at the meadow.*

JEWEL LEADS us directly to the point where two Allaran ships materialize to take us the short distance to the Bahamas. Chara, the scientist whose DNA gives me my unique abilities, descends from the ship on the right to welcome our family. I fight to control my revulsion, while Pax rushes toward her.

"Welcome, Star Children," she bellows. To be fair, she doesn't speak loudly, but her voice grates on my nerves. Allaran females have that effect on human ones.

Pax practically fawns as he informs Chara that Jewel and her family will be riding with us in her ship. The Allaran scientist nods and smiles, disappearing into the ship as Storm lifts our baggage behind her.

Vega calls out from the other ship, triggering my human female reaction to the Allaran males. I take control of it, even as everything in me wants to ride in Vega's ship, where Storm, Juliana, and Murphy would be with Sequoia and Wolf.

Thankfully, the impulse fades as soon as I float up the beam of light into the interior. We get comfortable in the bubble seats and watch as fish and dolphins swim in the reef on the observation screens.

Moments later Chara's voice informs us we've arrived. They drop us off at the same location as the last time, in a patch of scrub, out of view of any homes or roads. Only this time, Tony and Meg are there to greet us with two jeeps.

"It's about time you made it back here," Tony says while we take turns hugging Meg. "Your dragon has been making quite a stir with his frequent visits."

4
SKY

"What do you mean?" Dad asks, at the same time Jewel's dad pipes in with, "Who saw Triton?"

Anxiety peaks as we consider the ramifications. If Triton is making appearances, who has seen him and what will they do about it?

Sequoia suddenly moans and doubles over, holding tightly to her abdomen. She takes deep, slow breaths and holds up her hand to stop us when we move toward her.

When she can speak again, she says, "It's a simple contraction. There is still plenty of time, but we should get to the house right away. Has Lucaya been notified?"

"She and Donny are on their way," Meg responds. "You'll be in the same house you had before, and we've notified the Nicholls Town Clinic in case of emergency. We can get you there quickly with our boat, but I'm sure you have the Allarans on stand-by."

"It won't be necessary." Sequoia's voice is calm. "Thank you for your thoughtfulness."

Wolf helps his wife into the back of Meg's jeep and hops in beside her, with Analiese next to Meg. Charles, Mom, and Dad get into Tony's jeep, driving ahead while Pax and Jewel lead the way on foot, with Storm and me behind them. He concentrates on a row of floating luggage, effectively ignoring me. Juliana and Murphy bring up the rear, holding hands. It isn't far to the cabins.

Joy surges in me when they come into view, and I spot the glint of wavelets lapping the beach through the pylons holding them high off the sand. I can hardly wait to hit the water and swim as far as I can toward the deeper blue of the trench.

Storm and his sister send some of the luggage sailing toward our aqua house in the middle. They're sharing the yellow house on the right and Murphy is staying with Jewel and her parents in the coral house on the left. The speedboat we share sits on its trailer under Storm's house, next to their jeep. Our jeeps are also parked under our respective cabins.

I breathe deeply, envying Pax his ability to scent every delicious molecule of the sea air. I dream of living in a place like this after we save the world. I hope it isn't a pipe dream.

"We'll meet in our house in half an hour, kids," Wolf shouts from his veranda. It'll give us time to get the bags into our rooms and open the windows for the breeze.

I run up the stairs and burst in through the front door. Mom and Dad have already opened the house. Pax comes in more slowly, sniffing the air with a grin on his face.

"This is the life," he says, stretching his arms wide. "We should take advantage of every minute we have before…" His voice trails off. He's more worried about Jewel than he is about saving the world. To be fair, Jewel's and Terra's fates are tied together, but he isn't in love with Terra.

"TRITON HAS BEEN SPOTTED in this area by the U.S. Coast Guard. I've picked up their radio transmissions, and they're very concerned," Tony says once we're all gathered on the O'Connell's wide veranda. Sequoia is resting on a beach lounge chair.

Tony glances at Sequoia then turns to Wolf. "I suspect the Navy has been testing acoustical weapons in the depths of the Tongue of the

Ocean, and unless Triton stays away from here, he might become their target."

"We'll do our best to contact him. He has an affinity with Sky and might listen to her," Wolf says.

"Do they know he's a dragon?" I ask. "How much of him have they seen?"

"According to the transmissions, not enough to know what he is, but they've picked him up on sonar. All they say is, he's longer than a blue whale and swims with an undulating motion."

"Has anyone spotted him from land?" Storm asks. "The natives know about him, and wouldn't say anything to the authorities, but what about the tourists?"

"Someone has, and word is getting around," Meg says. "A couple hired us to take them out in Michaels' Dream just to spot the 'sea monster' they've been hearing about. We took them to the opposite side of the island, hoping we wouldn't run into him."

"I'll contact Atlantis, ask if they know anything," Murphy says. He's been quiet lately, which worries me. Not that he's normally talkative, but he does often interject clever quips into our conversations. Juliana is concerned, too. I hope everything is okay between them. But then, no relationship is perfect.

Meg and Tony don't know about our ability to communicate mentally through the wristbands, so we can't do anything about Triton until they're gone. Meanwhile, we have this beautiful beach and calm waters in the cove, and I'm dying to get in there.

"We can't do anything now, so who's up for a swim?"

5

PAXTON HUNTER FLETCHER

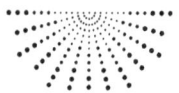

As tempting as the water is, I can't keep my eyes off Jewel as she shyly unwraps her towel to reveal a turquoise bikini matching her eyes. I can barely breathe at the sight of her. She's beautiful.

Her blush ignites a fire in me, and I rush to sweep her up in my arms and run into the surf, where we both fall into the swell. The lagoon is too calm for any real waves.

Her squeals suddenly stop as the warm water closes in over our heads. *This is wonderful, Pax. Can't we stay here forever?*

Every cell in me wants to stay here with her, raise a family, and make a living like Tony and Meg, with a boat and diving gear.

We'll talk to the Michaels tomorrow about getting you certified to dive. I can't wait for you to explore the reef with me. As I'm saying it, a dull ache fills my chest. If Sequoia weren't already in labor, we might not be here long enough for the baby's birth, much less diving instruction. My main concern now is protecting my girl from that miserable lizard. I wonder if Triton can help us.

Sky announces her arrival with a shout and a lot of splashing, Storm right behind her. Murphy and Juliana walk along the water's edge, holding hands as usual, and I wonder if they can swim. Are there pools in Atlantis?

Distant cumulus clouds turn salmon-orange as the sun sets behind us, its angled rays hitting them just right. Jewel stands beside me, waist-deep in the gently rolling sea, mesmerized by colors only she can see. Sky splashes up close to us, while Storm floats on his back, eyes closed and oblivious to the beauty.

My sister taps on her wristband, opening the link to all of us. *He's coming*, she says. *Triton is about to breach the surface.*

Storm flips over and watches the horizon with the rest of us. Murphy and Juliana have also come into the water.

"There," Murphy says, pointing to a dark shadow against the brilliant sky. The head of the dragon rises out of the water and turns in our direction. He's too far away to make out his features, but his shape is unmistakable. So is the massive wave of joy he sends our way. I'm nearly knocked over by it and can't help laughing with the others. It's a far cry from the anguish we first felt from him.

Quick, Sky says. *Help me focus. I'm sending him pictures.*

We've learned to loan our mental energy to each other when necessary. It's second nature to us as we push her focus toward the dragon. She sends pictures of ships tracking him, along with a warning to stay out of their range.

We don't get the reaction we'd hoped for. He's amused, so she projects fear and a picture of them hurting him with weapons. More amusement mixed with love comes back to her.

This isn't working, she says. *He's not afraid of them, and he should be.*

Why don't you tell him about the artifacts? Storm asks. *Weapons won't matter if the world is destroyed.*

She sends pictures of the six of us linked arm-in-arm, of the Mantoids and Formicians and the artifacts we fixed in South America. Then she shows him a crude map of the earth surrounded by ley lines, and the dots clustered at the junctures all over the globe, numbering millions. She zooms in on one of the clusters and shows him each dot is like his egg, in need of healing.

In turn, he shows us his "egg," the tetrahedron happily spinning in its force field. He sends contentment and gratitude for fixing it.

The tone of her transmission changes when she shows him what will happen if we don't fix the rest of the artifacts.

The dragon's roar sends the lagoon into a flurry of choppy waves. Legend has it, the Greek god Triton has the power to raise and lower the ocean and to affect the weather. His namesake, the dragon, had stopped hurricane winds from sweeping us out to sea. I'm glad he's on our side.

Triton sends a picture of Atlantis in its protective shield. His head dives into the ocean, followed by two humps of his long body. The forked tail is the last to disappear.

Wait! Sky's mental shout falls on deaf ears. The dragon is a fast swimmer.

"I meant to ask him about Cruiser and the sea folk," she says.

"We'll be hearing from Atlantis soon enough," Murphy says. "They know we're here, and Thuban is expecting Jewel to come to the city."

The thought of her around any Dracans makes my skin crawl, but I know she'll want to go, and I can't stop her.

"Not without me," I announce. Murphy nods.

"We will all go. You will all visit our beautiful city."

Thank you, Pax, Jewel says over our personal connection. *I've wanted to go back to my friends, and we'll need their help to find and defeat Shaula.*

"I'm not going anywhere until my cousin is born and I know she and Sequoia are safe and healthy," Storm says.

"That goes for all of us," Sky says, sending him love. He turns away and heads back to shore. When this is over, no matter what the outcome, he and I will have our reckoning. I'm sick of the way he treats my sister.

She sends calm my way, and I ignore it, unwilling to let the anger go.

"Criminy," she says, stomping off. We've both made her mad.

STORM

A small dark body tackles me as soon as I walk through the front door of our bungalow. Curly black hair covers a head buried in my waist where strong, thin arms are tightly wrapped.

"Hey, Storm! I'm nine now!" Donny's brown eyes focus on my face, his face split by an ear-to-ear grin. I hug him back, and then peel him off me and set him back at arm's length.

"You're taller. You must be eating a lot of your mom's super food."

"Yeah, and you're still as slow as a coconut crab. I've been waiting here for hours. Mama wouldn't let me come to the beach in the dark."

I don't remind him it's only been dark for a few minutes, remembering how slowly time moved when I was his age. Murmurs and a moan come from Wolf and Sequoia's bedroom. Lucaya is here, which makes everything right with the world, for the moment.

"Are you hungry? I'm starved. Come help me make sandwiches."

Donny places his hand in mine for a second and then takes off running toward the kitchen. I flip open cabinets and float plates and glasses out to the table for us. He stops in his tracks and stares, eyes white against his dark skin.

"We have lunch meats, cheese, peanut butter, and jelly. What are you hungry for?" I'm thankful Tony and Meg stocked our pantry.

"All of it," he answers, taking a seat to watch the rest of the show.

Between mouthfuls, he tells me about life in the village after we left.

"Mama sells batik tops and scarves to the tourists, who all want to see the dragon. We haven't told them anything, but some of our people are making carvings of Lusca to sell. The tourists hear about him from other tourists, but we only sell the trinkets and don't talk."

Lusca is their name for Triton. "Has everyone recovered from the fire?"

Their village narrowly missed being burned down by a brush fire that destroyed some outlying cabins. We met Lucaya and Donny when we rescued them. It's hard to believe it happened only four months ago.

"Yes. We live in the village now, and I like it better there. My friends live on my street, and school is closer to walk to. Mama is busy, and everyone who was hurt in the fire feels much better now."

He finishes his second helping. As I'm cleaning up the kitchen, Wolf comes out of their room and says, "Donny will bunk with Storm. Lucaya has Juliana's room. Sequoia wants to see you, son."

"Where's Juliana going to sleep?" I ask.

"The girls are going to stay with Sky, and Pax is moving in with Murphy at the Adams house."

Wolf stays with the boy while I go to my aunt. Lucaya greets me with a hug and leaves the room to see to her son. A rush of pain surprises me. My baby cousin is projecting her distress. It never occurred to me a baby being born is aware of the pressure that causes her mother pain.

"Are you okay, Auntie?" I ask, knowing she feels the baby's discomfort along with her own. I wish I could help.

"I'm fine, son," she says. Her voice sounds weak, and I reach for her hand and sit in the chair next to her bed.

Sequoia sighs. "I didn't expect to experience what baby is going through, but I know where she's positioned and how she's progressing. It won't be long, and you'll be able to hold your cousin in your arms."

I gently squeeze her hand. "You'll hold her in your arms, Auntie, both of you strong and healthy." I send up a quick prayer, hoping Creator is paying attention.

"She sleeps between contractions. It's a mercy." Sequoia's voice trails off, and her hand goes limp in mine. I stay for a minute longer, and then I feel the baby waking up with another contraction. It's time to get Lucaya.

DESPITE THE FOLKS' planning and bedding assignments, everyone has gathered here to spend the night. The girls set up a makeshift campsite on lounge chairs and air mattresses on the veranda for us. Analiese and Coral are keeping Lucaya and Sequoia company, emerging now and then to give us a report on the progress, while the men have taken over the living room. Wolf paces the length of the room and back, his face stoic, like the animal he's named for. Dylan and Charles talk quietly, trying to reassure him.

"Why is she so quiet?" I ask Coral when she comes out to get some water. I wonder if they've given her something for the pain.

"Lucaya is working with her on focus and breathing exercises. Your aunt is a strong woman, and the baby doesn't like the squeezing but isn't in pain. It takes time, but everything is going smoothly."

"Wolf, would you like to spend some time with her?" she asks. "I'll stay out here or sit on the veranda with the kids."

"Thank you," he says as he heads into the room.

I can't imagine how I'd be if it were Sky in there. I push the thought aside. It'll never happen.

SKY

The sky has lightened, and distant clouds turn orange as the sun peeks over the horizon when we hear the first piercing newborn cry. Storm throws off his blanket and jumps to his feet, frozen in place, his eyes wide and bewildered. Juliana runs to the door, grabs his hand, and pulls him inside.

Pax mumbles, "Finally," and stretches. Jewel laughs and heads into the living room, followed by Murphy.

Pax notices the tears rolling down my face and waits for me. "Are you okay, little sis?"

I usually have a comeback when he calls me that. He's only minutes older than I am, after all, but this is too important.

"She's like me." I don't have to elaborate. He knows.

I send my love to the baby in welcome. My sister empath has arrived safely.

GABRIELLA O'CONNELL HAS AN ENORMOUS APPETITE. Her mother sits nestled among pillows and blankets in the living room, perfectly content to nurse her beautiful baby and receive the accolades of friends and family. Her proud father snores faintly on the couch, having dropped off to sleep an hour after his daughter's birth.

I send soothing calm to mother and baby, reaching for her as soon as she's done nursing. I lift her to my shoulder and gently rub her back until I get a loud baby burp, then I sit and lay her face up in my lap, surprised she's awake. Her mother immediately drops off to sleep.

Donny stands next to me, leaning over Gabri, intently checking her out. "She's tiny."

He stretches a finger toward her face, and I stop him. "Have you washed your hands really well, like I showed you?"

He rolls his eyes and nods, reaching to stroke her impossibly soft cheek. "She felt bigger before she was born."

"What do you mean, Donny?" I ask.

"She wanted to play, and now she's too little to play."

"Did she tell you that?"

"Not in words, but I knew what she meant."

So, I'm not the only one who feels her emotions. Is Donny an empath, too?

I relax and gaze at her. I don't understand genetics the way Jewel's mom does, but it's odd that Gabri, as I've decided to call her, would have Storm's amber eyes and my red hair when she isn't related to me. Auburn, rather, the color of burnished bronze. Not as red as mine. She regards me seriously and projects delight, moving her face through a series of expressions. I believe she's trying to smile but hasn't figured out which muscles will do the trick, yet.

"You're only a couple of hours old, sweetie. You'll get the hang of it soon enough."

"The hang of what?" Jewel asks, reaching for the baby. I transfer Gabri to her lap and watch my friend make faces and cooing sounds. I laugh at her antics, and Gabri joins in with another happy surge.

"She's trying to match her face to her emotions. Do you realize how privileged we are to experience how aware she is as an infant? Why don't we remember those early years? Maybe Gabri is more alert than most."

"I'd say that's likely," Juliana says. "She's been interacting with her mother for months now, and it's obvious she's been aware of you. Remember how she alerted Sequoia something was wrong when we met with the giants in Peru? Dracan technology cut off your gift, and Gabriella felt it."

"True." I didn't know about it until after we came back, but it struck me as miraculous when I found out.

I reach for her tiny hand, and she tightly grasps my finger. She stares at Jewel's eyes, while I speak directly to her.

"We are a bunch of odd ducks, aren't we?"

I'd be content to stay here forever, but Murphy chooses this moment to poke his head through the front door.

"Thuban has arrived."

I hope there aren't any boats around to see the Dracan ship hovering over the beach. Jewel hands the baby back to her now-awake mother and rushes to the door. I follow and spot Pax and Storm already on the sand with Charles and Dylan, speaking to the King of Atlantis.

The only time I'd met him, he was in his Dracan form. Now as a human, he's still very much a king. Broad-shouldered, standing taller than my six-foot-two brother, he reminds me of a highland warrior, in trousers instead of a kilt. His golden hair, tied back in a tail, is nearly the color of his tanned skin. High cheekbones, tapering to a powerful jaw and dimpled chin, frame imposing features. Piercing blue eyes under bushy eyebrows stare regally over an imperious nose, and his full lips are set in a straight line. He's dressed in tan pants and a green collared shirt, open at the neck, and he's wearing sandals. I wonder if Marla's mother, Queen Avery, dressed him. Like Murphy, he makes an extraordinarily handsome human.

By the time Juliana, Murphy, and I reach the group, Jewel is hugging Marla, who appears older than the last time we saw her. Max, holding the hands of two young children, calmly floats down the light from the open portal. As soon as they get their footing on the sand, the ship takes off silently, moving so quickly it seems to have disappeared.

Except for their different outfits, the girls are clearly identical twins. How much time has passed in Atlantis during the last four months?

"Are they yours?" I ask, trying not to show my astonishment.

Thuban's voice rumbles as he says, "Allow me to introduce my grandchildren. My princesses, Khatryn and Sha'lat, were born to Marla and Max three years ago. I understand only four months have passed here since Max said goodbye to his father. It has been four years for us. I am happy to report the rogue wormhole causing this time anomaly is gone. Atlantis time is now the same as yours."

The men escort Thuban to the house, talking to him quietly while Max follows, carrying himself with the confidence of a man whose place in society is assured.

Marla hangs back with Jewel, who tells her about Sequoia's baby.

"How wonderful!" Marla exclaims. She'd spent time with Sequoia and our moms while we were in Peru. With the time anomaly, she probably thought the baby had been born four years ago.

I approach the twins and introduce myself. "I'm Sky, and the big guy over there," I point to my brother, "is my twin brother Pax." They glance at him and back at me and shake their heads.

"That is not possible," says the girl in the yellow tunic.

Her sister, dressed in blue, nods her head vigorously. "He is a boy and taller than you. How can you be twins?"

Marla steps in, gives me a hug, and whispers in my ear. "Sha'lat is the one in blue and Khatryn is partial to yellow. It's how Max tells them apart."

She addresses the girls. "I'll explain it to you later, my darlings. Now go with your father to meet our other friends."

They run to catch up with Max and the others.

We walk more slowly, hanging back deliberately. "Can you give me an idea of what Thuban wants?" Jewel asks.

"He wants to help you save the world, of course," Marla answers. "You have an idea of what it would take to fix all the artifacts at once, but we may have a way to accomplish it."

"Are you serious?" Juliana asks. "How?"

"Let's wait until we gather together, and Thuban will explain."

"Will it require separating us?" I ask, afraid of her answer.

"I hope not, but if so, it'll only be for a while," Marla answers.

8
JEWEL

"Absolutely not," Dad says, with a finality I haven't heard before. "I will not allow you to take our children to Atlantis, where you kept my daughter captive for five months, and where their abilities are nullified by your technology.

"Our baby Gabriella was extremely upset when Sky disappeared into a Dracan dome and lost her ability, and that was before she was born. I can't imagine how we'd be able to calm her if she lost connection to all of them at once," Wolf adds.

Both men are on their feet, while Thuban remains calmly seated. I'm impressed by his composure until I notice his eyes narrow and his scales darken slightly. He's up to something.

When Sky alerted me he's in his human form, I wondered how he looks. He never changed to his human persona while my gift was suppressed. Now, I can only see his true Dracan form no matter what he does. I've learned to read the aliens' moods by the shades in their scales, and his darker shade shows he doesn't like being stood up to. I hope he can control his temper.

He turns to me. "Do you understand why we must meet in Atlantis? Triton and the Sea Dwellers will be an important factor in implementing the plan to save Terra. They cannot meet with us here."

Marla speaks up. "Father, perhaps they would all understand if you explain what the plan is. The parents must also agree. Their stake in this is as great as ours."

"My daughter is as wise as she is beautiful," he says, his expression tender.

Marla appears as much an alien as her father to me, although she's half-human on her mother's side. Her children, on the other hand, are as human as Max. I wonder if the shapeshifting is something they grow into.

"Very well," he replies. "We share your concerns, Wolf and Sequoia. Their gifts are needed to fix the artifacts, and nothing can be allowed to interfere. Allow me to assure you, Murphrid's mother, Dr. Ashley Jenkins, has devised a way for each of your children to maintain their abilities while in our structures. It is a device small enough to be implanted, or it can be worn externally.

"Charles and Analiese, we did not treat your daughter as a prisoner, although she had to remain with us for a time. We regret the pain her absence caused you. I hope you understand we could not reveal her whereabouts to you for reasons we then considered to be valid. We have learned much about you since then."

Wolf and Dad both sit, their faces tight. With Dad's raised eyebrows, and Wolf's lips pressed into a thin line, they appear unconvinced.

"Please continue," Dylan says. "Catastrophic weather is escalating in frequency and strength."

Coral adds, "The same is true for seismic and volcanic activity. We're running out of time."

Thuban stands but quickly sits down. It's crowded in the O'Connell living room. Sequoia disappears into the bedroom when she hears her baby stir. Lucaya and Donny have been in there with Marla's twins since Thuban landed. I'm surprised at how quiet the children are. Lucaya must be keeping them occupied.

Thuban glances at each of the men. "The plan requires the cooperation of all sentient species inhabiting Terra who know the truth. As the largest undersea city, we will lead the ocean kings. Sea dwellers around the world will be ready to act when the time comes. Then the healing can begin."

"What role will our children play in this plan?" Dad asks.

"That is something best discussed in council."

"Who is in this council?" Dylan asks.

I remember very well who's in it, and the thought of facing those hostile aliens again makes my stomach churn. Not all Dracans are like Thuban, sensible and aware the destruction of Terra means self-destruction for their species. Some of them, thanks to Shaula, are convinced they can fix the planet after humanity has been killed off.

"Thuban," I break in. "Won't the council argue, and aren't some of them willing to do anything to stop the plan?"

"You stood before the Council of Kings, Jewel. This assembly does not include those opposed to saving humanity. It includes Cruiser and leaders of the other races who know the consequences of not working together and are willing to set aside their differences for this purpose. You will be surprised by those in attendance."

Thuban stands. "We must go quickly. Wolf, Dylan, and Charles, I hope you will accompany us. Juliana and Murphrid, please help the others collect what they need. I leave the women behind only to care for Sequoia and the child."

He heads out the door, followed by Max, while Marla goes to fetch her daughters. She emerges from the room followed by the twins, each holding one of Donny's hands.

"Lucaya has given him permission to come along," Marla explains. "He'll be safe among us, and Khatryn and Sha'lat enjoy his company."

Donny will be the best-educated nine-year-old on the planet after visiting Atlantis, the city for which archaeologists and historians have spent centuries searching. Lucaya gives him a hug and sends him off, beaming through her tears.

"I have their assurance he will be treated well," she explains to Sky and me, the only ones still here. The others have scattered to get ready. "I trust the dragon to watch over him."

I hug her tightly and say, "I've been there, Lucaya. It's a marvel, and he'll have the time of his life."

Sky heads to her cabin while I go to mine to pick up anything I might need. I change into the one Atlantean outfit I kept, a pair of loose pants, a blue tunic, and sandals.

9

PAX

As soon as we enter the Dracan ship, I take a sniff. Nothing. My scent guard mutes what I smell to a certain point, but this is more profound. The guard is down, and I'm getting nothing, other than what most people smell. It's claustrophobic.

Sky grabs my hand. I can't read her emotions, but I know she's worried about the baby. Will Gabri scream until she and our moms are exhausted, or will Ashley get us those implants before she gets to that point? There's no way to know. Our wristbands don't work in this ship, either.

Jewel? I test the special connection I have with her. She nods and squeezes my other hand but doesn't respond mentally. She's reluctant to use it in case Shaula might be listening in. Though I'm glad it still works, I can't wait to throttle that lizard. If he can hear her thoughts the way I can, he needs to die.

A guard escorts us to a room where benches line the walls. It's too bad they don't have bubble seats like the Allarans. Max and Marla take Donny and their girls to a different cabin. The rest of us make ourselves as comfortable as possible.

Storm sits across from us, next to Murphy, who holds Juliana close to his side. He leans back against the wall and closes his eyes. It'll be a short nap. These ships are fast, even in the water. Their skin repels anything that causes friction, allowing for a smooth ride no matter where they travel. We aren't aware of the takeoff, the trip, or the landing, but in a few minutes, we're disembarking at the docking bay in Atlantis.

Thuban leads the way into the first of a convoy of vehicles waiting outside. It doesn't hit me until we're in one of the cars that "outside" is completely encased by a dome over a mile below the ocean surface. There is nothing to suggest we're underwater or enclosed by anything but earth's atmosphere.

I barely notice when we start moving. The ride is smooth. Too smooth.

"Why don't we feel the engine vibration, or even the road?" I ask.

"Levitating cars," Juliana says. "They use electromagnetism, along with mercury as a superconductor. Their fuel supply will never run out, and they can stay afloat indefinitely."

Will humans ever catch up to this level of technology? I'm surprised by the scale of the landscape. Thankful for the large windows in our vehicle, I watch as we pass through a town with plain buildings, several stories tall, and no people. I wonder where they are. I breathe easier when the vista opens to farmlands, stretching to a curved horizon, again reminding me we're under a dome.

We cross a bridge over a wide river, where some boats carry cargo and others appear to be fishing. Now we're in an area full of imposing mansions and manicured gardens. We pass quickly through to another bridge and over a canal full of boats.

The next section is far more interesting than the others. Humans and Dracans co-mingle in a marketplace resembling a small-town farmer's market. I can't smell the food from here, but my stomach growls at the sight of vendors next to their carts and the people buying and eating their goods.

As we approach the next bridge, we drive past shops displaying clothing and jewelry. It must be the upper-class section, like Rodeo Drive in Beverly Hills.

We cross a canal lined by parks and shaded by stately trees of all sorts, and straight ahead, the crown jewel of Atlantis fills the view. It reminds me of drawings of the hanging gardens of Babylon, with rows of columned tiers rising to a central golden dome atop a circle of blue-marbled columns. Vines and flowers spill over the sides of each layer.

"I never saw it from this angle," Jewel says, her voice filled with awe. "I knew it was big and like a maze inside, but this is magnificent. I hope Ashley's invention works. I'm dying to see this in all its colors."

～

JEWEL WASN'T KIDDING about the maze. After Max's family takes Donny to another part of the palace and Thuban takes his leave, the rest of us, led by Juliana and Murphy, head into the building, making turn after turn, and passing rooms and other corridors along the way. I wish I had a map of this place.

Instead, I ask Juliana, who's lived here nearly her entire life. "Where are we going?"

"To Ashley's lab. Thuban wants us fully functioning for the council meeting. After we get our implants, we'll be assigned rooms, have a meal and sleep. The meeting is tomorrow."

"Maybe there's a way to wear the device rather than have it implanted," Charles says, glancing at his daughter, with concern in his eyes. I agree we need to explore the alternatives.

Jewel counters, "I trust Ashley with my life. If an implant will counteract the block against our gifts, I'm all for it. She'd never give us something that could hurt us."

When we reach a white marble door carved with plants surrounding an Egyptian Eye of Horus, Juliana covers the onyx pupil with her hand, and the door slides open. As soon as the last of us passes through, it slides shut again.

This hallway is more utilitarian than the others. Instead of marble, the floors are white tile, and the plain beige walls are decorated with a simple frieze of hieroglyphs extending the length along the top, only interrupted by doors with symbols on them. When we reach a heavy metal door, Juliana knocks, and it swings open.

Ashley hugs each of us as we pass into the laboratory. When Charles comes in, she says, "Please let Analiese know I miss her. Wolf and Dylan, your wives are like the sisters I never had. Please tell them."

"I hope you'll tell them yourself," Charles says, giving her hands a squeeze before moving into the lab.

Her son Murphy is the last one in, and she hugs him a bit longer. While they talk, my eyes are drawn to a creature floating in a large clear-glass tank in the middle of the room. Sky and Storm move closer. The men hang back and watch.

As soon as it spots Jewel, it bangs on the glass and titters madly, like a crazed dolphin. She runs and throws her arms out, hugging the glass and laughing.

This must be her friend Cruiser, the Sea Dweller who held her and swam alongside our submarine when Triton escorted us into his cavern. He saved her life while others of his kind saved Juliana, Max, and Murphy. Their faces appear more fish-like than human, but otherwise, they fit the description of merfolk passed down from earliest known civilizations, with human-like torsos atop fish tails and webbed hands with opposable thumbs.

I link with her and watch the rapid pictures flowing between the two. It's how they've learned to communicate, the way Sky communicates with Triton. I send them both a picture of Jewel with my arm around her waist, and Cruiser shows me his family. My heart swells with gratitude that such beings share our planet.

10

PAX

"Please come into the next room with me," Ashley says, loud enough to break our concentration. "The sooner we calibrate the devices to each of you, the sooner you'll be able to use your abilities here and in any Dracan structure. I must ask you to keep your abilities concealed. No one must know. You don't know when the element of surprise might be vital, and we can't be sure there aren't spies in the palace."

More tanks line the walls of the smaller lab, each with a small plaque describing the contents. I recognize the names from some research I did after Jewel told me about the strange deep-water animals inside. Her description didn't do them justice. Someone should cast them in a horror movie. Bug-eyed hatchet fish stare from a tank. Others display ogre fish, fang-tooth, and viperfish. Snakeheads and dragon fish make my skin crawl. Sharks are puppy-dogs next to these.

The largest tank holds a frilled shark with a head shaped more like a rattlesnake than a fish, and a tail like the fins of a Siamese fighting fish. Scientists believe they've been around for eighty-million years.

"Fascinating," Dad says. He reaches out and touches the tank holding the frilled shark. "I wonder if it's genetically related to land snakes. It sure resembles one, doesn't it?"

"Dad and Pax," Sky calls. "Ashley needs you over here."

When I reach the group around the table, Ashley's holding up a glass bead the size of a grain of rice. Are we supposed to swallow it?

"This silicate glass capsule contains a web of micro-circuitry to cause your energy to mimic that of a Dracan," she explains. "When it touches your skin, the barrier will recognize you and give you free access to use your abilities without hindrance.

"It requires contact with you to activate, which is why I'll have to calibrate each one. You have a choice of wearing it or having it implanted under the skin. I will caution you, wearing it is riskier. It can be removed either way, but it is a little harder to detect and to access below the surface of your skin."

"How easily can the Dracans locate it once it's implanted? Will they know we have it?" Charles asks.

Murphy answers, "Thuban has kept this research secret from the other kings, and only those who work directly with my mother know about it. They can be trusted to keep silent."

"Where would you put it," Sky asks, "and how hard would it be to remove it?"

It sounds like they've decided against wearing it, and I agree with them. Still, there are those, like Shaula, who wouldn't hesitate to dig it out of our skin with their claws.

"We'll place it on the inside of your wrist, under those wristbands you all wear. The band would make it harder to detect if someone were to search for it," Ashley answers.

I wonder if our moms let her in on our secret when she helped develop the mark for me from a vial of Jewel's blood after Shaula marked her. Charles made us promise never to tell anyone about the technology he developed. A device that allows for telepathic communication is too dangerous to share with others. It hasn't been easy to keep it to ourselves. He gives no sign she knows anything.

"What other technology is in there?" Storm asks, with narrowed eyes and a deep frown. "How do we know we aren't giving the Dracans control over us and our abilities? They track dogs and cats with these things. They could track us, just as easily."

"Trust the source. Jewel can tell you about my mother," Murphy replies.

"I don't trust anybody," Storm retorts. "Especially someone working with the Dracans." He pushes back from us and marches into the other room. Wolf quietly slips out behind him. I doubt either of them would be allowed to leave without an escort. They'd be lost in the maze of hallways if they did.

"I'll go first," Jewel says. "I do trust Ashley, and I want to see the colors in here."

11

STORM

"Why aren't they suspicious?" I ask my uncle. "The Dracans could have weaponized the implants. They could kill us with the push of a button from anywhere, or they can control our brains through those things."

"Some things are worth the risk, son. You must decide if this is one of them. I'm going back in, and I will take the implant if it means being able to communicate with Sequoia and you."

"How do you know it'll work with the wristbands? We can't exactly ask Dr. Jenkins unless she already knows about them." I massage my temples to soothe a dull pain throbbing behind my eyes.

"She might, but we can't take the chance. Murphy has one, and whether he told his mother or not, he would have included our ability to use our technology among the criteria for creating her device."

I scratch my head and stretch. It's already been a long day, and I'm ready for a meal and a bed. "I hope you're right, Wolf," I say as he goes back to the room.

I try opening the metal door to the corridor, but it won't budge. What the heck, I wouldn't know where to go if I did get out. I find a spot in a corner, behind a lab table, and sink to the floor.

"Storm?" Sky sinks down next to me.

"Let me guess. You felt my distress, and you've come to push some comfort on me." Even as I say it, I realize how snarky it sounds. What am I. Twelve? I glance over, surprised by her grin.

She draws her knees up and rests her head on her crossed arms, her soft, red hair draping over her face. "Nope. I don't have the implant yet, remember. Can't feel a thing."

When she glances back up at me, her eyes spark with amusement. Shaped like cat eyes, they're a shade of blue I've never seen in anyone else. Only Sky has those tiny silver flecks in her irises that dance and sparkle like magic. I avoid looking at her most of the time because each time I do, I'm a fish on a hook, and happy to be there. Since she doesn't have her ability now, these emotions are not a reflection of hers, and I'm forced to own them. As much as I fight it, I'm in love with her.

"If we were in danger in a Dracan city or tunnel, we'd need your ability," she says. "After this is over, you can get it removed. If it ever came to a showdown with Shaula and his goons, wouldn't you want to use telekinesis against them?"

Okay. She's going to get me with reason.

"I'll get it, but I don't like it. If the monster can use them to track us, it'll save us the effort of finding him. One way or the other, that lizard is going down."

Her smile is worth my easy surrender, even if what she said makes sense and I would have come to the same conclusion, eventually.

"I can see!" Jewel's shout brings us to our feet, and Sky runs into the other room. I stop at Cruiser's tank, where he's watching the door with his mouth stretched wide. Assuming it's a smile, I tap on the glass. The smile instantly vanishes, replaced by a grimace full of sharp teeth as he turns and slams his webbed hands flat against the glass in front of me. I jump back, startled, and he bends over, slapping the side of his tail as if laughing at me. Jewel told us he has a sense of humor.

I hit the glass with my hands, flattening them and baring my teeth back at him. That stops him, his expression grave for a second or two.

Then he starts laughing all over again. It looks like we're going to be friends.

~

WHEN JULIANA LIFTS a table and some chairs in the air, I go in for my implant after everyone else has received theirs. Sky's right. I'll need my ability to protect her, if necessary. I ignore the sting as Ashley injects the capsule into my wrist.

"It might itch some but be gentle if you need to scratch it. It'll take a while to settle in, and then you'll forget it's there," she explains.

"Easy for you to say," I grumble. "You don't have a potential self-destruct weapon in your arm."

"No, but if it is one, I stand to lose some amazing friends," she says. Her smile makes me want to trust her. I must be getting soft.

The floor begins to vibrate. Suddenly, everything is shaking, and a wall of sound smashes through us. Sirens wail over the roar, and emergency lights flash above the doors.

"Everyone be calm!" Ashley's shout is barely a squeak over the noise. Reaching out with my mind, I lift everyone in the room off the floor, creating a stable cushion underneath us. Juliana concentrates on the ceiling to keep it from collapsing while we clasp our hands over our ears and duck to protect our heads.

The sound rolls off into a distant rumble, and the room stops shaking, but I don't.

"What the heck was that?" I shout, barely hearing myself, while I make sure everyone is here. Anyone in the next room would have experienced the full brunt of the quake, assuming that's what it was. The only one missing is Cruiser.

Ashley ignores us and disappears into the other room. Jewel follows her.

"Murphy, do you know anything about what just happened?" Pax asks.

Before he can answer, the door to the hallway opens, and two guards rush in, followed by another Dracan dressed in loose pants. An open lab coat exposes his bare scaled chest.

"Where is Ashley?" he demands, marching past us to the back room. Murphy follows, saying something in their language. Sky runs to me, and I hold her close. What just happened?

I tap my wristband to open the link to the others. Will it work?

1 2

JEWEL

C *an anyone hear me?* Storm's strong voice rings in my head.

Loud and clear, Pax says. *Glad our connection's back.*

We're here, too, Juliana pipes in. Murphy comes out of the small lab and wraps her in his arms. They're next to Cruiser's empty tank. I hope he got out okay. The way we were shaking, the tube leading into the ocean might have been compromised.

Sky? I ask, and she answers with *Here!*

Will someone please explain to me what that was? If it was an artifact, then we need to stop wasting time. Storm's anger pulses through the link, and I worry about Sky. If we can feel it, then it's worse for her. *And who is the Dracan who stormed in here looking for Ashley?*

I'm sorry, I should have told you right away. That's my father, Leonis. Murphy sounds contrite, but I don't know why. Until now, he was with his parents and didn't have a chance to explain anything to us.

Back off, Ryder, Pax says. I don't need his ability to smell pheromones to know there's a rise in male hormone levels in here. Ashley's timing breaks the tension as she comes through the door with Leonis behind her.

"The earthquake did some damage to a remote section of the dome, and our technicians are already at work repairing it," she explains. "I'm sorry you had to experience it, but they've been happening more frequently, and they're getting stronger. These labs are safe rooms, reinforced with their own protective shield, should this part of the dome collapse."

"It sounded like an artifact, although not one we're close to," Dylan notes.

"Our pyramid, which gathers and stores our electromagnetic power, sits at a congruence of ley lines. Could it have something to do with the artifacts?" Leonis speaks with a deep, pleasant voice. "Forgive me," he says with a slight bow. "I have not introduced myself. I am Leonis, Ashley's mate and Murphrid's father. I have been working with them to design the devices you now have implanted."

How do we know we can trust him? Storm says through the link.

Murphy answers, *I've known him all my life. I trust him.*

Calm flows through me and I smile at Sky, happy she has her gift back.

"The map in Patagonia showed us the locations of all the artifacts. They cluster at the ley line junctures," Dad says.

"They?" Ashley asks. "How many are there?"

Wolf speaks up for the first time. "Millions." I watch her face go pale.

The door slides open, and Marla comes in. "Is anybody hungry?"

I CAN'T BELIEVE Thuban gave me my old quarters back, only this time there are three beds in the vast room, making it cozy.

"We thought you'd be more comfortable sharing with Juliana and Sky," Marla says. "At least, they might feel more at home sharing a room with you. I hope you don't mind."

The girls' faces light up in wonder. Sky claims the bed closest to the bathroom and sighs as she relaxes against the many pillows. Juliana comes out of the bathroom wearing loose pants and a soft baby-blue tunic that complements the blue in her aura, as well as her brown hair and eyes.

"It's very thoughtful of you and your mother. Thanks." It's only been four months since we last met, but for her, it's been four years. The last time we saw each other, only one month had passed for me, but she'd aged four years then, too, and she and Max were already married. That makes her eight years older than me. It's a little awkward.

"No worries," she says, her familiar phrase sending me right back to my first time here. "You know where the clothes are. Juliana has found her size, and I believe you and Sky will also find outfits to your liking."

As she turns to leave, I hug her. "Thanks, Marla. I've missed you."

"I'm happy you're here. I hope we can soon visit for pleasure, without the fate of the world hanging over our heads," she says, her eyes sad. I think of her two little girls. I have no words to comfort her.

"Your meal will be here shortly. Thuban will send for you tomorrow morning, so get a good night's sleep." She leaves the room and several servants wheel in carts loaded with dishes. Juliana watches them, sitting still on her bed.

Do you know them? I ask her in our private link.

One. She was twelve when we left, the daughter of a friend who served with me. She's grown up.

Don't you want to ask her about your friend?

Not now, Juliana answers. *Not until I have better news for her.*

Sky is sitting at a bigger table than the one I had before. "What are you waiting for? I'm starved!"

13

JEWEL

A sharp knock on the door, followed by the creak of the breakfast cart, and the tantalizing smell of fresh coffee, motivate me to get out of bed.

"Let's go, young ladies." Marla's mother practically sings. She claps her hands and nods at the young woman pushing the cart, who promptly pours coffee into mugs.

"What time is it?" I ask. "Are we late?"

"You have time to get ready for the council if you don't delay. Breakfast first, then a quick shower, and dress in the clothes we've laid out for you."

She must have been here earlier, or someone was, to lay out some of the beautiful formal clothing Atlanteans wear for these occasions. My dress is a gauzy aqua with a blue sequined bolero and silver sandals. I can't wait to put it on.

Sky grabs her outfit and heads to the bathroom. The rest of us dig into the delicious Dracan food.

Twenty minutes later, a vision in emerald green emerges. Sky'a flaming hair and matching aura bring out the jewel tones of the dress. Its style makes her appear taller, more imposing. I'm impressed.

Juliana's blue dress is perfect for her coloring. She models it like a professional on a catwalk, and Avery applauds with us. I know she's never worn anything like this in all the years she lived here.

As soon as I'm dressed, Avery leaves to get herself ready. Marla comes in then, in her Dracan form and dressed in gold from head to foot. I gasp, and she laughs.

"I might as well impress them," she says, "and so will the three of you. They have no idea what they're up against."

"Do they need convincing?" I ask. "I was under the impression Thuban has their cooperation in this plan he's cooked up."

"Some agree with him, but the others need convincing. Thuban intends to make them think they need us. In truth, we need each other to save the world."

Wiping my hands on the beautiful fabric of my dress is not ideal, but it's better than shaking sweaty hands with anyone. My thoughts run back to the last council session that involved me, and I'm terrified. The knots in my stomach make me regret eating breakfast. I should have known better. Standing in the grand foyer, waiting for the massive doors in front of us to open, doesn't help.

Sky gasps and I turn to see Max leading the men toward us. My heart stops and then beats furiously as Pax meets my eyes. A blush surges up my neck until I'm sure my face must be bright red. I can barely catch my breath.

They're wearing loose white pants and wide gold belts. Shirts with bloused sleeves ending in decorative bands around their wrists, are buttonless and open, exposing their bare chests in the Dracan fashion. Long, sleeveless vests add a touch of formality. To me, they're straight out of "Arabian Nights."

"Close your mouth before you drool," Sky says, close to my ear. When I turn toward her, she's staring at Storm.

"Take your own advice," I whisper back.

Pax's shirt matches my dress in color, with added gold filigree designs woven into the fabric. His vest is the same fabric as my bolero.

Storm's outfit matches Sky's, too. In fact, Juliana and Murphy, and Max and Marla are also matching couples. I love it, but Storm is clearly uncomfortable.

Wolf, Dylan, and Dad are dressed in gold and silver to reflect the dignity of their position as family elders. At least, that's the impression they make on me.

The two guards standing at attention in front of the doors suddenly move to open them wide. Marla steps through first, with Max at her side.

"Father, Mother, and esteemed guests," Marla says, imperial in her bearing and poise. "May I present the four who have been given the task of saving Terra, and their honored companions." She waves us in and directs us to fan out behind her, with the four of us at the center, and then steps aside to stand next to us. Apparently, King Thuban planned for us to make a grand entrance. It might become a spectacle with my jelly knees and upset stomach. I pray I don't get sick in front of this crowd.

Polite applause fills the room, followed by the murmur of ongoing conversations as we make our way to our seats. My nerves calm down.

The chamber is laid out more informally than the courtroom-style cavern in Uluru. Tables line three walls, leaving the entrance side open. High-backed chairs are filled with representatives of the sentient species we've met. Many of them glance at us as they talk among themselves.

I'm not surprised to find Meissa, Queen of North America, sitting on Thuban's left while Queen Avery sits on his right. The chair next to hers, which should have held her now-disgraced husband Malgol, remains empty. Eleven seats to Avery's right are also empty, apparently waiting for us. In the last council, I faced interrogation by the thirteen Dracan thrones. This time, we're the guests of honor.

I count five other Dracan rulers. That makes seven, including Meissa, in favor of saving the world, while the seven absent ones, including Malgol, would wipe out humanity. Meissa and Malgol would normally be counted as one, but divided as they are, they make the split even. Of course, it's possible some who are in favor simply couldn't make this meeting, but it doesn't seem likely considering Thuban's influence.

"Is that Cruiser?" Pax asks, nodding toward three seats occupied by Sea Dwellers.

"Watch how they're moving. They're floating," I say. "They must be attending remotely, and we're watching the projection." I wave and Cruiser waves back. "They can see us, too."

I search for familiar faces and wonder how many others are here by remote feed. If they can attend that way, why couldn't this meeting have been held somewhere else? I'm not complaining. It's good to be back.

"Gienika and Jayman are over there, next to Jaina Chen, but they're all the same size and she's in her human form," Sky exclaims. "They must have shrunk them to fit the chairs."

Storm snorts and then seems to think better of laughing out loud. Why is he so cheerful? Magenta blobs floating among the red and black streaks of his aura clue me in. He must have realized he's in love with Sky.

"I don't suppose they would have fit in the Dracan ships," he says. "Where would we be without technology?"

Across from us and near the door sit five Allarans, two silver-skinned males and three golden females. My hackles rise until I recognize the scientists from our Sentinels. Vega was the first Allaran we'd met, and the one who told us Terra is a tetrasphere, a geometric shape formed by joining many tetrahedra. He's Storm's DNA donor, and Baran is Pax's. I share Belena's DNA, and Sky's donor is Chara. Maia was assigned to guard Juliana, whose abilities came from her mother's mutated DNA.

A flurry of activity in the center of the room catches my attention. Five ant people are setting up a piece of equipment. How will Thuban pull this off with diverse species communicating in different ways?

A picture forms in my mind, accompanied by a loud buzzing, and I turn to see Jaina staring at me. I close my eyes to hear better.

A Mantoid appears, dressed in diaphanous fabric with a magnificent collar resembling an open peacock's tail vibrating behind her head. It stops shaking, and so does the buzzing. Her slanted eyes, positioned along the sides of her triangular head, stare at me intently, and the collar starts shaking again, only this time each word is punctuated by a jolt, with the static of a bad radio station as background noise.

Jewel Adams, do you remember me? I am Jaide Laurelei, Queen of the Mantoids. Her mental voice sets my teeth on edge.

Of course, your Highness. You gave me great comfort when Shaula held me captive, and my friends were in trouble. I've wanted to thank you, I answer.

No need. We will now speak in images to reduce your discomfort. She's as gracious now as she was then, and I hope she knows I'm grateful.

Blood drains from my face when Shaula leers at me in my head. What is Queen Jaide showing me?

14
JEWEL

Thankfully, his evil face disappears, and I'm rapidly approaching a field of ice with jagged peaks in the distance. I don't know how I get there, but I'm suddenly under the ice and dropping into a vast cavern over a lake. Shaula's ship sits on a narrow beach. I watch his guards herd a small group of people into the ship, and it takes off, entering a wormhole swirling over the water. I hover over the sand where his ship stood and read a message he left for me. "You for them."

Why are you showing me this? Are you his ally?

No. I stiffen at the jolt and brace for the static. *You must go with the Allarans. They will take you there.*

I've already read the message. Shouldn't I follow that ship?

The queen's face begins to fade, and her collar makes a rattling sound as it shakes. *The Allarans will take you there.*

"Jewel? Snap out of it!" Why is Pax shaking me? Faces around the room stare at me and I'm disoriented for a moment. Jaina catches my eye and nods before looking at her folded hands. I wonder if the Allarans have been in communication with Queen Jaide, too.

Who was that? And where is that ice cave? I'd forgotten Pax can share my mind when I let him.

You met her while I was in the glacier stronghold with Shaula. She sent the vision of the tunnel collapse that led you to me.

She was the Mantoid queen? You know you aren't going without me. I squeeze his hand and then turn my attention to Thuban, who's risen to his feet.

"Friends," he says, raising his cup. Those who are not holograms or projections, also stand and raise their glasses.

"A toast to the success of our four young heroes in saving our beloved planet Terra."

He's being overly optimistic and premature. He should have saved the toast until after we succeed. If we do. I believe we can do it, given what I've learned, but I haven't figured out how, yet. I hope he has.

When he sits, a hologram of Earth appears in the center of the room. This must be what the Formicians were working on because it's exactly like the one Jaina showed us in the cavern of the third artifact in South America. Leonis stands next to the floating globe, appearing more powerful in formal clothing than in his lab coat.

"Terra is dying," Leonis says, projecting grief in his deep voice. "As you are aware, ley lines cover our planet in a grid of electromagnetism, a grid from which we power our cities."

We watch as the net depicting ley lines covers the globe, and then the red dots appear, millions of them, clustered at the points where the ley lines meet.

"The dots represent Terra's organs, tetrahedra which have, until recently, kept the planet in balance. The red indicates those that are deteriorating. The humans call them artifacts. You are witnessing the rapidly approaching end of the world. We have among us four humans who have repaired five of the artifacts and have a plan to repair them all." Leonis turns to Thuban and bows at the waist.

Did he just say we have a plan? I thought the Dracans did.

"Jewel Adams," Thuban begins, his voice silencing the disturbed murmurs circling the tables. "Will you please tell us how you four intend to fix all the artifacts at once?"

I can't move. I can't breathe. We came with him believing he knew what to do! Why is he asking me? Pax puts his arm around my shoulder, and my trembling transfers to him.

His voice in my head soothes me. *Breathe. In and out, slowly. Now, tell them about the ley lines. You know how it can work. They can help with the logistics.*

He taps the wristband and Sky's voice reassures me, *We're here with you.*

I spot Jaina staring at me. The unpleasant buzz of Queen Jaide's communication invades my thoughts, this time without an image. *Resonance.* One word, and then she's gone again. *Resonance.* I repeat silently. Then Pax and I stand together, and he steadies me with his hand on my back.

"Resonance," I say aloud. "Terra's resonance has changed, becoming more discordant as the artifacts sicken. We must tune the planet."

I stop there, because, how do you tune a planet? It's not like you can tighten the strings, unless that's what the ley lines are.

I wish I could say I've been saved by the bell, but the distant rumble isn't a good thing. It grows quickly into an ear-splitting roar, accompanied by violent shaking. Thuban rises and quickly leaves the room with his wife and daughter. Pax and I slap our hands over our ears and fold up together under the table. Max dives in next to us to ride it out.

The guests are pushing over chairs and trampling each other in their rush to get out of the room, even as the massive doors close, keeping most inside. Where do they think they can go? Not every room in the palace is reinforced, but surely this important meeting room would be.

The roaring rolls off into the distance, leaving screaming people and wailing sirens in its wake. This is the second quake in as many days. Are these quakes caused by failing artifacts, or could this be the work of Triton? If the artifacts are causing them, how much longer do we have?

When it subsides, I search for my friends and spot Storm holding Sky. He helps her into a seat and then joins Wolf and our dads as they help people get off the floor, moving tossed furniture and debris from the ceiling off them. Pax and Juliana join Murphy and work the other side of the room. I can't help but notice how easily Storm lifts heavy furniture, and I hope no one else makes the connection to his gift.

The holographic earth is gone, and so are the remote guests. I'm guessing the conference is over, and we still have no idea where to go from here.

The clanging bells and sirens stop suddenly, and the doors once again open. People push to make their way out of the room in a hurry. Sky gets up to comfort those who've been hurt and are waiting for medical attention. I doubt they'll know she's soothing them with empathy. I'm surprised I can see where the injuries are even in the Dracans. They have no detectable auras, but injuries are darker than their normal coloring.

When the medics arrive, I tug on my friend's sleeve. "Come on. Let's wait in the foyer. There's nothing more we can do here."

She nods, and we head to the door, where the group of Allarans stands waiting.

"Sky Children." Warmth pours through me at the sound of Vega's voice.

I'm right here with you, Pax reminds me. *Don't let him affect you.*

"We agree with your assessment," Vega says. "We are aware everything in creation carries its unique resonance, and dissonance can cause disruption that can lead to chaos if left unchecked. We had not considered it in relation to the tetrahedra until now."

"We can think of two ways to accomplish what you may have in mind," Baran says. "One solution would require a degree of cooperation among Terra's inhabitants that has never been achieved before."

I nod, thinking how impossible it sounds.

"Would you help us to enlist the other races?" Sky asks.

"If necessary," Vega says. "However, we believe we have a solution that will not need the other races if you are willing to work with us."

The men have joined us in the foyer, their auras swirling with shades of brown, while Storm's is blacker than usual. They really don't like the Allaran males.

"We're listening," Storm says.

"You Star Children must find the most powerful source of electro-magnetism on Terra. From there, as you heal an artifact, you must project your healing energy along the ley lines."

Wolf asks what I'm wondering, "How will they find the source?"

15

PAX

I don't like Vega's suggestion at all, but Dad and Charles think it may be the quickest way to fix millions of artifacts at once. Wolf is undecided but wants to return to Sequoia and their new baby, and all of us want to get Donny home to his mother. They might have to peel him away from Max and Marla's twins.

Meanwhile, we're getting ready to go to Antarctica with the Allarans.

"We don't have any winter clothes," Jewel complains, "much less mukluks and furs. What were we thinking?"

I tap the wristband to include the others. Murphy and Juliana insisted on coming with us, and I'm glad. We'll need all our strengths if this half-baked plan goes wrong, and it's bound to.

Belena assures me they have cold weather gear for us. She says the cavern is warmer than we think. She sounds confident.

What do they think we'll find there? I'm not sure why we're going, Storm says.

I don't mention the vision Queen Jaide sent to Jewel. I saw the same things she did. Shaula had Storm's parents and a few others with him in the cavern, and he took them through a wormhole. Will we be able to follow? I don't want to get his and Juliana's hopes up.

Jewel joins the conversation. *If what the Allarans have planned doesn't work, they promised to help us gather the races for another plan. I'm not clear on either one, but saving Terra is in their best interest, so we might as well trust them. No one else has any ideas.*

Time to go, Murphy says. *We'll meet them at the docking bays.*

BELENA WAS RIGHT. Dressed in heavy thermal clothing, the cavern is almost too warm for comfort. Who would have thought a fresh-water lake could exist under Antarctica's thick layer of ice? Blue light filters in through the ice forming a dome overhead. It must be artificial because the sun doesn't shine during the Antarctic winter. The ice would be too thick for sunlight to penetrate in any case.

I hold Jewel's gloved hand in mine as we search the sand for Shaula's message.

"There." She points, and there it is, exactly like in the vision. "You for them."

"What's that supposed to mean?" Storm asks suspiciously. "You knew it was there, didn't you? How?"

Sky and Juliana examine the words and spot human footprints nearby as Jewel explains, "The Mantoid queen, Jaide, spoke to me while the council was being seated. She showed me this place. Shaula herded people into his ship, left me this message, and then disappeared into a wormhole."

"Where was the wormhole?" Murphy asks.

She points to the lake. "Somewhere out there. It's gone."

"I shared her vision. Jaide insisted Jewel was to go with the Allarans," I add. "We hadn't planned to, but here we are."

"Now what?" Sky asks. "This is a dead-end."

"It is not, Sky Children." Chara and Baran have followed us down to the sand. Her voice is like silk, but she no longer attracts me.

"We now have the signature of the wormhole and can track it. We also know Tom and Salali were among the people he took."

Baran says, "My crew and I are going after them. Chara and Vega will take you to our city under the ice. Heliade sits on the juncture of many ley lines, powered by electromagnetic and geothermal energy."

"Murphy and I are going with you, Baran," Juliana cries. "He has my parents."

"I'm going too," Storm says. "That lizard has messed with us for the last time."

"He's mine." I pipe in until I remember I won't leave Jewel, and I won't take her anywhere near the snake.

A sudden sharp jolt knocks us off our feet into the sand. A boom reverberates through the cavern, followed by crackling and popping sounds that nearly stop my heart and make me want to curl up in a fetal ball. The ground trembles as a hunk of ice the size of a small car shatters on a rock a few yards from us.

"It's breaking!" Sky screams. I roll over, scramble to Jewel on all fours, and collapse on top of her. It's futile, but at least the ice will hit me before it gets to her. Thuds rock the sand as parts of the ceiling crash farther down the beach, and chunks splash into the lake. The ceiling is intact directly above us, but it's only a matter of seconds before we're all goners.

"Oh God, oh God, oh God," she says, over and over, just loud enough for me to hear over the din. I hope he's listening.

A shadow blocks the light, and I stiffen for the impact. Instead, yellow light surrounds us, and we're lifted into one of the ships. A crew member pulls us to the side to make room for the next rescue. The ship rocks violently while it scoops up Sky, Juliana, and Murphy. I watch the portal close and hang on to Jewel. We're in a rock tumbler for what seems like forever. When we finally stabilize, I send a quick "Thank you" to God for her.

"Where's Storm?" Sky asks, tears pouring down her cheeks. "He isn't here, and I don't feel him!"

16
STORM

My teeth are about to chatter themselves into slivers with the force of my shivering. Bone-chilling cold pierces through my polar-explorer clothes. My head throbs and I reach for a sharp pain on the back of my head. With my heavy gloves and the parka hood pulled tightly around my face, I can't touch it. How did I get here? Where is here?

My vision and brain clear as adrenaline rushes through my body, warming me enough so I can sit up and get to my feet. I'm in a familiar cavern I can't place. The high ceiling tapers down toward an opening in the distance, where pale, reddish light illuminates a river pouring over the edge. When my eyes adjust to the dim light, I notice the river divides the cave down the middle. Odd figures move slowly on the opposite bank. I have no idea how far away they are, and can't judge how big, or even what they are.

The floor is a jumble of boulders tossed together, some covered in a brown moss-like growth and others are bare gray. I'm on one of the bare rocks, still off-kilter from whatever got me here in the first place.

Testing the surface, I'm happy to discover the boots I'm wearing have good traction. I head toward the river, hoping the water isn't full of strange microbes.

It's farther than I thought. By the time I hear its roar, several of the creatures I'd spotted on the other side are heading in my direction, on this side. What are they? The largest approaches me, moving as if floating.

A pale, beak-like head measuring around three feet from tip to the back, with no apparent eyes, nose, or mouth, sits on a thin, fragile stalk, It stands about eight feet tall. Thick, shiny leaves grow in a spiral to within a foot of the head. A mass of delicate, moving tendrils curl and uncurl around the stalk near its throat. It isn't floating, but moves on an undulating mass, like a tangle of octopus tentacles and roots. Plant? Animal?

I assume a defensive stance, not knowing if it's friend or foe, or even if it has any intelligence. It stops just outside my kicking range. Four others arrange themselves in a half-circle just behind it, effectively blocking me from the water.

Not wanting to hurt them, I gently lift one in the air and set it down to the side, using nothing but my mind. Another one slides in to take its place.

"It is useless, Star Child." A silken voice startles me. "They are protecting you and will not clear the path, no matter how often you move them."

When I turn, a beautiful woman smiles, immediately disarming me. The reddish light glints off her golden skin and colors her white hair pink. The word "Allaran" pops into my mind, but I don't know what it means. I have the strangest impulse to bow at the waist. Who is she? Why is she dressed like it's the middle of summer?

"Aren't you cold?" I ask. I'm no longer shivering, but still glad to be wearing cold-weather gear. She has on a sleeveless tunic over some light-weight pants, and she's wearing sandals.

Her laughter is like wind-chimes on a breezy day. She approaches the plant thing and cups her hands under the tip of its head and hums. It nods and clear liquid drips into her palms. She lifts her hands to her mouth, then waves me over to stand beside her.

"The river water is unsafe to drink, Star Child Storm. The Aracai give us nectar to satisfy our thirst. Hold out your hands as I did. You will find it to be more than refreshing. First, please remove your gloves."

I do as she asks, and the skin on the back of my hands pebbles in the frigid air as soon as the gloves are off. I cup them and hold them toward the plant's beak. She hums a note I can barely hear as the plant drips its nectar. As soon as the liquid touches my palm, my hands grow warm.

The woman giggles and my body instantly reacts to the sound. Sky would kill me if she were here. Sky?

A picture forms in my mind of a small woman with a mane of wavy hair in many shades of red standing with hands on her hips, her blue eyes flashing in annoyance. This must be Sky. The thought of her grounds me and I take a lick at the tiny pool in my palms.

The taste is mildly sweet, with a touch of citrus. Warmth spreads through me, pleasant until sweat makes my jacket, leggings, and boots uncomfortable. Removing the jacket, I'm glad I have a tee shirt on underneath. I quickly peel off the leggings, relieved my jeans are under them. I don't have any other shoes, so I put the boots back on. I understand why the woman is dressed like she is. The temperature in the cavern is like early summer.

"I am Lilyana, singer to the Aracai. I will be your guide and protector as long as you are here, Star Child Storm."

For a second, my head spins with vertigo, and I suddenly remember who I am and how I came here. An Allaran ship rescued my sister and friends from the sand while the ceiling of the ice cavern came crashing down. I blacked out watching it speed away, convinced I wouldn't make it out. The second ship must have brought me here, but where am I?

"Just call me Storm. I doubt I'll need a protector, but thanks for the offer." It sounds snarky, even to me, so I quickly stammer an apology. "I mean, if you know who I am, then you know what I can do. I'd love to have your company while I'm here."

Lilyana nods and repeats, "Storm." When she smiles at me, her green eyes crinkle at the corners.

By the way," I add, glancing around, "where are we?"

"You are on my farm. Come with me and meet my family. My mate and I will explain why you are here," she says.

17

STORM

Lilyana gathers my discarded jacket and leggings and hands them to a plant which extends several leaves to hold them. I follow her over boulders and along narrow pathways in-between them. The five Aracai glide silently behind us. What a spectacle we must be. I wish the others were here to see this.

My stomach is growling by the time we reach a wall where several arched cave openings lie along a path winding up toward an opening as large as an airplane hangar door. It's the only one I see with doors.

Two children spot us and shout, bounding down the path to barrel into my guide and nearly knock her over. Their combined laughter is like a bell choir at Christmas, and I can't help but laugh, too. In fact, I'm giddy.

The smallest girl turns to an Aracai and hums a familiar melody. I can't quite remember where I've heard it. She offers me the nectar the Aracai produces in her cupped hands. I cup my own, and she pours her handful of liquid into mine. I quickly lap it up, surprised when the growling and hunger stop, and my head clears. I could market this at home.

The other child grabs my hand, oblivious to the sticky dampness, and pulls me up the incline to the third opening where curtains are pulled back and anchored to each side. These must serve as doors, more for privacy than protection.

As soon as I see the Allaran male, I brace for the reaction I know will follow, but it doesn't happen. There's no instant aversion to his silver skin and white hair, no impulse to fight, and when Lilyana speaks quietly to him, I don't feel the need to protect her. When he speaks, his voice sounds like any other guy's. Did the nectar do this?

"I am Hamal. Welcome." He waves me inside and points to a low table where plates of fruit and cheese are laid out. I wait for Lilyana and the girls to sit, cross-legged, on colorful cushions, and when Hamal sits, so do I.

"I gather I'm not on Earth anymore," I comment. The girl to my right giggles and the smaller one on my left snuggles close, filling me with peace. Both children have their parents' white hair, and I detect a hint of gold in the rosy tone of their skin.

Hamal picks up a cracker, tops it with some cheese and a slice of a fruit resembling a melon, and says, "The little one is K'ary, whose gift is like your Sky's. Her cheerful nature spreads joy to all. Her song draws the best from the Aracai."

The taller girl's eyes sparkle when her father introduces her. "K'amryn is our curious explorer. She wishes to become a scientist and visit your Terra. She has no doubt your mission will succeed, and our planets will continue to thrive indefinitely."

"We'll do our best," I answer, "but I have to get back, or it will never happen."

"You are on Allara for a purpose," Lilyana says. "Tonight, you eat and rest. You will soon be reunited with the others, stronger and more equipped for your task with what you receive here."

After a delicious meal, Hamal leads me through a couple of tunnels to a room with a view of the cavern. From this perspective, I remember why it's familiar. This is a scene from the dream I had, where all of us become separated from each other. What is happening to my friends?

I remember what Baran said in the ice cavern, about tracing Shaula's wormhole. Did it lead here? Are my new friends in danger? I laugh. Of course, they are. They're living on a planet that, like Earth, is about to blow.

I lie down on a comfortable bed, facing the window, and remember nothing until soft light coming through the curtain wakes me.

1 8

SKY

P ax had told me satellites have detected an object under the
Antarctic ice large enough to bend gravity. None of the satellites
have been able to make out what it is because it's blocking every
attempt to map it, whether by radar, sonar, or any other mapping technology. The terrain is too harsh to send explorers down, and so it sits,
safely out of range, miles below the ice. We are about to see it.

Vega offers us a cup of water before we leave the ship. Everyone is
as thirsty as I am, and we eagerly drink. I'm grateful it tastes fresh and
faintly sweet.

"How do you happen to have a base here? You told us Creator
banished your race to the skies, while the Dracans were given the
Earth." Pax questions Vega as he leads us down a corridor in a docking
area like the one in Atlantis.

"Heliade is one of two Allaran bases on Terra, the other being
Hyperborea near the North Pole. Each city is encased in a sphere that
can, if necessary, move into space," Vega says.

"Creator allowed us the two poles, with the provision we aid those
who would repair the artifacts when necessary. We are aiding you, Star
Children."

Automatic doors at the end of the stark corridor slide open, and I gasp at the sheer beauty laid out before us. Tall spires and delicate structures sit among banyan and palm trees, and gardens of green and striated plants overflow with blooming flowers.

"The colors…" Jewel's voice trails off in wonder.

"The buildings look as if they're made of lace," Juliana comments.

"More like filigree," Murphy says. "The material must be stronger than anything we use in our cities. The towers must be a half mile high."

Vega says nothing, but there's satisfaction on his face, which doesn't normally show any emotion.

"Come," Chara says, taking the lead. "You have friends already here and waiting for you."

"Storm?" Jewel asks.

I could have told her he isn't here, but Chara does it for me. I would know if he were anywhere on our planet.

Pax says, "We would love to explore your city, but where is Storm? You've assured us he's fine and with Baran, but where did they go?"

My brother is showing remarkable restraint, considering I'm feeding my worry to him and everyone else.

"I have assured you, Baran rescued him. They followed the wormhole signature, as he clearly told us he would do. They are out of communication range, but Baran and his crew will keep him safe," Chara explains.

I'm not convinced she's telling the truth. Storm, where are you?

Pax sends me calm, and this time I accept it. There's nothing we can do about it now, and we need to be fully present to solve the artifact problem.

A vehicle rises from somewhere below to our level, large enough for all of us to enter and sit comfortably on bubble seats. I notice there's no one driving. Is everything automated in Allaran society?

We fly to the tallest spire in the center of the city and then fly upwards, past floor after floor of two-storied windows visible through openings in the filigree design. We stop when we've reached the tower's mid-point, where a landing platform encircles it like a wide, flat ring. Inside, we walk through a botanical garden filled with plants from all over Terra. Pax sniffs and grins.

"They have honeysuckle," he says, pulling Jewel close to his side. "It smells like you." He meant it for her ears alone, I'm sure, but the acoustics are amazing in here.

Allarans move among the plants on paths that light up with each step. As they talk to each other, their musical voices blend in a pleasing harmony. Somehow, their voices have lost the power to either attract or repel us. I wonder if the dome has something to do with it.

"What are those?" Juliana asks, pointing to the oddest plants. We stop, and Vega and Chara come back to watch with us, saying nothing.

Huge beaks sway on stalks seven or eight feet tall. Planters full of roses and lilies block my view below their tops, but the vines curling in and out just below the beaks make my skin crawl.

An Allaran female approaches one and hums, holding out a small bucket. The beak bends down and pours liquid into it. She caresses it, hums something else, and walks away. The plant thing follows her, and I see all of it when it clears the planters. Below the creepy vines, huge fleshy leaves grow in a spiral down to a mass of roots. Are those octopus tentacles under there?

"What are they?" Murphy asks, not at all grossed out.

"The Aracai," Chara answers, her voice soft. Why doesn't she sound as strident as she did before?

"Their nectar is our water, our sustenance. They live only on Allara and here, in our cities. We do not yet know what effect the nectar may have on humans or Dracans, but we believe it will be beneficial to all races."

"I'm not willing to put it to the test," Murphy retorts. "Not until I know more about the nectar's chemical makeup. I hope this isn't your answer to the artifact problem."

I love the sound of her laughter. Why did I ever think she sounded like nails on a chalkboard? Is there something in the air here?

Pax taps on his wristband. *I have a theory about the nectar and the fact the Allarans aren't affecting us like they do topside.*

Spill it, I say. *Will we hate them once we're out of this place?*

The pheromones in here are different from anything I've scented until now. There's a vibration in the air, like the ones the Ant People make when they're communicating with Jaina. Do any of you feel it?

I don't know if it matters, Jewel says, *but the colors here have a quality I can't name. They're more vibrant than on the surface, and their frequency is different.*

The soles of my feet are vibrating, Juliana says. *I thought it might be from an engine or power source.*

You may be right, Pax says. *If it is a power source, then it's altered the frequency in here.*

So, what's your theory about the nectar? I ask.

Did you see the Allaran hum before the beak gave her the nectar? Whatever is in it might be affected by frequencies.

What if the nectar is what's changing the frequencies? Juliana asks.

Let's observe, for now, Murphy suggests. *We're about to arrive at our destination.*

We come to a set of double doors, carved like the multiple trunks of banyan trees, with actual vines growing between the trunks. We don't have time to admire them, because they swing open to a vast room. It must take up three floors, which is a good thing because three giants are standing on a platform in a glass enclosure in the middle of it. Are they prisoners?

"Gienika! Autumn! Jayman!" I shout as I run to the glass wall. It opens as soon as I reach it, and Gienika, the Truth-Sayer, enfolds me in a gentle, and quick, hug.

"Sky Fire Hair, it is good to see you again," she murmurs, bending down to kiss the top of my head.

Jayman steps forward, while Autumn pats me on the head, silent tears flowing down her pink cheeks. Happy tears. I can feel their emotions, and I send love to each of them.

"We are glad you are here. Where is your brother, Juliana?" he booms.

Vega speaks in a soothing voice. "We trust Baran is keeping him safe, Jayman."

"We can't know for sure," I pipe up. "They went after Shaula."

19

PAX

T his isn't right. Why are giants in the Allaran city when they live in a place built by Dracans?

Something is wrong with this picture, Jewel says through our connection.

What, exactly, was the first plan the Allarans shared with us? I ask.

We'll find the most powerful source of electromagnetism on the planet and project our healing energy along the ley lines as we fix an artifact.

Did they mention how we're going to find the source? If they did, I don't remember it.

Not exactly, but I think I'm figuring it out.

I remember the dream Storm and Sky had shared. He's missing, and now I'm afraid my sister will take off with the giants. I will not leave Jewel's side for anything. Not willingly.

Her frown reflects my concern, and we turn to watch Sky. I tap to open my private link with Juliana.

Is the vibration still under your feet?

Yes, and it's increasing, she says. So is my suspicion.

"Sky," I say, using my calmest voice. "Come here for a second."

She turns toward me, and everything happens at once. Jayman lays his hand on her shoulder, grabs Gienika's hand while she holds her daughter's, and they shimmer and disappear. All of them.

I run toward Vega, intent on killing him.

He says, "Stop!" and freezes me mid-stride. The last time he did this was at the sacred cave in Blue Mountain, North Carolina. It was for our benefit that time, but this is different.

"Listen before you act impulsively, Paxton. If we are to find the one place where the power is great enough to reach around the planet, we cannot do it as a group. Time is running out. Please understand, Sky is in the best of care."

He releases me, and I growl, gathering myself for another attempt.

"Wait," Jewel's voice stops me. "Hear him out. He has a point."

"What are you talking about? You know I won't leave you."

"Perhaps we can send Juliana and Murphy to one location and you and Jewel to another," Chara says. "Would that be an agreeable compromise?"

"Where are you sending us?" Murphy asks.

"Pax and Jewel will accompany the Mantoids and Formicians to Mount Shasta in California, where many ley lines cross. The volcano is on the verge of eruption, according to your scientists, and the artifacts frequently cry out."

"What do we do when we get there?" Jewel asks. "We can't fix anything without the others."

Vega answers, "You are in tune with the artifacts. You will know if it is the right place because they will tell you."

"That makes no sense," I counter. "They don't speak to us."

"The Formicians and Mantoids hear and understand them. They will tell you."

"What about us?" Juliana asks. "Where will you send us, and who will interpret for us?"

"A cluster of artifacts exist in Mauritania. You and Murphrid will go there."

I'm about to ask the next question, namely how we would get there, when the air shimmers where the giants were moments ago, and Jaina and her guard appear.

She's in her human form, but the guard is an imposing man-sized mantis, complete with helmet, body armor, and a spear. We met him in Peru, where Al would have killed him if he could have. Al is in love with Jaina. I wonder where he is.

"I'm sorry about the way this is playing out," Jaina says. "Since it may be impossible to unite the races for the harmony Terra needs, this may be the only way to achieve it."

I pull Jewel close and approach the Mantoids. "Let's get on with it then. The sooner we do this, the sooner we'll be together for the grand finale."

20

JEWEL

As soon as we materialize at the cave entrance on the side of Mount Shasta, I know Shaula is close. My eyes burn with tears, but I force them back and pull away from Pax. I can't distract him now, and I won't draw the monster's attention to him. I can't lose him.

One of the giant ants appears at the entrance and beckons us inside. Black eyes regard me solemnly as I examine the creature. An iridescent brown face, wide at the head, narrows down to a pair of serrated mandibles nearly the length of the face itself. Antennae wave from its forehead, and it stands upright, holding its forelegs like arms bent sharply at the elbows. Even with its other four legs firmly on the ground, it stands taller than Pax. I'm glad it's friendly to humans. I hug the wall and give it plenty of space as I slide past, only to find four more waiting in the tunnel, each wearing a glowing orb on its forehead, like headlamps. My eyes quickly adjust to the dim light.

A slight buzzing sounds as Jaina transforms into her Mantoid form and stops to talk to the Formician. Her guard stands next to her, holding his spear like a walking stick.

Their pheromones change rapidly as they speak, almost too quickly for me to detect the subtle changes. Learning their language won't be easy. Pax's voice in my head both comforts and alarms me. He doesn't know Shaula is close by, and it isn't right for me to keep him in the dark. He needs to be alert.

"We can't use our connection now," I say, nearly in a whisper.

He turns me to face him, his eyes questioning. I nod. He pulls me close and murmurs, "Let him come. Once I get hold of him, he's dead."

The first Ant person walks past us and takes the lead, flanked by two others with headlamps. Jaina lines up next, and the last two wait for us to stand behind Jaina. The Mantoid guard takes the rear. I feel strangely safe with these creatures.

We descend at an easy angle, heading deeper into the mountain. An occasional rumble and vibration in the floor and walls remind me we're in an active volcano that could blow at any minute. I should be terrified. Are the Ants projecting peace? Are they empaths?

Jaina changes into her human form and motions for us to fall in ahead of her. We can still walk side-by-side in the wide tunnel.

She speaks loudly enough to hear over the rumbling mountain. "You should know more about Mt. Shasta." I nod, and Pax squeezes my hand.

"The mountain is a Creator-made temple, sacred to ancient inhabitants and still sacred to Native Americans today. They believe it was one of the first earthly places the Great Spirit created."

"Was it?" I ask. "Weren't the Formicians and Mantoids here before Creator made humans?"

"We were, but Terra was ready for us before he made us. We don't know how the planet was formed."

The path grows steeper, and Pax walks slightly ahead of me, reaching back to help me down a slick incline flanked by rocks. The insect people have no problem navigating, even when they use only four of their six limbs.

"Climbers today will tackle any summit, including this one," Jaina says. "Until modern times, only medicine men and women climbed up the mountain beyond the tree line, where they performed ceremonies to appease the dangerous spirits inhabiting the high places. We are the ones they feared, along with our Dracan and Allaran friends. We hoped to keep them out of danger. The mountain is an active volcano which has been dormant for a time. It will soon awaken with catastrophic force unless you and the others are successful."

I interrupt, "Unless we're together, we can't fix a single artifact, much less millions of them. How likely is it we'll succeed by separating?"

Jaina continues as if she didn't hear my question. "This mountain is a generator, at the center of a congruence of ley lines. The electromagnetism here produces powerful energy, like the Stargate in Peru and the Gate of the Sun in Bolivia. The natives tell stories of people who have disappeared into portals that might open to other planets, other dimensions, or other places within Terra. If you and the others can heal all the tetrahedra within the planet, it would start here."

I ask again. "Then why separate us if you already know this is where it will happen?"

"The others are not convinced. Your companions have gone to explore other places where many ley lines intersect." We have nothing further to say, and we proceed in silence.

With as many tunnels as we've been in lately, I should be used to the fear of being crushed by trillions of tons of mountain by now. If it should happen, I tell myself, then the world will end, and I won't have to watch my loved ones die. If we can't pull this off, an eruption would be a mercy. Pax squeezes my hand.

The mark we share makes us hyper-aware of each other's thoughts and emotions. I'm the first human in history to share the mark with two men. Shaula bit me in my sleep, injecting me with a biochemical marker used for only one purpose. The chemicals saturate the female's organs, marking her as the Dracan's mate. He marked me without my knowledge because he knew I'd never agree to it. The process is irreversible, and only the death of one of the paired can break it, or the deaths of both.

In Dracan society, Shaula's bite on an unwilling female is the equivalent of rape, and he'll die for it, especially if Pax and Storm get to him first. They won't wait for the Dracan law to run its course.

Thanks to Max and Marla being the first couple with a human male and half-Dracan female sharing the mark, Murphy's mom and mine figured out a way to link Pax with me through my blood. Because I'm in love with him, our bond should have been strong enough to break Shaula's hold on me. It hasn't. It's only complicated matters.

If I should willingly give in to Shaula, he wins, and Pax and I will live with the tragedy of loss for the rest of our lives. If we can't fix the artifacts, it will be a mercifully short life.

I can think of several scenarios where Shaula could force me to surrender. All of them include trading my life for someone I love. Pax squeezes my hand, his face twists in grief. He's been watching my thoughts.

I lose track of time as we trudge down the winding tunnel. The only sounds, other than scary mountain noises, are the clicking of Ant feet on stone and a hum in my chest, too deep for my ears to register. I'm like a zombie, carefully placing one foot in front of the other in a dazed, mechanical walk.

I nearly run into the back of an Ant when Pax pulls me back. "We're stopping to rest."

We're in a small cavern, wider than the tunnel. How are we still breathing fresh air at this depth? I stumble to a wall and slide down, sitting with my back against it.

He pulls out his canteen and hands it to me. I drink metallic-tasting water, thinking it's the best I've ever had.

"Look at the walls."

A greenish glow emanates from the walls. When my eyes adjust, moving shadows startle me and I recoil, until they come into focus. Trees. Vines growing, twining among the branches. Underbrush. Everything swaying and blowing in a phantom breeze. What is this? A dream?

"Shadow Forest," Jaina says. She sinks to the floor next to me and points at the canopy of a tree spreading overhead.

"A gift from Creator to the Formicians. Eons ago, they saved mankind from a catastrophic event above-ground, one caused by the war between the alien races. The Ant People brought humans to a land deep in the earth, where they nurtured and taught them survival skills they would need when they emerged into the sunlight. The ground above was uninhabitable for generations, but the Formicians gladly shared their resources and lives with a race not their own."

"It's a beautiful story, Jaina. Why haven't we heard about it before?" I ask.

"The Hopi share the legend with their children, but few believe it anymore. It was carved in caves and on canyon walls after the people returned, but those carvings are no more than a curiosity now. How sad for all mankind to forget such a rich history. If they hadn't, tolerance for other races would have a completely different meaning now. It would include every race inhabiting Terra."

"Unfortunately, too many humans can't tolerate differences in each other, much less be open to intelligent species, such as yours," Pax says, yawning widely.

"Is the forest a projection?" I ask.

"It is, in a way," Jaina says. "This forest exists in Terra. It grows, moves with the sun, feeds on rain, and sways in the wind. It changes through seasons, produces new growth, and sometimes suffers fires and earthquakes, tornados, and floods.

"The Forest provides the fresh air keeping us alive at this depth. The rain, although not felt as such, feeds freshwater streams throughout the mountain."

"How are we watching the vines growing? You wouldn't see it in a real forest," I say.

She answers, "Where this forest exists, time is accelerated. The Formicians can come and experience a season in a matter of hours."

"Amazing. Beautiful," I whisper.

"Where it exists?" Pax asks. "Is it in a time warp?"

"Perhaps I will show you someday when you and the others have completed your task and Terra is safe," she answers.

She gets up, brushes herself off and turns toward her guard, who has removed his helmet and breastplate and piled them next to his propped-up spear. She grabs her backpack and returns, pulling out some sandwiches.

We thank her and tear into the bread. When was the last time we ate anything? We roll up the paper they were wrapped in and hand it back to Jaina, who puts it in a pouch on her pack.

"Get some sleep," she says. "The Formicians will let us know when to move out again."

I watch the dance of shadows on the ceiling for a long time before my eyes slowly close.

2 1

SKY

CRASH! BOOM! I press my hands over my ears and shut my eyes in a futile attempt to keep out the brilliant flashes streaking every few seconds. When Gienika told me I'm going to Lake Maracaibo in Venezuela, I expected something like Lake Titicaca in Peru and Bolivia, with its sunny skies and colorful people. I first met the giants near there, at the Stargate.

Lightning illuminates the lake in the distance. We're somewhere above the banks of the Catatumbo River, sitting on the side of a mountain under an overhang.

"They call this the Everlasting Lightning Storm," Jayman says between crashes of thunder.

Everlasting? How are we supposed to get anywhere if this never stops? Autumn wraps a warm blanket around me, draping it over my head. I smile, glad she came along and relieved we left Gienika with her tribe. I doubt she would have managed some of the steep trails we've had to use to get down the mountain. Now I wish we'd stayed in the cave we emerged from.

"It only lasts about ten hours most nights," Autumn shouts when a sudden wind moving down the valley turns the light rain horizontal. God chose that moment to turn on the spigot, sending a sudden torrential rain pouring like Niagara Falls over the narrow roof of the overhang. Water blows into our measly shelter, soaking us to the skin right through the protective blanket.

When the rain eases, I'm transfixed by the spectacle in the towering clouds. Fireworks have nothing on God's light show. Jagged streaks of magenta and blue jab from cloud to cloud, ending in forked branches of blinding white, lighting up the layers of clouds in bright colors, like a gargantuan stage set with multiple props. Thunder crashes and rolls, an undulating noise that doesn't stop. The flashes reveal Jayman, eyes half-closed and a huge grin on his face. If he's enjoying it, I might as well relax and watch the show too.

As wet as I am, the air is warm, and I'm not shivering with cold, as I expected I would be. I forget my discomfort while I watch the spectacle. Never ending? I'll ask about it in the morning.

I'M IN A SAUNA, getting ready to jump into a nice, cool pool when Jayman gently shakes me awake. The sauna is real, with mist rising in the heat. Oh, well. At this rate, we should be dry in an hour or so.

Autumn hands us some bread from her well-stocked backpack. She hasn't said much since the Allaran tower, but her frequent smiles and the way she knows what we need and when we need it make her invaluable. I hope to break through her shyness during this trip.

"Please explain why we're here." I had dreamed this before we left home. I wonder where the others are and if they've found anything useful.

Jayman answers. "A cluster of artifacts lie deep below us at a powerful juncture of many ley lines. There is so much power, it must discharge into the atmosphere to keep from blowing up this land."

"Is that why this storm is everlasting?"

Autumn has cleared up our campsite while Jayman and I talk. It's time to leave. She takes the lead, our silent guide, while I follow with Jayman behind me.

He explains, "It is called that by the natives and the few storm-chasers brave enough to spend time here. The lightning can be seen four hundred kilometers away. Ships navigate by it. The storm produces hundreds of strikes per hour and lasts at least ten hours. During especially explosive displays, it can produce more than forty-thousand strikes in one night. However, it does not happen every night of the year."

My foot slips, but I catch myself and move on. I hate climbing steep paths but going down them is just as bad. I hope we get to where we're going soon. I'd hate to fall into the river roaring in the gorge below.

"If it were discharging the energy from the power grid, wouldn't it fire up every night?" I ask.

Jayman grunts as he navigates a boulder I easily climbed over, and answers, "Atmospheric conditions must be right so the power can feed into a storm that has already formed. During times of drought, or the few times a year when conditions are not ideal, the ley lines do not discharge. If too much time passes, the people in this region are in danger of earthquakes and underground explosions."

Autumn waits for me, pulls me close and sets me on the path beside her, away from a steep drop. I'm grateful it's wide enough to walk together. The clearing mist still sends wisps obscuring the path in places, and the sound of the river is a constant reminder a slip now could mean drowning.

"Has it happened to them before?"

"Not yet, but they came very close to catastrophe when the storm stopped for six weeks a few years back. We could not warn them to leave because they don't know of our existence, but we were prepared to help as many as we could after the fact. Thankfully, it did not happen."

"So, where do we go now? You can't allow anyone in the villages to spot you."

Autumn steps ahead of me and turns into the mountain. Not until I follow her do I realize we've walked through a holographic curtain. When Jayman appears, I ask, "What happens if someone stumbles into this?"

"It is unlikely," Autumn answers. "It remains solid unless one of us approaches. We resonate at a different frequency than other humans and animals."

My mouth drops open. It's the most I've heard her say at one time, and she isn't as simple as I thought.

"Who guards the artifacts in this part of the world?" Every tetrahedron we've fixed has had its assigned guards. The one in North Carolina had its watchers, a sub-species of the Allarans. Triton guarded his "egg" in the Tongue of the Ocean. The Mantoids had charge over the three artifacts in Peru and Patagonia.

"You may recognize the little gray people in these mountains, Sky Fire Hair," Autumn replies.

I'm glad to hear the Allarans have given their watchers guard duty. The four who had guarded the tetrahedron in Blue Mountain gave their lives protecting us after leading us to the cave system where it lay hidden. Marla had then taken us to the actual cave.

"Were you fond of slides when you were a child?" Jayman asks.

"Why do you ask?"

He points toward a dark opening ahead. "The only way is down from here. The builders must have considered stairs to be inefficient, and instead, left us this."

Three highly polished handrails curve over the edge of a drop. Thinking we'll have to climb down ladders, I grasp the handrail, lean over and gasp. The blood drains out of my face. Light-headed, I back away shaking my head.

"There is no way I'm going down that."

22

STORM

I'm wasting time here. Why did Baran drop me off and just leave me here? I use telekinesis to lift the mattress off the bed and fly it around the room. The furniture is carved from the same stone as the floor and walls. Lilyana couldn't change the room around if she wanted to.

I could destroy it, but I wouldn't do anything to hurt this family. At least I know my ability works fine on Allara.

Again, it strikes me I'm on an alien planet, many light years from Terra. When I tell my grandkids about it, will they believe me? Will I ever have grandkids? Neither planet will survive long enough for that to happen if I don't get back home.

Peals of musical laughter draw me to the window overlooking the farm. Lilyana is walking toward the river, her daughters running and tumbling beside her, and two of the Aracai trailing her.

A shadow blocks the light from the distant opening. I watch the ship glide in, not bothering to cloak itself until it hovers near the path leading up to the dwelling.

I watch Baran descend the portal beam, while K'ary and K'amryn run to wrap their arms around his legs. It's the first time I've heard him laugh. Lilyana hugs him and waves to her husband, now standing on the path to my left.

I found my winter clothes, clean and neatly packed in a small backpack, when I got up this morning. I grab it and head out to meet Baran.

"Storm," he calls, striding toward me. "My sister tells me you have been a gracious guest."

Why don't I react to him the way I do at home? Rather than animosity and the desire to rip him apart, I find I can tolerate him. Where his voice was like a cheese grater on my nerves before, he sounds normal now.

"I've been drinking the magic nectar," I say, as we shake hands. "What's in it?"

He glances at Lilyana with raised eyebrows. "The change in him is remarkable. Is the Aracai nectar responsible for this?"

"When you left him, he was freezing, even dressed as he was for the cold of our planet. The nectar instantly warmed him. Baran, we have never given it to a human to drink until now. The Aracai sang it would not harm him, but I did not anticipate this."

He walks around, looking me over, like a mannequin on display. At home, I would have reacted with resentment and anger. Wait, have I lost the monster inside?

"Did you find Shaula? My parents?" I ask.

"We did not," Baran responds.

There it is. A growl starts at the back of my throat as the rage stirs. I'll need it to kill the lizard.

Baran's eyes narrow. "We traced him to an island we had not been aware of here on Allara. It was on none of our maps, and our cold temperatures had killed the vegetation. It held traces of habitation, but no one was there."

I remember how insistent Sequoia had been about the island that disappeared from the Tierra del Fuego archipelago. She knew it was important to us, somehow.

"I'll bet a wormhole brought the island here from South America. Allara would have been the perfect place to hide my parents and Thuban's crew if they're still alive."

Baran gives me an intent look and says, "They are no longer there. We were not able to recover your parents."

"Then he's taken them back to Terra," I say with complete conviction. "He's after Jewel, and they would make a fair trade, in his twisted mind."

Baran hugs Lilyana and his nieces. "Please give my regards to Hamal. We must return to Terra immediately. Come."

"Thank you for your hospitality, Lilyana, and for allowing me to sample the Aracai nectar. I hope you'll visit us on Terra when this is over. Please say goodbye to Hamal for me."

She and the girls hug me, and I follow Baran into the ship. The Allarans are much less alien to me than before. If the nectar changed my perspective this way, what would it do to other humans on Terra? And what did she mean by "the Aracai sang" it wouldn't harm me?

I WATCH from the observation room as we descend through the worst blizzard I'd ever experienced toward the Antarctic ice. Our ship slips through the buffeting winds with no resistance. I hope we humans get our act together and develop technology like this. I hope our planet survives long enough.

We're in the midnight season of the pole, where the sun never rises above the horizon. Belena comes into the room and sits next to me.

"Don't they need you to drive this thing?" I ask.

"I'm a scientist, not a pilot," she answers and laughs in her musical voice.

"How are we seeing this so clearly?" I've always wanted to know how things work. When this is over, I want to study with the Allaran engineers.

Belena answers, "The ship uses a light band which turns the night to daylight, like your night-vision goggles, but without the green color. It does not project light but receives it through an array of coated lenses. We do not disturb the environment."

I think of the applications we could use those lenses for, and then I remember the implications. We haven't told anyone about the wrist-bands because the tech can be used for military purposes and by unscrupulous people who would try to take over the world through mind-control. The same could be said for Allaran technology. The world isn't ready for it, yet.

We approach a large opening in the side of a mountain, partially covered by a round object, either a crashed spaceship or a gigantic metal door. I've seen photos of this and wondered if it might be an alien base. I'm about to find out.

We drop into a shaft and keep dropping. The walls, alternating between ice and rock, move by at the pace of a mechanical elevator. Why?

Belena answers my unspoken question. "We are approaching our Antarctic city Heliade. Sensors in the shaft trigger electromagnetic mechanisms to keep the landing ship at a steady speed and away from the walls. We shall arrive shortly. Your friends should be there waiting for you."

The city is nothing like I expected, an ice palace surrounded by ice-everything. Instead, it's an engineering wonder, a city defying logic. The towers alone shouldn't be able to stand with nothing but a filigree design around a circular core reaching at least a half-mile in height. Isn't this inside Antarctica, deep underground? Wouldn't the land above a cavity this large have caved it in?

We fly to the central building in a floating car. The Dracan vehicles also move suspended above the ground, and again, I wish we had this technology. Nikola Tesla knew about this, but no one listened then, and they wouldn't listen now.

Vega meets us on the ledge midway up the spire. Where are the others? Where's Sky?

"Greetings, Storm," he says. "Let us go inside where we can talk."

I don't like this. Something is obviously wrong. Sky wouldn't have missed a chance to jab me with her annoyance.

Images from the dream flood my brain, starting with the cavern on Allara. If that part happened, then the others must be where I saw them in the dream.

23
SKY

S torm's back! Thank you, God! While he was gone, it felt like someone had carved a hole in my chest. He and my brother are the only two people I can feel at any distance. The first time I lost him was in Blue Mountain when he and my brother both disappeared while they were exploring Dracan tunnels. It's when we first realized Dracan technology blocked our abilities.

Since Ashley and Leonis fixed the problem, I never expected it to happen again. Wherever he disappeared to doesn't matter now. He's back!

Where were you? I shout into his mind. I guess it does matter.

Hello, Sky. It's good to hear your voice in my head.

I detect a hint of sarcasm and breathe a sigh of relief. He isn't hurt.

Where are you? We both speak at the same time, causing a jolt of brain freeze. I press my thumbs into my temples to ease the sudden pain. It subsides in a few seconds.

You first, he says.

I tell him about my trek with the giants to this cave in Venezuela. The storm is still raging outside, so I open my senses and let him experience it.

Those are some bright flashes, he says. *And loud. Are those ladders leading down from where you are?*

No. Slides.

Like in the salt mines in Germany? He asks.

Worse. These plunge into bottomless darkness. They're steeper too, almost vertical. I can't do it. Waterslides scare me, and they have water resistance to slow people down, and you can see where they end. This is highly polished wood, and we'll have to sit on leather pads. We'll fly down those things, and I just know I'll fly off and get killed.

I can't control my anxiety, even knowing my fear is probably infecting him. I need him to assure me I'll live through this.

We've been in this cave for hours. It's urgent we get down there, but I can't do it.

Is Jayman with you? He asks.

Jayman and Autumn are here, I answer.

Why don't you sit on his lap? He's strong enough to restrain you with his arms. Make sure your hair is covered, so it doesn't suffocate him on the way down.

I picture my mass of hair standing straight up as we fall. Wouldn't it be ironic if the giant dies by the Fire Hair his people had been searching for when they found me? The thought makes me giggle. I send Storm gratitude and turn to Jayman.

"There may be a way out of our dilemma," I say.

WITH MY HAIR and shoulders wrapped in Autumn's Peruvian shawl, I cling to Jayman like a burr on a dog, squeezing my eyes shut and fisting my hands on his sleeve. His tree-trunk arms hold me tightly, leaving me just enough room to breathe.

"Do not hold your breath, Fire Hair," Autumn cautions. "You will run out of air long before we arrive."

I glance at her and then shut my eyes again. She's perched on top of the slide next to us, legs dangling over the edge.

I hear a grunt and a swishing sound, and then Jayman pushes off with his left hand and the contents of my body hover in space while the rest of me plummets with him.

My drawn-out scream echoes back to me, making me scream more. If we survive, I hope Jayman's ears recover quickly.

At some point, my stomach catches up with us, and I pry my eyes open, expecting total darkness. Instead, a light keeps pace with us, enough to give us views of about twenty feet of speeding stone walls. The sight makes me dizzy, and I close my eyes again.

After an eternity, the angle of the slide changes.

"Are we slowing down?" I ask Jayman, my voice shaking as much as I am.

"It appears so. I believe the worst is over." The rumble of his voice calms me. I also hear Autumn singing a cheerful song in her language and shake my head. How can she sing at a time like this?

Finally, we slide to a stop, the light now stationary around us, sparking off millions of crystals, like in the Cherokee cave in Blue Mountain. I'm being lifted to my feet, but no one is touching me. Are these watchers invisible?

No. Three small gray beings are standing off to one side. They must be using telekinesis.

Once the three of us are safely off the slides, a familiar buzzing fills my head.

Star Child. You alone cannot help Terra's organs.

Jayman answers for me, "Sky Fire Hair is here on a mission to understand how she and the others can repair more than one artifact at a time. Perhaps you can enlighten her."

We are responsible for those in this region. We do not have contact with others.

The three of them become rigid.

"What's wrong with them?"

Autumn answers, "They are communicating with the fourth, and perhaps with someone who is giving them instructions."

"Are the Allarans the ones they answer to?" I ask. Vega had told us the grays, as humans call them, are Allaran constructs assigned to specific tasks. They have had more human contact in recent history than any of the other hidden races.

Before she can answer, the buzzing resumes. The speaker says, *Follow us. You may find what you are seeking.*

He leads us along a pathway clear of crystals. I can't help but think of diamonds, which reminds me of Storm. Storm! I didn't let him tell me where he'd been!

I tap my wristband but get no response. He could be sleeping. I'm comforted by the fact I still feel him. Criminy. I'm curious now.

2 4

STORM

Vega and Belena lead me through a lush garden where I spot several Aracai and their singers. I long for some of the nectar, but my hosts aren't stopping.

I haven't heard back from Sky, and don't want to distract her now she's decided to take the plunge. The walk gives me time to contact Wolf and give him a quick update. Then I reach out to Sequoia.

How is our Gabriella? I ask. In answer, she sends a surge of contentment. *She's as powerful as Sky, isn't she?*

Sequoia responds, *Much more so.*

I laugh out loud, causing some of the Allarans to stop in their tracks and stare at me curiously.

Remind me to never get her mad, I say. *I can barely survive Sky's jabs, as it is.*

Where have you been? she asks.

Let Wolf explain, I say. *I have to contact the others. Auntie, I experienced my part of the dream. Sky is living in her part now. Please pray the others aren't in trouble they can't get out of.*

Sequoia pauses and I sense a tinge of wonder in her mental voice. *That's the first time in a very long time you've asked me to pray for you or your friends. I will gladly do so. I love you.*

She's the first to break the link. We arrive at a set of intricately carved double doors. Vega opens it and gestures for Belena and me to go into a ballroom with vaulted ceilings. Groups of Allarans are talking around tables scattered throughout the room, but Belena heads for the center, where a raised dais is enclosed by glass. The glass slides open when she reaches it, and she beckons me inside.

"Storm," she says, and I realize her voice has grown softer, like caramel melted over an apple. The effects of the nectar must be wearing off. I'm surrounded by Allarans, at least half of them males. If any of them speaks after I'm back to normal, the beast will get loose, and I might kill some of them. Or be killed. Maybe that's why she led me into this enclosure.

She croons, "We are sending you to your sister and Murphy. They are in Mauritania, beneath the Eye of the Sahara, where many artifacts are clustered. They need you."

She steps out, and the glass slides closed, leaving me inside. The air shimmers, and I'm standing in yet another tunnel. I hate tunnels.

I run toward a light in the distance, toward the din of metal clashing against metal, shouts, thuds, and screams, ready to tear chunks out of the wall to toss into the fray when Juliana shouts, "Stop! Don't kill him!"

When I slide to a stop at the entrance of a cavern full of blue light, I realize I shouldn't have bothered.

Six bearded men in traditional Arab robes are pinned to the wall, feet dangling six feet or so from the ground. Juliana stares at them with her hands on her hips, while Murphy, in his human form, holds the point of a spear toward the throat of the only one still standing. The Arab brandishes a dagger and circles the half-Dracan with fury in his eyes. I lean back against a rock, arms folded, waiting for someone to make the first move.

The Arab feints and jumps back. Murphy jabs but doesn't connect. He has the longer weapon and the advantage of his larger size, but he's holding back. Why?

For no apparent reason, the Arab steps back, places the knife in a sheath hanging from a loose sash, and folds his arms across his chest.

"You have proven yourself," he says in heavily accented English. "We will accompany you to the sacred chamber."

When he spots me, he whips the knife out, faster than my eyes can follow. It embeds itself in the rock, a quarter inch from my ear.

"You missed," I say, moving slowly away from the knife, impressed with his speed.

"Of course," he says. "If I had wanted you dead, you would be dead. Who are you?"

"He's with us," Murphy says, grinning.

You think this is funny? I open our link. *Just wait, brother. I'll get you.*

A flying body nearly knocks me over. *Storm! You called him brother!* Juliana's arms squeeze me in a tight hug. *We were worried about you.*

I peel her off after hugging her back. The six wall decorations are on the ground, brushing themselves off.

"What's going on here?" I ask aloud. No need to make them suspect our mental link.

"We are Rae, the Guardians of the Eye," the leader says, bowing from the waist. "We were told to expect four of you."

"I'm one of the four," I say. "Juliana and Murphy are not, but they're with us. Do you know why we're here?"

"To repair the ailing pyramids," he says. His black eyes glitter in the blue light. Where's it coming from? I look up at several random translucent areas on the ceiling, blue where the light is coming through.

"What is this place?" I ask.

"Didn't you see it when the Allarans dropped you off?" Juliana asks. "It's the Eye of the Sahara, of course."

"Never heard of it," I joke. This is one of the places I've done some research on, fascinated by photos taken from satellites and the International Space Station. From space, it's a giant Eye of Horus, complete with shadings that resemble lines of kohl around the eye. The eyeball is made of blue concentric rings of different shades, and to this day, no one knows who made it or how it happened to be. They call it the Richat Structure and, as with most mysteries on Earth, scientists have tried to explain its origins, but their theories have yet to be proven.

"We're under the fifth ring out from the center," Murphy says.

The lead Arab gestures for us to follow him, and he takes off with long strides down a slanting corridor. There's only room to go single file, so Murphy goes next, then Juliana. I follow my sister and the rest of the men fall in behind me.

I wasn't dropped off, I say through the link. *The Allarans transported me from their city, Heliade.*

It's a beautiful place, Juliana gushes. *They flew us here. I think they wanted to show us the Eye from their perspective.*

The terrain is deceptively flat, Murphy says, *and although we Dracans knew it was here all along, humanity only discovered it when they developed space flight for themselves.*

We stop several times in round chambers where benches line the walls and clear water bubbles up in fountains in the center of the rooms. It tastes fresh, but I long for the Aracai nectar.

Vibrations increase as we approach another chamber, and when we reach it, the artifact is spinning without a single wobble.

"At least there's no urgency to fix this one," I say aloud.

"This is one of many," the Rae leader says. "The deeper ones are becoming unstable. It is urgent they be repaired as soon as you can do it."

"That's why we're here," I explain. "If there is sufficient power here, we may be able to reach all the artifacts at once."

I approach the spinning tetrahedron, careful not to get too close. The force-field around it is invisible to me and touching it would send me flying across the room.

How would I know if this is the place? I ask Juliana and Murphy while I circle the artifact.

Vega said the artifacts will tell you, Murphy answers.

I'm not hearing anything. Sky is the only one of us who can sense these things. Something isn't right about this.

2 5
JEWEL

We remain in the Shadow Forest as we move deeper into the mountain, its soft glow making the path visible in the narrow tunnel. When the path widens, Pax grabs my hand and walks next to me.

The certainty Shaula is close grows stronger the farther we walk. Is he already here, in the artifact's cavern? I wouldn't put it past him. He's managed to stay ahead of his pursuers. I'm afraid nothing will stop him, as determined as he is to have me.

"How much farther?" Pax asks Jaina.

"Not far," she says, pointing straight ahead to a change in the light down the tunnel.

Colors dance in the light, and when we reach it, rainbow shafts bounce off millions of crystals embedded in the walls of a large cavern. The floor vibrates under my feet, strangely comforting. An egg-shaped energy field in the center of the cavern holds a spinning tetrahedron. The field is intact. Nothing is wrong with the artifact. Aren't they all failing?

Pax sniffs, grabs my arm and backs up into the tunnel opening.

What's wrong? I ask him.

Shaula, he says, and my stomach drops to my feet, joining the blood draining from my head, leaving me dizzy and sick. I glance back at the dark tunnel as the hairs on the back of my neck stand up.

Even though I knew he was close and expected something like this, questions fire through my brain. How did he get in here? How did he know where we were heading? Is it his connection to me? Did Jaina turn on us?

Pax pulls me farther into the tunnel, using his hands and nose to guide us. The tiny bit of light penetrating from the cavern behind us is enough for my vision, but it won't last long, and the bend coming up will block it entirely.

Where can we go in the pitch dark? Someone shouts behind us and I try to close my ears against the horrible squishy noises that follow, as if someone is stepping on the Ants. I fight nausea by focusing on my heartbeats, the rapid pulse pounding in my ears.

The sound in the tunnel ahead of us gives me little warning as a large body pushes me into the wall and rips Pax's hand from mine. Growls, groans, the crack of a breaking bone, and curses fill the air while the faint light of the cavern outlines vague rolling shapes.

Run! Pax's voice cries in my head. *Run! Hurry!* His fury and pain and a primal need to kill overwhelm me. I send him mine, pouring my hatred for Shaula into him, my need to shatter the monster and end him.

Go! I can't hold him... his voice trails off. He shifts his full concentration to the battle. I turn, send him every bit of love in me, and run.

At the bend, my hands brush the tunnel walls until my eyes adjust to the faint glow of the forest. Pounding footsteps running from deeper in the tunnel send me scurrying into a dark alcove. I hold my breath until three fully armed Dracans rush past, carrying weapons.

The alcove is just large enough for me to sink to the floor and wrap my arms around my legs. I don't hear Pax and can't feel him. Did Shaula kill him? I swallow the wail threatening to burst out of me in fear and grief, letting the tears flow unchecked. Sobs wrack my body in long shudders, as silent as I can make them.

The sounds of battle fade, and I wait to be discovered, but no one comes. Shaula knew I was there. He can see in the dark. Why hasn't he come for me?

Pax? I reach out for him, hoping for a hint of the connection we share, but I get no response. He's gone.

I crawl out of my hiding place and shuffle back to the cavern. Blood, debris, bits of torn clothing, and discarded weapons litter the tunnel where Pax battled Shaula, but there are no bodies, human or Dracan.

I dread the gore splattered all over the cavern, once pure and brilliant, but I must know if anyone is alive. Ant carcasses lie broken on the path, some impaled on jagged crystals in the walls. The artifact spins as if unaware of the violence that occurred here.

A movement on the far side of the cavern catches my eye. I can't muster the energy to run, but I shuffle there as quickly as I can.

A pile of clothing I recognize as Jaina's moans and stirs. When I reach her, she's pushing against the floor with one arm, trying to sit. I'm surprised she's in her human form, which must be dominant since she wouldn't have been able to maintain a secondary shape in her condition.

I reach her and help her up, propping her back against the wall. Her left arm hangs limp, obviously broken.

"My guard?" she asks, grimacing in pain. I shake my head. She hangs hers, and I realize she thinks I meant he's dead.

"I didn't see him, Jaina. I'll look for him and find us some water."

Avoiding the Ant remains, I search for the Mantoid, retrieving Jaina's mangled backpack along with another he must have carried. There's no sign of him. Either he was obliterated, or Shaula took him.

I open a bottle of water from the pack and hold it to Jaina's mouth. She sips and leans back, closing her eyes.

"How did they find us?" she asks, her voice croaking.

I don't answer, but the Mantoid's absence is suspicious to me. Of course, Shaula may have simply tracked me through the mark. Isn't that how Murphy found Juliana when the giants had her? I hope that's what it was. I like the Mantoids.

I'm trembling and realize I'm going into shock. Without help, we'll die here. I'm okay with that if Pax is dead.

I sit close enough to Jaina to share our warmth and watch the spinning artifact. If hatred is the thing destroying them, shouldn't this one be especially wobbly right now? Fatigue makes my eyes heavy. I fight sleep, knowing I'll have nightmares, but I lose this battle, too.

~

SCRATCHING, clicking sounds jar me awake, slamming my heart with a rush of adrenaline. Shaula? I scramble to push closer to the rock at my back, and then I remember Jaina and grab her good arm to pull her with me.

My head buzzes with Queen Jaide's voice. *We have found you. The Formicians will take you to the surface.*

Relief mixes with grief, and I break down sobbing. I'm boneless, a blob, just one of the gooey puddles littering the cavern floor. I'm barely aware of the gentle lift as one of the Ant People picks me up and cradles me close to its carapace.

A picture of a waiting Sentinel fills my mind, and I drift off to oblivion.

SKY

"Enter," a frail voice, crackling with age, invites us into a dim alcove. A small figure, completely swathed in a shawl, sits on a pile of cushions on top of a boulder, putting it at Jayman's eye-level.

"Why is only one of you here? Where are the other three?" I can't tell if the voice is male or female, but it isn't a watcher because it's using sound rather than telepathy.

I step forward and say, "I'm Sky. The giants call me Fire Hair. I'm looking for the best place for the four of us to meet, to project healing to all the artifacts at once."

"You are quite ambitious," the figure says. It reaches up and pulls the shawl off its head, revealing a craggy face topped by wisps of pale red hair, with more wisps sprouting from its prominent chin.

"I am Trueno, God of Thunder." His cackles bounce off the walls. Amazing acoustics in here.

I laugh politely, not getting his joke. Seated, he's no more than two feet tall, and he's ancient. His strange mix of emotions whirls like a mad vortex around me. I throw up a wall against him. Whatever he is, he's quite insane. Still, he represents authority to the watchers.

"Do not let my stature fool you, Sky Fire Hair. I may be small, but

I control the lightning raging over the lake. Here, I am indeed the god of thunder."

"Forgive us, Trueno," Jayman says, his booming voice echoing in the chamber, like the strange creature's laughter did moments before.

He lowers his volume. "Sky and her companions are searching for the one place powerful enough to project their healing around the planet. Would this be the place?"

Before he has a chance to reply, intense pain streaks through me, doubling me over. I scream as my heart rips apart. Autumn wraps her arms around me, sinks to the floor and pulls me into her lap.

"What is it? What is wrong?" she keens and rocks me while I gasp in agony, unable to control the moaning.

"It's my brother," I whimper.

Pax! I felt something break in him. I heard him cry out to Jewel, and suddenly, he was gone. Where he was, there's only a void. This is nothing like when the Dracan technology blocked our connection.

"He's gone," I wail, clutching my stomach, rocking in pain.

"What happened to him?" Jayman asks, his face going pale with shock.

I can't speak, can't answer him. Half of me just disappeared into nothingness.

My grief pierces through the giants, sending Jayman to the floor, face buried in his hands weeping. My hands automatically cover my ears when Autumn's howling grows painfully loud.

"Stop!" a voice like thunder cuts through the cacophony, shocking me and the others into silence. The little man has thrown off the shawl and stands on the boulder, hands fisted on his hips, his short, heavily muscled legs spread wide. He's dressed in armor, and thick red hair, with an orange tint, now covers his head and bearded face. Coal-black eyes glare at us. His ancient persona was an illusion or a disguise.

Jayman gets to his feet, staring at the little warrior.

"Jazwel?" he asks, his voice cracking. "Alive?"

Trueno cackles and answers, "Yes, brother. More than alive. I am king of the mountains."

"But, how?" Jayman stammers. "How is this possible? We buried you. Our mother grieved your death until her own."

"You buried a coffin filled with earth, stupid giant. I was never one of you. What I lacked in stature, I more than made up for in brilliance and power, but none of you saw beyond my physical limitations. I am no longer limited. I am who I want to be, and I control the storm."

"No!" Jayman roars. "We did not reject you, nor mock you for your lack of height. You were loved, Jazwel, and sorely missed when we thought you gone forever."

"Liar!" Jazwel shouts. "I have had enough of you."

He turns, pointing at me. "You do not need a place of power to project to all the artifacts, human. You do not know your own power. Leave me. Leave my mountain and my lightning. This is not the place you seek."

His lips curl up in a sneer when he adds, "And you, brother, never return, neither you nor any of your tribe."

"We go. I am deeply sorry you felt the need to separate from your people. It was a mistake to come here. Please accept our apology, Trueno. Sky has suffered a great loss. The entire planet has suffered this loss. Enjoy your domain while you have it. Earth will not recover from this," Jayman says, his voice thick with tears.

Autumn picks me up and carries me in her arms, cradled like an infant. Grief, hers, Jayman's, and my own, squeezes the energy out of me, like an ever-tightening net. Without my brother, the world will end, and I don't care.

The watchers are gathered in the tunnel, waiting for us. I'm barely aware of them as they lead us down endless tunnels.

I curl up in Autumn's arms. She holds me close as she hums a soothing melody, reminding me of my mother.

Oh, God. How will I tell my parents? Tell them what? I don't know what happened to him. Only that he's gone.

The combination of grief and Autumn's humming lull me to sleep.

When I wake up, we're outside, in a secluded valley. I'm lying on Autumn's shawl, but the giants are somewhere out of sight.

Sky? Storm's voice is anxious in my head, but I don't answer. I don't want to talk to anyone. He doesn't get the message.

I know you're in the link. Listen, then. Sequoia told me Gabriella has been inconsolable. Something happened to set her off, and she hasn't stopped screaming for hours. Whatever has happened, you need to calm her down.

Oh, no! I forgot Gabri is closely tuned to me. Could I comfort her from this distance? I hope I can muster up enough to help her.

Can you patch me in with Sequoia? I don't know if it will help, but if anyone can pass my emotions on to her baby, it's your aunt.

He answers, *send it to me while she and I are linked. She should receive it.*

I don't know if I have it in me, but as I concentrate on my love for Sequoia and her baby, its power increases.

Sending now, I tell him, and I push a wave of love to him, and through him to the baby.

His wall is down and he's vulnerable, but I can't handle it now. He doesn't know about my brother yet. I break the link.

The Allaran ship appears in the distance. The giants float into the light and I wait for it to pick me up, not caring if it does or simply flies off and leaves me here. No. I need to know how my brother died.

STORM

W e're in the third chamber with a healthy artifact when Sequoia contacts me, asking me to reach Sky. I can hear the baby's screaming through the link. It takes several tries before Sky's link opens. Her grief hits me like a fast-moving train, and I want to know what's wrong, but Gabriella is a more pressing issue.

I can tell how much it costs her to send peace to the baby. As soon as Gabri calms down, Sky shuts the link.

I try to contact her again, and the link opens. Pain washes over me, and she shuts it again without saying anything.

I tap Pax's code but get nothing. Then I tap Jewel's code, but she's silent, too. What is going on?

"Juliana, have you tried to contact any of the others?" I ask.

"No," she says. "Is there a problem?"

What is it? Murphy asks through the link.

We need to get out of here, I answer. *I have a bad feeling.*

Murphy turns to the Rae leader and bows, saying, "We thank you for your hospitality, and for showing us what we came to see."

The leader also bows. "Have you determined if this is the place the four will use to save Terra?"

I reply, "I can't be sure yet. We're exploring all possibilities. After we talk with the others, we'll let you know if we'll be returning here."

They lead us out, past the chamber where I came in, to an opening in the side of a cliff a distance away from the Eye. I walk to the edge of the cliff and gaze out over the desert, moonlit under a star-filled dome. The Milky Way slashes through the sky like a wide road. I send up a quick prayer for my friends, hoping Creator is helpful tonight.

I'm surprised at the dark triangle overhead blocking out some of the stars. I was expecting an Allaran ship, not the Dracans.

The portal opens, and light momentarily blinds me as I'm drawn up into the craft. When Juliana and Murphy are safely inside, Murphy greets the waiting Dracan. I watch the expression on his face change from his usual optimism to sadness.

"Talk to me, Murphy. What's happened?"

"Let's find a seat," he says, throwing his arm around Juliana's shoulder and leading her out of the portal room.

The rage I've tried hard to control goes from a simmer to a boil. If someone doesn't tell me what I want to know, I won't be responsible for the damages.

"There has been an attack. Jewel and Pax were in an artifact chamber deep inside Mount Shasta in California when Shaula and a group of renegade Dracans attacked."

"Did he get her?" Juliana asks, her eyes filling with tears.

"No," Murphy answers. He pulls her close and clears his throat before continuing.

"Pax is gone."

"Did they find his body?" I can barely croak out the words. No wonder Sky won't talk. She can't.

"She found much blood, but Pax and the Dracans were gone when she came out of hiding. She's lost her connection to him. She believes he's dead."

"I don't," I say with conviction. "In fact, I may know where the monster has taken him."

"Where?" Juliana and Murphy say at the same time.

"Do you remember when Sky thought I was gone for good because she no longer felt me? When the ice cave collapsed, Baran's ship picked me up. He was on a mission to find Shaula, but first, he dropped me off on his sister's farm, on Allara."

"You were on another planet?" Juliana's question comes out in a squeak. "I want to go!"

"In due time. While I was there, Baran found the island that had disappeared from Tierra del Fuego. When it happened, Sequoia thought its disappearance was connected to our parents somehow. Baran told me they'd found evidence it had been inhabited for some time."

"Do you think it's where Shaula has taken him?" Murphy asks.

"I doubt it. The Allarans will be monitoring it, now they know it's there, but I suspect he and our parents are somewhere on Allara."

"Why would he have taken Pax, and not Jewel?" Juliana asks.

"Leverage. She's too strong for him," I answer. "He couldn't break her when he held her captive under the Perito Moreno glacier. He'll use Pax as a bargaining chip to get her to surrender. Once she does, he won't matter to him, and might not matter to her. The mark would be fully activated."

"If he were dead, Shaula would have nothing to trade, except for our parents," Juliana says. Her brows draw together in a deep frown.

"We know she would give herself up for our parents, too, but if Shaula doesn't know that…do you think he's killed them?"

"I doubt he knows much about her," Murphy says. "He probably thinks Pax is the only way to get to her. Besides, they share the mark. Once he has her, he'll kill him."

"What about our parents?" Juliana asks.

"Once Jewel is his, I suspect he'll use them to buy his freedom," I answer.

"What now?" Murphy asks.

"We regroup. I say we go back to Andros and figure this out. Besides, I want to make sure our cousin is okay. She and Sky share a special bond, and when Sky lost Pax, Gabriella wouldn't stop screaming."

～

THE HOUSE IS dark and quiet when I open the front door, careful not to make noise.

"Welcome home, Storm and Juliana." My aunt is sitting in a chair, surrounded by cushions and with her feet propped up on the coffee table. Gabriella is lying quietly in her arms.

"Were you waiting for us, Auntie?" I ask.

"Every time you leave the house, I wait for you," she answers, with a soft chuckle. "Gabri was hungry, so we came out here. Wolf is finally sleeping, and I didn't want to disturb him."

"Where is Donny?" I ask, missing my little friend.

"He and Lucaya returned to their people several days ago," Sequoia answers.

Juliana reaches for the sleeping baby, and settles on the couch, holding her close. I kiss the top of Sequoia's head and go sit by my sister, touching my cousin's soft cheek. She turns her head toward my touch and makes little sucking sounds.

My heart expands and fills with a protective instinct I've never experienced before.

"You will be a good father," Sequoia says, watching us. My eyes burn with unexpected tears. I must be exhausted, I reason, knowing there's more to it than that.

"The baby is calm," I say. "Does it mean Sky is doing better?"

"She's here. The Allarans brought her to her parents this afternoon. She's asleep now, but when she first arrived, a hollow existed where her spirit normally dances. Gabri felt it too, and cried, even when Sky held her for a few minutes."

"We don't believe Pax is dead," Juliana says.

"No. I couldn't bring myself to believe it, either," Sequoia answers. "If your parents are still alive after all these years, when I thought them gone, then surely he is, too."

28
JEWEL

I t's over. I wonder how long it will take for the planet to die. Please, God, do it before Shaula comes for me.

No. I'm being selfish. Rather, give Gabri a chance to grow up. Take your time, God.

The sun warms my body, and I let the sound of waves kissing the shore lull me into a semblance of calm. If Shaula does come for me, there's no reason to resist him anymore. I won't make it easy for him, though. He'll have to return Salali and Tom to their family.

I take a deep breath, wishing I could smell the fresh sea air the way Pax did, surprised at how good it feels to breathe. Then pain stabs my shredded heart once again.

The brilliant colors of the sun rising over the ocean sparkle and move in the water and sky. For the first time, I wish someone would block my vision. My ability mocks me, a betrayal of my lost love.

I wonder if my folks brought the glasses Dad invented to help me manage my first and only weeks in high school. As soon as I find them, I'll wear them for the rest of my life.

Sky emerges from their house, walks down the steps and heads out to the beach. She's in as bad shape as I am. I get up to follow her.

"Wait," I call, the cool sand slowing me down as I run to catch up with her.

She stops ankle deep in the wavelets but doesn't turn. I get she wants to be alone. So do I, but now is not the time.

Her sadness draws me in, and when I reach her, she turns to hug me. Our tears pour out from an endless void, our offering to the boundless sea. We walk together, pushing aside the water until our feet no longer touch, and then we swim.

I stop to catch my breath, treading water. The trench is close, and it's much cooler here than in the shallows. I imagine how wonderful it would have been to dive along the coral reef with Pax. Perhaps I'll get a glimpse of it as I sink. I'm not going back to shore.

We swim, aching in soul and body, until a wall of water rises into a wave powerful enough to push us back.

She turns and flattens. I copy her motions, and we ride the wave back into the lagoon. I'd never body-surfed before. When the water recedes, the lagoon is as calm as when we started. I turn to look out where aquamarine meets deep-water indigo, and I spot the dragon.

His keening matches ours as we shout our grief to the ocean. He's sad, but there's something more. He's projecting love and concern for us, and hope?

"He isn't grieving with us. Do you feel it?"

"I do," she answers. "He's grieving because we are. Maybe he doesn't know about Pax." She chokes on her brother's name. "Since you were there, let's open our link and tell him what happened."

I open my link to her, not wanting anyone else to join us in this private moment, and send her images of the attack and what I found when it was over. She sends them on to Triton.

The dragon sends back an image of Pax, hurt but alive.

"He doesn't understand," she says. "I'll try again."

The image she sends rips into both of us. My Pax in a coffin. Gone.

The dragon's roar brings Storm and Murphy running to the beach, with Juliana right behind them. We're far enough in the lagoon to see, but not hear them.

And then everything stops. My breath, my heart, my brain – all stop when Triton sends the next image. Pax in a cell, in pain, but *alive*.

The next beat of my heart fills me with a heady combination of joy and fear. My body tingles as I come alive again. I feel Sky's joy and realize we're both shouting, "He's alive!"

We lift out of the water and fly toward shore, where Juliana and Storm are drawing us in. Did they see the pictures from Triton? Do they know?

When we reach the shore and gain our footing, we turn in time to watch Triton's forked tail sink into the waves, and then we hug our friends, crying with relief.

2 9

SKY

"What now?" I ask, after Storm explains how they concluded Shaula didn't kill Pax.

We're sitting in the surf, letting the warm water wash over our legs as we talk. Jewel stares intently at the water, watching fish swim below the surface, hidden from us by the reflection of the sun and sky.

"We can't rescue him if he's off planet and we don't know where the snake is keeping him," Storm says. I lay my hand on his arm, sending him peace. His wall is down, and he doesn't resist.

He glances at me. "Baran is hot on Shaula's tail. Thuban wants to find him, too. I say we leave the search up to the aliens. No offense, Murphy."

"None taken." Murphy grins, back to his easy-going self. Juliana, snuggled next to him, gazes at him with love in her eyes.

"What do we do in the meantime?" I ask. "Did any of you find what we were looking for? The Allarans sent us to the most powerful ley line junctures on Earth. What did you find there?"

Jewel answers first. "Before Shaula attacked us, Pax and I went into Mount Shasta. Jaina, her guard, and some of the Formicians took us through the Shadow Forest to a crystal cavern where an artifact was spinning, as healthy as ours were after we fixed them. The battle didn't affect it."

"In the dream I had, he was in the forest and you were sitting in a dark place, separated from all of us," Storm says.

"I dreamt the same thing," I remind them. "The forest was strangely beautiful, like a real one moving on the walls."

"It is the shadow of a real forest, only in accelerated time," Jewel explains. "You can watch plants and trees grow and follow the rapid passage of seasons. Creator gave it to the Formicians for their service to humans during the great war. The dark place must have been the alcove where I waited out the battle. I should have stayed and fought, but he wanted me away from Shaula."

"Before the attack, did you notice if there was enough power for us to heal an artifact and project it to all the others around the globe?" Storm asks.

"No," she answers. "The one artifact I saw didn't need healing."

Storm turns to me with warmth in his eyes, and for the first time, he doesn't withdraw when our eyes meet. The void Pax left is a little less cold.

"What about you?" he asks.

"The Allarans transported us to one of the Andean mountains along the Catatumbo River," I answer.

"Jayman said they took Gienika home during transport. She would have had trouble walking down the steep rocky paths, soaked to the skin in a blinding thunderstorm. It was no picnic for any of us."

I shudder, remembering how drenched we were. "They call it the "never-ending lightning storm" with good reason. It lasts ten hours a night almost every night of the year. Jayman thought the power from the congruent ley lines was so great, it had to discharge into the atmosphere or risk blowing a hole in the area."

Murphy asks, "Did you find it to be true? Is that the place of power we're searching for?"

"No," I answer. "We went past several healthy artifacts in crystal chambers, probably like the one you saw, Jewel. When we told the watchers what we were looking for, they took us to their boss."

"Boss?" Storm asks, sounding indignant. "Was there an Allaran down there?"

"Hardly," I say. "We met some crazy little guy claiming to be the god of thunder. At first, he appeared weak and frail, and he sounded ancient. After my brother disappeared and I had a meltdown, he changed into a raging warrior, small but powerful."

"Could he have been what he claimed to be?" Juliana asks.

"Jayman recognized him as his brother Jazwel. Apparently, he had felt out of place among his much larger family, and he'd faked his death to start a new life away from the tribe. His emotions churned like quicksand in a cement mixer. Mine were so raw, I couldn't have helped him even if he'd been receptive. He found a place in the mountain where he could pretend to rule over thunder and lightning. In any case, he kicked us out."

Murphy laughs, and Storm joins in. "Talk about delusions of grandeur," he says.

"What about you, Storm?" I interrupt, annoyed Jazwel's problems amused them.

"You never told me where you went after the ice cave collapsed. What did you find?"

He stops laughing and turns thoughtful, picking up handfuls of wet sand and letting it dribble into the wavelets.

"I went to Allara. When I came back, the Allarans sent me to meet Juliana and Murphy at the Eye of the Sahara. I found them fighting a bunch of men dressed in desert robes and turbans. The men weren't doing so well."

"Wait a minute," Jewel interrupts. "You went to Allara? Aren't you going to tell us about it? What was it like being on another planet?"

I nod, eager to hear about the time I felt his absence as keenly as Pax's absence now. He didn't have a chance to say anything when I was in the mountain.

"I'll tell you everything later, but right now, we're comparing notes for one purpose. We need to figure out how to save our planet."

If he had the wall up, I'd be sending a jab right now, but I see his point. He isn't trying to hide anything. I send peace instead. His smile surprises me.

Murphy takes up the story. "Once we proved we were stronger than they are, they told us they're the Rae, the guardians of the Eye. They led us deep beneath the desert into a series of well-maintained sand caverns, in which tetrahedra were spinning."

Juliana pipes in, "They were healthy, so we asked if any others might be sick. They said the deeper ones are, and insisted we stay to fix them. They were upset when Storm told them we couldn't help, but they already knew. I think they wanted us to call the rest of you."

"I didn't get the impression there was any great power," Storm confides, "but I still don't know how we're supposed to know, one way or the other. The whole thing made me suspicious. I think the Allarans sent us on a wild-goose chase, and I want to know why."

I add, "Aren't the artifacts supposed to be dying? Why are we witnessing so many healthy ones? I thought the destruction of Earth was imminent."

30

PAX

Cold. Freezing. I fight the thing wrapped around me, snap my eyes open and struggle to get free. When I come fully awake, I realize I'm fighting a rough blanket and stop, pulling it closer. My teeth chatter, and I can't stop shivering. I'm lying on cold stone ground. Sitting up, I scoot back until I hit a wall, and make myself as small as possible to conserve what body heat I still have.

Faint pinkish light streams through cracks in the wall, not big enough to squeeze through, but enough to illuminate the small, dank room I'm in. Metal bars open to a narrow space ending in another stone wall.

"Hang in there, son," a whisper, just loud enough to hear, comes from beyond the bars.

I open my mouth to speak and realize it's so cold and dry, my vocal cords are frozen. I desperately need water. Who whispered, and where am I?

I groan silently as memories flood in. Shaula, breaking my arm, trying to kill me. Jewel. Did he get her too? How did I let him take me by surprise? I knew he was nearby. Why didn't I just take her and get out of there? What made me think I could kill him?

My arm. I flex it, expecting pain, and realize it isn't broken. I felt the bone snap. Heard it. What the heck?

"Am I dead?" I whisper, unable to make a sound.

"No. You're alive. A prisoner, like my wife and me." The voice is clearly human. How?

"How long have I been here?"

"A week or so. We don't know anymore."

"How is my arm fixed? It was broken."

"Nectar. The guard smuggled it in."

What is he talking about? I don't have the energy to find out. Basic stuff, first.

"Who are you?" I ask.

"Tom Ryder."

"Your wife is Salali? You're Storm's parents."

"Yes, and Juliana's. Have you seen them? Are they well?"

I think back to Storm's disappearance and weigh my answer.

"They're searching for you. Never stopped believing you're alive." I wish I could tell my friends I found their parents.

"Our boy is truly alive?" This whisper is softer. Salali.

"He was the last time I saw him," I answer truthfully. Shaula had told them he'd died when he abducted them. Jewel was able to communicate with them through Morse code when Shaula held her captive under the glacier. She told them Storm is alive but wasn't sure they got the message. Their last response was simply 'Thank you.'"

"Where are we?" I ask, wondering if they know.

"Allara," Tom says, and my hope shatters. How do I get us home from another planet?

I hear quiet weeping, until someone shouts, "Shut up!"

A DRACAN in chains delivers water and food once a day, if the light coming from outside is any measure. He makes his rounds as the light dims.

I spend the light hours pacing and doing push-ups and squats at

Tom's suggestion. Keeping warm is a priority, with the added benefit of strengthening my muscles. I intend to get out of here.

The Dracans leave their cells for several hours a day, their chains clanking as they leave and return, but I don't know who lets them out.

During those hours, I exchange whispers with Tom and Salali. The second day, Tom told me Shaula has planted listening devices. He figured out the electronics only pick up sound vibrations. Whispers don't trigger them. When I asked how he knew, he simply said he'd found out the hard way. I didn't question him further.

Tom told me Shaula had put them together in one cell to save room. I wonder if they're sharing one ration of food and water, but I don't ask them.

"What is the nectar you mentioned the day I woke up?"

"Allarans have plants that produce healing nectar. The Dracans are forced to work on a farm. One of them has access."

Forced labor? Are we in a prison camp?

Tom hesitates and says, "Without a tiny bit of nectar in our water every few days, we would freeze to death here."

Where is Shaula? Why hasn't he come to gloat? If he has Jewel, wouldn't he want me to suffer? Why didn't he simply kill me when he had the chance?

Frustrated, I move through one of my katas. The cell is small, but I adjust my exercise accordingly. If nothing else, I'll put up a fight the next time. If there is a next time. With every passing day, I let rage grow.

31

STORM

The more I think about it, the more I suspect the Allarans are deceiving us. First, they tell us the artifacts are dying. They didn't say "all of them," but they implied it. Second, they refused to help find Jewel when the Dracans had her. They said Creator wouldn't allow it. Third, they tell us the only way to fix the millions of artifacts is to heal one in a power source and, somehow, project it to all the others. They never did say how we'd do it. Fourth, they separated us, allowing Shaula to take Pax. Are they in league with Shaula? Do the other races know, or are they blindly trusting, like we did? I never trusted any of them, but my friends don't share my skepticism.

Gabriella regards me solemnly from her perch in the highchair. I send another spoonful of mashed carrots toward her mouth, and she opens wide, and smashes her lips around the spoon, smearing half the carrots over her cheeks and down her chin. Gabri is developing too rapidly, but Sequoia isn't bothered by it. How does an infant sit up by herself at less than two months old?

She laughs as if she's playing a big joke on me. There's nothing as contagious as a baby's laugh, and I join in the fun. She pushes, the way Sky sometimes does, but I don't understand the emotion she's sending.

"What are you saying, little one?"

She frowns and then laughs again. Again, I laugh with her, and she sends another push. What the heck?

I wipe her mouth and reach to pick her up. Her sticky hands pat me on the cheeks before I pull her out of the chair. The love she sends is unmistakable. I'm her favorite cousin, and I know it.

Sequoia comes in from the beach, a towel wrapped around her wet bathing suit. She's humming one of her Cherokee songs, and Gabri coos, reaching for her mama.

My aunt takes her from me and holds her close, not caring she's getting her damp. "After your nap, we'll go down to the water together, my baby."

Gabri claps her hands as if she understood every word. I wouldn't put it past her. She's been fully aware since long before her birth, and the way she's growing, she'll be a toddler by three months.

I kiss them both on the cheeks and head out to the beach, spotting snorkels near two of the kayaks in the water.

Grabbing the kayak that came with our house, I paddle out, getting there just as the two girls break the surface.

"It's incredible," Jewel says. "It's like being in a living aquarium, and the colors…I could stay down there forever."

"You'd better grow some gills then," Sky says, laughing. "And an extra layer of protection over your skin. Mine is like a prune." She throws her mask and snorkel into the kayak, and using her flippers for extra momentum, flops inside without tipping it.

"Tony and Meg are coming over later to take us on our first dive," Jewel says after she successfully gets into her kayak. "I've passed the written test, and so have Juliana and Murphy. We'll have our dive certifications in a couple of days."

Part of me hopes she'll have time to complete it. The other part wants to find and rescue Pax now. The Allarans have been telling us for three weeks now they've been searching, but I wonder if they're in on it and only putting us off. If so, what hope does he have?

"Juliana and Murphy took the speedboat out to the mangroves. They'll be back in time for the dive with Tony and Meg," Sky says.

"There's no telling when we'll be able to rescue Pax. We might as well keep busy while we're waiting."

Sky's voice in my head sounds angry. *You don't have to remind us. We feel his absence every second. Jewel is dying inside. She needs this.*

Sorry, I answer. *We need to be ready to drop everything the minute we know where he is and have a way to get to him. I'm not implying you'll be too busy. I know better.*

The love she sends lets me know I'm forgiven.

Oh, wow. It just dawned on me, I haven't had my wall up once since my time on Allara, and I haven't missed it. Did the nectar do this? Its effects started wearing off just before I was beamed out of Heliade, so why is the wall still down?

As we reach the shore, the sound of a speedboat going full blast reaches us, and we turn to see Murphy at the helm and Juliana waving frantically from the bow. What's their rush?

She points back, out toward the open ocean. A waterspout undulates across the horizon like a slow white tornado. They must have spotted it from the mangroves before it moved into our line of sight.

Even with the throttle wide open, their boat doesn't make it to shore before three gray triangles shoot out from the waterspout, coming right at us. A wormhole.

I lift Jewel away from her kayak and drop her off on her veranda. Then I lift Sky and set her next to her friend, watching as Analiese pulls them inside. Charles comes out, running down the stairs. Wolf emerges from our house, while Dylan rushes down the stairs from his. They're all carrying rifles.

I brace for the battle, wishing we had some rocket launchers, despite knowing they wouldn't do any good anyway. I wonder if sand will be enough to block their lasers. I could use the kayaks and speedboat.

"Split up!" Murphy yells, running the boat onto shore a distance away from us.

We're an easy target standing together.

Juliana shouts, "Storm, flank them!"

I run to the opposite side of the beach. We might each take a ship down, but it would still leave one, and Murphy and the men don't have our ability.

I get ready to throw half the island at them, and they stop. What are they up to, hovering in the middle of the lagoon, no more than a hundred feet over the water?

JEWEL

I slap my wristband, opening our communal link. *It's Shaula. He's in the middle ship. Pax isn't with him.*

Let's take him down, Storm responds.

If he's the only one who knows where Pax is, shouldn't we try to get him to talk? Juliana asks.

No, Murphy responds. *We won't get the truth out of him. For Jewel's sake, he must die.*

Stop talking! Just survive! Sky sounds terrified, and I know her fear is for Storm, not herself.

She and I press our faces to the window, where we have a full view of the beach, as well as the verandas of the other two houses. I don't worry about being spotted. Shaula can find me anywhere through the mark. Murphy explained it's like a GPS tracker, only interplanetary and inter-dimensional. There is literally nowhere to hide.

The door of Wolf's house opens, and Sequoia steps out onto the veranda, holding Gabriella on her hip. What is she doing?

She stands tall, every bit a Cherokee warrior. Then she opens her mouth and sings.

The rhythmic tune reaches through the walls and into our house.

Everyone on the beach whips around to stare at her, while she focuses on the Dracan ships. Then we turn back to watch the Dracans.

The middle ship begins to wobble, and the others follow, as if on a choppy sea. Her song is doing that? They move higher, but the waves catch them there, too. Suddenly, the sound of Gabri's laughter spreads through the air, magnified beyond belief. The ships move violently, crashing into each other. First one peels off and flies for the wormhole, and then the others follow it in.

Gabri laughs again, her laughter riding on the waves of Sequoia's song, and the giant white tornado simply evaporates.

"HOW DID YOU DO THAT?"

"How did you know to do what you did?"

We all speak at once, surrounding Sequoia and her baby on her veranda, where we ran as soon as the wormhole vanished.

"Let me sit, and I'll do my best to explain," she says, taking Wolf's arm as he leads her to a lounge chair. He takes Gabri and sits in a chair next to his wife.

Storm leans against the railing, and the rest of us drag seats in a circle around them.

"I was as shocked as you are. When the ships came into our lagoon, rage burned me to the core," Sequoia says. "I now understand what has tormented you since your parents were taken. I'm sorry you've carried it inside you all these years." He nods, his face set like stone.

"Gabriella sent me a picture of the two of us standing outside. The song began at that moment, but I waited until we were outside to let it loose.

"Power surged from my baby, carrying the war song to the ships. Gabriella's laughter pushed the sound waves, amplifying both the song and her voice until we became a weapon."

"She tried to tell me," Storm says. "This morning, when I was feeding her, she laughed and pushed a feeling toward me, one I didn't recognize. Twice. When I didn't understand, she went back to her normal self."

Right now, normal for the baby is napping in her father's arms. How can such a tiny thing have so much power?

"She's much more than an empath," Sky says. "Remember Meissa's prophecy?"

Storm closes his eyes and recites it from memory. "Your child will cross the bridge of hope, built by another to save the nations. The light she brings will never be extinguished, so long as Terra survives."

As he says it, a light goes on inside my head. This is how we're going to fix all the artifacts at once. Gabriella's laughter will cross the bridge of hope, meaning the bridge will amplify her laughter to somehow, bring all the artifacts in line. Okay, I haven't put all the puzzle pieces together yet, but this feels right.

"I believe Gabriella may be a key to fixing all the artifacts," I say.

"How?" Sky asks.

"I don't know, but you're the bridge, so once we figure out your part, then hers will fall into place."

Dylan shakes his head. "First, we need to rescue our son. Without the four of you working together, nothing will save Terra."

"Shaula will be back," I say. "He'll have Pax with him to trade for me. Unless you guys can figure out a way to save us both, I'll gladly trade myself for him."

Sky hugs me tightly. "We'll save you both. Pax couldn't live with himself if we don't. We'll figure it out."

33
PAX

A door slams, waking me out of a restless sleep. I sit up, back against the wall, and brace myself as heavy boots march toward my cell. It sounds like I'm about to get a visit from the monster, himself.

"What new weapon are your people using against me?" Shaula growls in anger. He attacked me in the dark, where he had the advantage, and when I "saw" him in my delirium as the chemical biomarker was linking me to Jewel, my imagination didn't do him justice.

The yellow eyes with the vertical pupils are exactly as I imagined them, only more sinister. His scales are duller than other Dracans here, although it's hard to tell whether they're gray or black in the pink light. Crocodile teeth protrude from his short snout, long, sharp, and jutting upwards and downwards outside his scaled lips. Six-inch claws grasp the bars for a moment, until he withdraws them, snorting in disgust.

The thought of Jewel with this ugly horror makes me want to vomit. I might have, had there been any food in my stomach.

"What, no hello?" I ask, feigning boredom, despite the quaking in my gut.

His yellow eyes narrow and he gestures with his head for the guards to open the bars and drag me out. He whirls and marches back the way he came in, and I catch a glimpse of Tom and Salali for the first time. They're holding each other in a far corner of the cell. Tom's long hair is as matted as mine, his face covered in a thick beard. Mine isn't as thick, but it's scruffy and itches like crazy. He nods at me as I pass. I hope he's praying for me.

I drag my feet, more in defiance than weakness, but it doesn't slow the Dracans down one bit.

The pale red sun nearly blinds me when we first emerge. My eyes had become adjusted to the few beams of light coming through cracks in the wall, which I now see is the side of a hill. Ice cold air sends me into a shivering fit I can't control. What kind of plants grow in this frigid atmosphere? I sniff, but the cold interferes with my ability, and I smell nothing but my own stink. I quickly put my scent guard up again.

My clothes are in tatters, held together by sweat and blood stains. I haven't had a shower in what could have been weeks, and the toilet in the cell was a noxious overflowing hole in a corner. I hope I stink up the inside of their ship. It would be a small revenge.

"Get him cleaned up," Shaula orders his men before he disappears into the ship. I'm afraid they mean to hose me down outside, turning me into an icicle, but instead, they march me inside where the heat warms my cold skin. It's short-lived.

They shove me into a small closet and blast me with cold water. I strip off my rags, find a soap dispenser and wash quickly. I do my best to comb through my matted hair and beard, working up some lather. I wish they'd given me a razor. Moments later, they pull me out and hand me gray pants and a gray tunic. I dress while they watch.

The heat makes me sweat, but I smell a lot better than I did. I'll get used to it soon enough. The two Dracan guards shove me in a tiny, windowless room with a bench bolted to one metallic wall. When the door slams, shutting me in, I stretch out on the bench and wonder what weapon Shaula was talking about. Who used it against him? The Allarans might have weapons we don't know about. I fall asleep thinking of all the ways I'd like to make the lizard suffer before I kill him.

~

CLAWS RIP AT MY ARMS, and I kick and squirm, trying to get out of their grasp. When I'm fully awake, I realize the guards have pulled me off the bench and are dragging me out of the ship. We're on the ground, with the ramp down. The cavern is tolerably cool, and I wonder if we're back on Earth. As I look around, I realize we're back in the Stargate cavern.

"You recognize the place." Shaula's voice grates across my nerves. "The giants live in a Dracan structure, which means you cannot use your ability here, although I cannot imagine how effective a hound's nose would be against us." He snorts in laughter, making my skin crawl.

He's right. What good is my keen sense of smell? I don't reveal his technology no longer blocks our abilities. I say nothing at all.

We exit the cavern to a familiar path that leads to Gienika's camp. After a short distance, we leave the trail and head down into a gully, which we follow in the opposite direction from the camp, along the cliff.

I drop my scent guard, eager to smell the trees and plants growing around us. I get a whiff of something else, something making my nose itch. Agateno. I remember her scent from when we rescued her and the others from the collapsed tunnel in Patagonia. She's as ripe as I was before my shower. Is she on Shaula's side?

For now, she's staying hidden, and the Dracans haven't been alerted. I keep my mouth shut. She and her scraggly friends are scouts. She could be on a recon mission.

I track her movements, parallel to ours. When we come to a door in the cliff, disguised to look like a boulder, I smell her retreating. If she were with Shaula, wouldn't she have let them know she was here? Will she get help? I have hope for the first time since my capture.

The door slides open, and Shaula leads the way inside, a guard shoving me after him. The tunnel divides, and Shaula goes one way while I'm led down the opposite corridor. Once again, I'm pushed into a cell. This one has a bed and a real toilet behind a small screen.

There's even a sink with running water. I'm moving up in the world. Unfortunately, there are no windows, and when the guards leave, they turn out the light. I can hear their laughter as they retreat.

I'm back on Earth, which means my wristband will work and I can contact Dad. I won't risk Jewel, and I can't speak to the others and leave her out. He'll tell them I'm safe, and they'll figure out a way to get to Shaula.

I tap his code and get nothing. I try Mom, with the same results. What the heck is wrong with the wristband? It isn't cracked. Did Shaula figure out a way to neutralize it? My energy drains out in a rush, and I sink to the floor. Rage and despair churn in my gut, immobilizing me.

When my muscles cramp, I get up, stretch, and feel my way around the cell, counting steps to the bed, to the toilet, and from one wall to the other. It's roomier than the dungeon on Allara. In the dark, I practice katas until the light flips on and a Dracan brings food and water.

I wonder how much weight I've lost on the once-a-day rations. When the Dracan comes to pick up my empty tray, he leaves my light on. I know all Dracans aren't like Shaula. This is the first one to show kindness. Or maybe he's just forgetful.

I stretch out on the hard, bare mattress and plan my escape. Agateno is my only hope now, providing she brings help, and they manage to break me out. I run scenarios through my head until my thoughts turn to revenge. Shaula must die.

34
SKY

The weather is perfect for the final two dives before my friends get their dive certifications. I can't wait to explore more of the reef and the trench wall.

The five of us crowd into Storm's jeep and head to the pier where Tony and Meg's dive boat, *Michaels' Dream*, is docked. They have all the equipment we'll need on board.

Andros sits on the edge of the third largest barrier reef in the world, which is also the third largest living organism on the planet. Coral has been dying in record numbers around the world in the last few years, but it's still thriving here, along with tons of other sea life.

Atlantis sits in the deepest part of the trench, the Tongue of the Ocean, more than a mile down. Thinking about these three just now getting their certification, after swimming in the midnight layer of the ocean with mermen and a dragon, makes me laugh out loud.

"What's so funny?" Storm asks. He's as eager as I am to get back in the water.

I open my link to him and show him the image of three Dracan-suited divers, and he laughs with me. In the back seat, Murphy holds Juliana close to his side, and Jewel has her eyes closed, head back against the seat. My heart aches with her. Pax should be here.

Storm parks the jeep alongside the thirty-eight-foot cabin cruiser. Meg waves us on board, and we help cast off the lines.

When we've cleared the other boats in the bay and are cruising safely in open water, we gather on the bench in the stern and Meg gives us last-minute instructions.

"Sky, you buddy with Juliana. Storm, you'll dive with Murphy, and I'll be with Jewel. We'll dive the reef in the shallower water first. Forty minutes will seem like five down there, so keep a sharp eye out for my signals, and check your watch and gauges every few minutes. Reef sharks are common. They won't bother you, right Storm?"

He nearly panicked the first time a reef shark swam nearby. I can't imagine anything scaring him now, after all we've been through.

Meg continues her instructions. "We won't use wetsuits for this dive, although we will when we get to the wall. The water temperature in the shallows is like bath water this time of year."

The girls and I are wearing one-piece bathing suits, instead of our usual bikinis, because they're easier to pull wetsuits over. There's less risk of losing a piece in the process.

When we reach the spot, Meg drops six dive flags in the water, while Tony raises the flag on the boat. We put our gear on, helping each other and checking each other's gauges and connections. We open our mental link as an extra safety precaution. The Michaels still don't know about our telepathic connection.

We'll only use it as needed, Storm says. *Let's experience the reef like everyone else, with our own thoughts. We can compare notes later.*

Agreed, we say, one after the other, and then we fall backward into the ocean.

It's nearly as warm as the water in our lagoon, silky on my skin as I kick the flippers and slide toward the bottom. Juliana's astonishment and Jewel's wonder wash over me. Watching sea life in an aquarium is nothing like being among that life in its habitat, and the reef is nothing like the depths Juliana and Murphy are used to.

We glide among branched coral, sponges, and brain coral. I watch a couple lobsters scurry under rocks as our shadows move over them. An octopus covers its bulbous head with flowing tentacles and squirms into a hole where its skin becomes the color and texture of the stone. I tap Juliana's shoulder and point to a reef shark. She pauses to watch the beauty of its motion, its tail propelling it effortlessly through the water. When I hear the chatter of dolphins, I spin around and spot them coming toward us. Juliana is looking the other way, too far for me to touch.

Dolphins, I alert her, and she turns to watch them come. They're swimming slowly for their species, as if curious about us. One stops in front of me, clicking loudly and nodding its head, while the other swims around Juliana. Could these be the same two I met last winter?

I reach out a hand, and the dolphin touches my palm with the tip of its snout, flips around, and the pair speeds off together.

It's time, Storm says in my mind.

I check my dive watch, and forty minutes have passed. Juliana and I break the surface a distance from the boat, but our flippers propel us there quickly. The smell of grilling fish is added incentive to get out of the water.

"You're nearly there," Tony says as he dishes up plates filled with grouper and grilled zucchini. "After the next dive, you'll be certified for scuba. If you want to go on to get your rebreather certification, we'll be happy to train you for that, too."

"Once we find Pax and save the world, we'll take you up on your offer," Jewel says. "I'll want to explore the blue holes with him." Her sadness brings tears to my eyes. She must know what he's going through. She was Shaula's prisoner, too.

It occurs to me I feel complete once again. Is my brother back on Earth?

35
JEWEL

Where are you, Pax? Sharp longing pierces my heart as I pull on the wetsuit. He should be doing this with me. I feel guilty for enjoying the ocean while he's languishing in one of Shaula's cruel prisons. I'm only doing this to stay occupied until we can take some action, and because Sky shares my pain. We both need the distraction, and this way, he and I can dive together as soon as he's home.

"No more than fifty feet, folks," Meg warns. "It gives you ten feet of leeway to the lower limit of our dive."

The water is noticeably cooler the deeper we go. Human scuba equipment is much bulkier than the Dracan dive suits. I wonder if the Dracans will share their technology once we save the planet. Diving would certainly be simpler, and people could go as deep as they want to.

The wall is as fascinating as the reef, with colors I've never seen on the surface glinting and flashing in the constant movement. I notice what the others are probably missing—cuttlefish flashing warning signs in their skin, and an octopus blending in with its surroundings. Their camouflage doesn't fool me any more than the Dracans in their human forms do. A Moray eel, halfway out of its lair, floats softly with the movement of the current. I reach out to touch it, and it lets me.

We come to a part of the wall that drops vertically below us, and when I look down, I nearly weep at the sight of two familiar forms. I start down toward them, but they wave me back.

Meg tugs on my shoulder, gesturing frantically. Have I gone too far?

Check your gauges, Sky says. *How deep are you?*

I'm back at fifty-five feet, but I don't know how far down I went. Sea Dwellers are watching us.

You've spoken with them before, Storm reminds me. *What do they want?*

I've only spoken with Cruiser. I'll try talking to them the same way. I send a picture of Cruiser, and two new faces pop up in my head. Before I can respond, one sends a picture of my face as a question.

I point to myself, knowing they're watching, and suddenly a flood of images come through.

Are you getting this? I ask the others.

Yes, Juliana responds, and I let the images come, while gliding along the wall pretending to be watching the sea life. I don't want to alert Meg to their presence. She might consider them a threat and cut the dive short.

The images, coming from both, are confusing at first, but then I recognize Murphy's mother. Once I'm in the flow of the conversation, I watch, sorting it out as best I can. Jaina is talking to Gienika, and suddenly, there's Pax being led into a cliff by a group of large Dracans. He looks tired, scruffy and sporting a beard, but he's walking on his own. There are no obvious injuries, but then I'm only getting what someone sent along a communication chain through the Sea Dwellers.

I send an image of Gienika back with a question. Is Pax in her territory, under a Dracan dome? They send an affirmative, and Sky projects joy mixed with concern.

Storm's mental voice interrupts the flow. *Time's up. Sorry, guys.*

I wave goodbye to my new friends and kick up to the surface.

Meg pulls off her mask and sputters, "What were you thinking, Jewel? You went below the sixty-foot limit."

"I'm sorry," I respond. "I got distracted. It won't happen again."

"You may have to repeat the dive to get your certification. We'll see what Tony says."

I nod and swim to the boat, no longer caring about getting certified. I'm relieved Pax is back on Terra, but he's still Shaula's prisoner, and I have no idea how we're going to rescue him. Why hasn't he contacted us?

We snack on crusty bread and cheese while Tony and Meg talk on the bridge. Tony's face is stern when they come down, but he says, "Congratulations. You're now certified scuba divers."

He turns to me and says, "Next time, check your gauges before you go deeper."

Dad, Wolf, and Dylan are at the dock when we return. Judging by their serious faces, they've heard from someone about Pax's move to the giants' territory.

"Jack Austin contacted us," Dad says.

"Why didn't my brother contact us directly?" Sky asks. "If he knows where he is, he'd know Dracan tech doesn't block us anymore."

"Maybe he doesn't know where he is," Storm says.

My gut clenches at the thought. Did they brainwash him? Did they blind him? I can't control the trembling taking over my entire body.

Dad pulls me into a tight embrace, and I tell him about my conversation with the Sea Dwellers. "He didn't appear injured, Dad, but that doesn't mean they didn't damage him."

"Ride with us," he replies. "We'll figure this out."

It's a perfect night for a bonfire on the beach. Sequoia and Gabri snuggle together on a lounge chair, wrapped in a blanket against the cooler night air, with Wolf sitting next to them. Mom and Dad share one blanket, while Coral and Dylan share another.

"These are incredible," Murphy mumbles through a mouthful of toasted marshmallow.

"Mmmmmm," Juliana hums, spearing another one and holding it over the fire.

When we came back from the docks, we needed rest. Murphy contacted Thuban and arranged for the Dracans to pick us up tomorrow. The Atlantis king wants Shaula as much as we want to rescue Pax. He'll come prepared for battle. If it goes badly, this may be the last time the rest of us will be together.

"Tell us about your time on Allara, Storm. We've been patient long enough," Sky says, offering him a marshmallow.

"Yes, tell us," I urge, craving any distraction from the fear and longing in my heart.

"I didn't know where I was when I woke up in an enormous cavern," he begins. He tells us about Baran's sister and her family, and about the Aracai.

"We saw some of them in Heliade," Sky says. "They followed some of the Allarans around."

"Those were their singers," he explains. "The singers hum and the Aracai produce a nectar with some amazing properties."

"What properties?" Sequoia asks.

"Allara is a freezing cold planet," Storm says. "I was dressed for the Arctic, and the cold bit right through every layer. One sip of the nectar, and it was like summer there."

"I suspect it's the reason the Allarans aren't affected by outside temperatures," he added, "but there's more. Lilyana's voice didn't attract me, and Hamal's didn't repel me. They were like normal people." He gazes at Sky, his eyes warm, and for the first time since he's been back, I'm aware of the magenta in his aura. How did I not notice how few of the red and black streaks remain?

"By the time I realized the rage was gone, the effects were already beginning to wear off. Allaran voices became irritants again, and the rage was coming back. That's when they sent me to the Eye of the Sahara to meet Murphy and Juliana."

He throws a piece of driftwood into the fire, stirring up a few sparks to spiral upward. "I liked not being angry for a while. I wasn't afraid of losing the people I care about. I felt normal until the nectar wore off."

"And now?" Sequoia asks. Her voice is soothing, encouraging.

"Now I crave it. The nectar."

Sky's love envelopes Storm. Gabri adds her baby love, too, and his eyes glisten, reflecting the flames.

"One thing didn't revert back when the nectar wore off," Sky says, almost too softly to hear. "Your wall didn't go back up."

He reaches his arm around her shoulders, pulls her close and says, "Nope."

Juliana sounds troubled when she asks, "Did you learn anything about our parents on Allara? And, Jewel, in all the images the Sea Dwellers sent you, was there a picture of my parents?"

Storm shakes his head. "Baran found the island that disappeared from Tierra del Fuego in a remote area on Allara. It had been inhabited and then deserted. If they were there, Shaula's moved them somewhere else."

"I'm sorry," I say reluctantly. "They weren't with Pax. If Shaula has them, and I believe he does, then maybe they're being held somewhere else."

We fall silent, and all I hear are crackling flames and swishing waves hitting the shore. I listen to the rhythm and wonder why the thought of plant singers sticks out from all the rest Storm shared. The sound of the sea, tunes that produce healing nectar, Sequoia's song and Gabri's laughter, all are connected somehow.

I'm lulled into a doze, and then it's like an explosion wakes up my brain. "Sound!" I exclaim, startling everyone. "That's it!"

"What are you talking about?" Sky asks, shooting me an annoyed jab.

I jump up, brush the sand off my legs, and head toward the house. "I have some research to do."

STORM

"What do you think she meant?" I ask.

Charles replies, "She may be right." His answer is as cryptic as Jewel's statement. He and Analiese take their blanket to the water's edge to shake it out and walk together back to their house.

Sound?

"We'll see you in the morning," Coral says as she and Dylan gather their blanket and leave.

Wolf takes his sleeping daughter from Sequoia and helps his wife get to her feet. "Bring the chairs back with you, please. Your aunt needs her rest."

Juliana and Murphy wander down the beach, out of sight, leaving me alone with Sky.

I float the chairs back to our deck and, craving the dark, I send a shower of sand and water to extinguish the bonfire. I pull her to her feet, take her hand, and start walking along the beach. The moon paints a path in the water, washing warm light in waves over our feet.

"What do you think she means by 'sound?'" I ask.

"I don't know for sure," she answers. "She'll tell us when she figures it out."

She turns to me, and even in the dark, her eyes shine, and I can't look away.

I stop and swing her around to face me, deliberately keeping the moon behind me. Its light turns her hair to burnished bronze and her skin to pale silk. I pull her close and run my hands down her smooth arms, aware of her surprising strength.

She glances up at me and then lowers her lashes, hiding the fire smoldering in her eyes. I touch her chin and pull her face up, silently urging her to look at me. No one has eyes like hers, with tiny silver flecks swimming in deep, brilliant, bottomless blue.

Without the wall, I'm defenseless against her. Heat flows like ocean waves, igniting the desire I've suppressed for too long. Everything in me wants Sky.

I lower my face to hers, taking in every detail, loving the beauty of her, loving her. She rises to meet me, and I kiss her, pouring my love and longing into the kiss. She presses close. I need her closer.

Clinging to me, she backs up, away from the water's edge, hooks her foot behind my heel, and pushes me flat onto the sand.

"Hey!" I respond, a little shocked she caught me off guard.

"You're not the only one with a black belt," she says, laughing. Then she kisses me.

Her heart pounds on top of mine in matching rhythm. I pull her head down, burying my face in her hair, breathing in the scents of wood smoke and moonlight, salt air and shampoo. She kisses my face, my neck, leaving a trail of fire, and I kiss hers, tasting her salty skin. I caress her arms, run my hands down her back, longing to touch all of her.

"Sky." I murmur her name, breathless, burning. "We have to stop. Now."

She pushes off and hits me. Hard. She also sends a sharp jab of anger to make her point. "Storm, you idiot!"

Jumping to her feet, she brushes herself off, turns and marches back toward her house.

"Wait! Come back. Talk to me." I run after her, and when she shows no sign of stopping, I lift her into the air and turn her around to face me.

She crosses her arms, suspended off the ground. Her wild red mane floats weightlessly around her head, and with the daggers she's sending through her eyes, she could be Medusa, turning me to stone. I'm too breathless at the sight to move. She's more furious than I've ever seen her, and her anger excites me beyond bearing.

"I'm sorry," I say, trying to look contrite.

"For what?" she says through gritted teeth. "For wanting me? For showing weakness? Maybe you're sorry for pretending to love me."

"You know me. You know what my wall was like, and you know it's gone. Everything I feel for you is real."

She softens and I press my point. "I've loved you since the moment I met you."

"Then why did you stop us? You don't know how long I've been waiting for this." Her arms uncross, and she brushes away tears. I lower her to the ground, pull her into my arms and let her cry. I want to cry with her.

"You deserve so much more."

"I do, don't I?" she chokes back a sob, and then she's laughing.

"What's so funny?" I ask, offended. This was a solemn moment, and I'd just bared my soul to her.

"Oh, Storm," she says, sending me soothing warmth and still laughing. "That wall of yours never stood a chance."

THE DRACAN SHIP arrives before sunup, and we're ready. Wolf, Sequoia, and Gabriella are staying here, but everyone else is coming along this time. I don't question why, figuring the women were tired of being left behind. I hope we aren't going into a war zone.

The ride is shorter than I'd anticipated. Are we in Peru?

I recognize the Atlantean dock as soon as we leave the ship. What are we doing here?

Guards lead us outside to waiting transports, minivans with glass bubble front ends. Bubble cars.

It takes a full half-hour to get to the palace, pushing slowly through crowds at the open market and in the fancier shopping district.

Max and Marla, with their two girls Khatryn and Sha'lat, meet us at the palace entrance. The girls throw themselves at me, nearly knocking me off my feet.

"One at a time," I say, laughing while I pick up first Sha'lat and then her sister, swinging them around while they squeal with laughter. The twins shout and beg for more.

"Down, girls," Max says, pretending to be a stern father. I lower them gently to the ground, and they run to grab his hands.

"We're so sorry you haven't found Pax and your folks yet," Marla says, hugging Juliana. "Giants' territory? Wouldn't it be a simple matter for an army of Dracans to rescue him and capture Shaula?"

"There are complications," Max replies. "Thuban will spell it out for you, and we'll make plans from there."

"If you will excuse us," Murphy says, bowing slightly to Max. "Juliana and I will visit my mother in her lab. She and Leonis have been working on a project that may help us with the artifact problem."

Marla hugs Juliana and waves her off, then she and Max lead us to a conference room, where Thuban and Avery stand to greet us. The king waves Dylan and Coral to sit next to Avery and invites Charles and Analiese to sit on his other side. The rest of us take seats around the table.

Marla and Max sit at the end, opposite her parents, while a servant leads the little girls out of the room. More servants bring in carts of tiny sandwiches and iced tea.

When we've all been served, Thuban says, "You eat, while I explain why you are here. We have heard from the traitor Shaula."

I nearly choke on a bite when he says the monster's name. Jewel's face has gone white, and Sky's face reddens with anger.

"He declares he is willing to give us Pax, but only in exchange for Jewel. I informed him we do not negotiate with traitors. If he releases his prisoners unharmed, we will show him mercy."

Charles says, "I imagine that didn't go over very well."

"No." Thuban snarls. "He laughed." A rumbling growl comes from the king's chest.

"To make matters worse, Shaula claims he has placed explosives inside the giants' protective dome, powerful enough to destroy everything inside. He claims the same explosives are planted throughout Atlantis and Superstition Mountain. He knows Meissa wants his death as badly as we do."

"How did he manage that?" Dylan asks. "Don't you have guards watching out for him?"

"We must have rats in the house," Thuban says. "Not everyone wants to save humanity." He bares his teeth in a growl. I wouldn't want to be the Dracans working on Shaula's side.

"How much time does he give us?" Dylan asks. Coral's face twists as she tries to hold back tears.

"Three days, beginning tomorrow. He claims he is merciful and would give her time to say her final farewells."

"As soon as I show up, he'll kill Pax," she says. "Pax and I willingly share the mark. We love each other. Shaula will never let it interfere with the bond he forced on me."

"You have a unique situation, Jewel," Thuban says. "You are the first female in history to share a mark with two living males. It is true one must die, leaving the other to be your mate if you accept him."

"What happens if I don't?"

"Consummation is necessary to forge the bond. Until you are a mated pair, he has limited control over you, and he cannot force you to mate with him. In a normal relationship, neither the male nor the female exerts control over the other. There have been exceptions, of course."

"What happens to the other male when one mates with me?"

I've been wondering the same thing.

"We do not know, but we believe the mark will not break. The other would either live a miserable life alone or would choose to kill himself."

Tears fill her eyes and spill down her cheeks. "Why me, Thuban?

Why did he choose to mark me?" She slams her hand on the table, rattling dishes.

"You were to be our ambassador to the humans. He wants humans destroyed. If our society had fully accepted you as I had planned, then humans would have an equal place of prominence in the world, recognized by all Dracans. His goal is to subjugate you, making it impossible for you to represent us."

"But I never agreed to your plan," Jewel says. "You had me testify before the Council of Kings, so they would conclude humans should be saved. Becoming an ambassador had nothing to do with it for me."

The expressions on his lizard-like face are harder to read than a human's, but he seems apologetic.

"You were confused. I tried to explain, but I understand why you did not comprehend. I hope you will reconsider in the future."

"What now?" Dylan asks. "We are not giving her to Shaula, and we are going to rescue my son."

"And our parents," Juliana adds. "We still don't know where they are, but we'll find them."

"We have soldiers searching Atlantis for the explosives. Meissa is doing the same, but it is unlikely we will find all of them before the three days are up," Thuban says.

Avery pipes in, "Gienika has been informed, and she will oversee the evacuation of her domain. Their dome is not as large as Atlantis, nor as thickly populated. Queen Jaide's people, along with the Formicians, are searching the forest."

"That leaves Pax in prison," Jewel says. "If Shaula's rigged the prison, then he doesn't stand a chance."

37

SKY

My emotions, dominated by fear, are all over the place. I know I'm affecting my friends and family and try to dial it back. I take deep breaths, but they don't help. My brother isn't here to send me calm.

Why hasn't Pax contacted us through the link? He should be able to. He's on Terra, and Dracan tech can't block the wristbands anymore. Did Shaula find a way to break it? Cut it off? Oh, dear God.

I stand up and announce, "I can't sit here anymore. I need to be doing something to save my brother. Shaula says he's planted explosives, but what if he's bluffing? What if it's all a ploy to get Jewel to surrender? Pax will still die."

"We cannot take the chance," Thuban says. "However, if the Mantoids and Formicians do not smell explosives in the giants' domain, and we do not find anything here by the end of the second day, we will consider it a hoax and act accordingly."

"What about using Sequoia and Gabriella?" Jewel's voice is almost too quiet to hear, but her desperation comes through.

"What do you mean?" Thuban asks.

"When Shaula and two other Dracan ships came to our lagoon, Sequoia's song joined with Gabri's laughter to form a powerful sonic weapon," Jewel explains. "It nearly destroyed the ships and would have, if they hadn't escaped into the wormhole they came out of. Then the wormhole dissolved."

His laughter reverberates through the room, so loudly I want to cover my ears. Too bad he can't weaponize it.

"A baby's laugh defeated the worm, Shaula?" He shouts in laughter again. At this point, everyone joins in, including me. We need a tension-breaker.

When the room grows quiet again, Charles says, "We can't ask Wolf and Sequoia to put their baby at risk."

"You are correct, Charles," Thuban says.

"I can ask Gabriella directly," I say, immediately wishing I'd kept my mouth shut. Storm shoots me a questioning look and I feel his astonishment and rising anger.

I've put my foot in my mouth this time, but what if I'm right?

"I would never put her in danger," I add quickly. "She and I have shared a unique bond since long before her birth. I use images to communicate with Triton. I haven't tried it with her yet, but why not? She's far more aware than any of us expected."

"She was never close to the Dracan ships," Jewel points out. "Neither was Sequoia. They stood at a safe distance and sent their voices out."

"If we're going to try this," my mother says, "then we'd better do it before Shaula's deadline. We need to get back right away to talk to Sequoia."

"She is a woman of the highest honor," Analiese says. "Coral and I will talk to her. If she's determined not to take the risk, we'll find another way."

"Yes," Thuban agrees. "I will send two ships with you, and if Wolf and Sequoia agree, then they will transport you to a place near the cliff, but far enough to hide you from Shaula's men. I will notify Queen Jaide, who will have her people meet you there."

On our way out, Storm taps his wristband, and I know he's letting Wolf know we're coming. Or maybe he's warning Sequoia.

Murphy and Juliana are waiting for us at the entrance.

"What are the scientists working on?" Storm asks them, pulling me close.

Juliana answers, "They're developing a device which will send sound waves through the ley lines."

"What for?" I ask.

"Something Jewel said resonated with them."

～

WOLF AND SEQUOIA are on the veranda, waving as we descend from the triangular craft. As soon as we're safely on land, both ships take off to wait for Murphy's signal.

I reach out to Gabri and find her asleep in her crib. I'll feel better about communicating with her after I have her parents' permission. She would do it in a heartbeat to save Pax, but the decision isn't hers to make, and she might not be able to do it without her mother's song.

Storm grabs my hand and pulls me up the stairs to join the others. I didn't realize I'd been holding back, making us the last ones on the veranda. We find deck chairs and wait, while the women talk to Sequoia inside. The men are telling Wolf everything that's going on, and I close my eyes, suddenly exhausted.

～

"SKY." Sequoia's voice draws me out of sleep as she gently shakes my shoulder. "Someone has been waiting for you."

I open my eyes in time to take the baby and lower her to my lap, where she sits staring at me.

I draw her close. "Hello, Gabri, my sweet baby girl," I say into her soft auburn hair. She squirms and places her hands on both sides of my face, staring with strange intensity into my eyes. A picture forms in my mind. Sequoia singing a lullaby. I form a picture of Storm, and she sends a bubble of love over his face. I show her Jewel, and she sends sadness.

"Yes, little one. She is sad, and so am I," I say aloud. "We miss Pax."

She sends a picture of Pax the way she last saw him, happy, and playing with her. A bubble of sadness covers his face, too. She's communicating using both images and emotions, and I understand her.

"We have talked about Jewel's hopeful plan," Sequoia says. "If Gabriella understands what you want her to do and why, then we will go with you."

"How will you know if she understands?" I ask her.

"I will know. When the evil one came in his ships, Gabriella made it clear to me we must go outside. The song, an ancient war song of my people, came to mind and I needed to sing it. She pushed a warrior spirit into me, amplifying my song, and then laughed.

"Because her vocal cords are not yet strong, her sweet baby laugh is what we heard, but her true laugh was one of power. It wove into my song and drove like a spear into the hearts of the Dracans flying the ships. They nearly crashed because the ones inside could not control themselves, much less their machines. If the wormhole had not drawn them in, they would have fouled our beautiful lagoon. I believe our baby closed the wormhole when they were gone."

I shut my mouth as soon as I realize it's been hanging open through Sequoia's story. "Wouldn't she recognize the enemy when we get near Pax's prison?"

"It's possible. The Dracan ships were an immediate threat, and she reacted to it. She may not consider the cliff a threat if she doesn't know the danger inside," Sequoia says. "What if she isn't able to separate Pax from the Dracans?"

"She senses him," I say. "She knows him as well as she knows the rest of us. She just sent me a picture of his face."

"So, you do communicate with her." Sequoia projects her satisfaction. "Your bond is a wonderful mystery."

I send her love and turn my focus to Gabri, showing her the cliff and the Dracans marching Pax inside. She screws up her face for a loud wail and shows me an image of Dracans falling and Pax holding her.

"She gets it," I say to Sequoia, who's taken her back and is bouncing with Gabri in her arms to try to soothe the baby. "She's crying in anger at the Dracans who took Pax away from us."

"Then we go in the morning," Sequoia says calmly, and my admiration for her grows even more.

38

PAX

The Dracans are active today, running up and down the hall outside my cell. I watch them carry canisters and wire, and I wonder if they're planning to blow us up. I wouldn't put it past them. Shaula would sacrifice all of them to gain what he wants. He'll only keep me alive long enough to trade me for Jewel. As soon as he has her, he'll kill me and everyone with me.

At first, I mistake the scratching noises in the wall for Dracans planting bombs, but they go on even after the lizards leave. I knock on the wall to scare off the rats, if that's what they are.

The wall knocks back. Sudden hope rushes into my head, and I knock again, this time in Morse code. There is no answer, but the scratching sound resumes.

My head buzzes and a voice, one I recognize from Jewel's communication with the Mantoid queen, says, *Stay away from the wall. The Ant People are digging for you.*

An image of ants busily digging is quickly replaced by an image of Queen Jaide, a praying mantis dressed in a cape attached to a high Elizabethan collar. It vibrates, and my head buzzes again.

You must be ready to move with them when the time is right. They weaken the wall and wait for my signal. Be ready.

Thank you, I send back, hoping this is a two-way conversation. *Does my family know where I am? Does Jewel?*

They know, she answers. *They come.*

I'm glad when the buzzing stops. My teeth felt it, and when I used my tongue to cushion them, it vibrated too. I can learn to read the pheromone-based language, although I won't be able to speak to them using it. The vibrational frequencies, on the other hand, are more than a little unpleasant to receive, even though Queen Jaide is adept at turning them into words Jewel and I understand.

I run through my katas to pass the time, and to make some noise when Dracans run past. I don't need to, because the Ants stop digging when they sense the vibrations of their feet on the stone. They can differentiate between my footsteps and the others.

When I get out of here, I'm going to hug Agateno, even if I have to hold my nose doing it. Then I'll hug whoever she told, everyone who got the word out to my friends and family.

Hope flows like a fountain, clearing out the cobwebs and drowning my despair. I am ready, Queen Jaide.

THE PURPOSEFUL STRIDE of my enemy alerts me, and I sit on the cot with my head in my hands, trying to look as dejected as I felt earlier.

"This may be your lucky day," Shaula bellows. "If not today, then surely by two days from now, when I set off the explosives I have planted here and in other places."

"What other places?" I ask, knowing he loves to brag. When the Ant People break me out of here, I'll share the information, and maybe we can save the people there.

"Atlantis will sink for the last time. Superstition Mountain will cover the Lost Dutchman Mine forever." His laughter is like a shredder on my nerves.

"How did you get explosives into those places? Aren't they searching for you? Aren't you a traitor on the run?" I'm goading him, my rage taking over my common sense.

His eyes narrow and he hisses through bared crocodile teeth, "I am the savior of my people. Those who oppose me are traitors. They intend to share Terra with your inferior race, vermin who took over the planet we settled before you had brains. You rats have overrun the surface. It rightfully belongs to Dracans. Terra will wipe herself clean of you, and then we will take it once again.

"And you, thief. You marked my woman, claiming her after she was already claimed. When your people come for you, they will witness what I do to those who take what is mine.

"Speaking of my woman," he says, his voice going quiet. "She waits outside. She has demanded to see you."

Already? What about my jailbreak? Is Jewel out there alone? Fear for her immobilizes me.

"Guards, bring him," Shaula says.

Two of them grab my arms, dragging me between them and marching so quickly I can't get my feet under me to match their pace. I don't want her seeing me like this.

As soon as they stop before two large metal doors, I get my balance, determined to walk out on my own. I failed her once when they captured me. I won't look like a coward this time.

When my eyes adjust to the light, she's there, her beautiful eyes examining me. I must look like Bigfoot with my beard and matted hair but the sight of her makes me want to run to her and hold her tightly. Then I picture her pushing me away and holding her nose, and I start to laugh. That would be just like her.

Shaula shoots me a warning look and draws himself to his full height.

"Where are the others?" he demands.

"I'm here," Jewel says. "You asked for me, didn't you? I'll come to you when you let him go."

"Hmmm. I expected a fight," Shaula says. "You are not as brave, or as smart as I thought. I can simply take you and keep your thief too."

She pulls a dagger out of a sash wrapped around her waist, and I notice she's wearing Dracan clothing.

"If you take a step toward me before you release Pax, I will use this on myself, and you will never have me."

"There is the spitfire I have grown to admire," Shaula says, placing his hands on his hips and running his tongue across his teeth.

"Very well. But you must come to me before I release him."

"Absolutely not," Jewel says, defiance in her eyes. She's a warrior princess, mimicking Shaula's arrogant stance.

"Then we are at an impasse," he says, trying to sound disappointed. "Let us try this again tomorrow, shall we? I would have my guards take you by force, but we both know your surrender must be voluntary. Besides, I know your people are hiding like cowards in the woods behind you. You have two days before I blow up Atlantis and Meissa's kingdom. And this one, of course, with every one of you inside."

He turns and struts back into the cliff. I struggle against the grip his goons have on me, but I can't get loose. I turn my head and she winks at me. Am I hallucinating?

She blows a kiss, and I watch her walk back into the forest.

39
STORM

That went well. Pax was filthy but appeared healthy. Knowing him, he's been working out, practicing his karate. Thinking about how he was attacked in a dark cave burns me up. He's a fighter, and I'll bet he did some damage before the monster took him down.

I want to rip up some boulders and smash those doors in, but I'll follow the plan. The Formicians will break through the wall and pull him out before Gabriella and Sequoia do their thing, and Juliana and I will take care of Shaula's leftover Dracans.

Jaina, whose left arm shows no sign of the break she suffered in the cavern, reports the giants and her people have scoured the country and haven't found any explosives outside. The Atlantean Dracans did their own search, using scanners, and found nothing. Still, they're helping Gienika's people evacuate, in case they missed something. Hopefully, the bombs he has inside the cliff aren't powerful enough to take the dome down.

Shaula was partially bluffing. I wonder if Atlantis and Superstition Mountain are really wired, or if that's a bluff, too. I guess we can't take the chance.

"I can't stand being near that monster," Jewel says, handing the dagger back to Jaina. It had belonged to her guard, who might be one of Shaula's prisoners if he survived the attack in the cave. "This had better work, or I'll need it back."

Sky hugs her friend tightly. "It'll work."

"I cannot wait to see what the baby and her mother do to the Dracans," Jaina says. "I must confess, I'm a bit skeptical."

"You didn't witness what they did to the invading ships on Andros," Wolf says, reaching for his daughter. "I have never been so proud."

"Might it have been a fluke?" Murphy asks. He was there. It looked deliberate to me.

"I don't think so," Sky replies. "Gabri is more aware than a baby her age should be. She knew they were enemies and dangerous, and she dealt with them. She also knows the same enemies are here, and as soon as we know Pax is clear, she knows what to do."

Jaina stiffens and gazes off into the woods. When she turns back, she says, "The Formicians can deliver Pax at any time, but they report they have found two more humans inside as well as an injured Mantoid who may be my guard. Dracan prisoners are in other cells."

Juliana jumps to her feet. "Can they get them out in time? They might be my parents. The Dracans would be Thuban's men."

"They have called more helpers. Should they bring Pax to us now?" Jaina asks.

"No," Jewel says. "Once they know he's escaped, there's no telling what they'll do to the others. It must be all or nothing. He would want it no other way."

Sequoia agrees, "We rescue them all. There is no other option."

"How long would it take the Formicians?" Charles asks.

Jaina responds, "I'm only estimating, but it could be an hour or two before the reinforcements arrive. In the meantime, the ones inside are already gnawing at the walls of the other cells. Queen Jaide thinks they will be ready by this time tomorrow."

"Then we'll have to put Shaula off one more time," Jewel says. "I don't know if I can do it again, or if he'll try to push things along by hurting Pax."

"We could rush him and grab Pax before he can make a move," I suggest.

"Yes," Sky retorts, "and he could have the detonator in hand when you do. Kaboom!"

"Didn't he wait to bring him out after you appeared today?" Sequoia asks. "Why don't we wait within earshot, and if he does not call to you, you won't have to face him again."

"If he does?" Jewel asks.

"Then we'll formulate a plan," Dylan says.

WE MEN TAKE turns standing guard, but it appears Shaula isn't interested in finding our camp. He's too arrogant to imagine we might have the upper hand. His pride will take a huge hit when we take him down. My grin turns into a yawn, and I scratch at a bug crawling in my hair.

"I wish Gienika and the giants were here," Sky says as she hands me a sandwich from the stores we brought with us. We're not setting campfires for obvious reasons.

"Where'd they go?" I ask, my mouth full of bread. Her nose wrinkles in disgust, and I grin.

"With Gienika and the Atlanteans, except for the ones left behind to search for bombs. I assume they'll follow the others. The mountains in Patagonia are full of caves where they can hide. They can live there, if necessary."

"What use would they be here?"

"Do you remember how big they are? The men are hunters, good with bows and arrows, as well as rifles. I'll bet the Dracans have no defense against arrows and sharpshooters."

"Other than their scales, you mean?" I take her hand and walk back toward the others.

"I believe the giants would easily find the chinks between the scales," Sky says. She's loyal to her friends.

I wish I could be as positive as she is. "The Atlantean Dracans will back us up when they return. They have effective weapons against their own kind."

Sky looks thoughtful and hesitates before answering. "We can't be sure they're all loyal to Thuban. They could turn on us."

JEWEL

P ax's aura was pale. The magenta appeared when he looked at me, but it was mostly black streaked with red. The blues and yellows were missing. It's more like Storm's aura now. I'm worried about the emotional toll this is taking on him.

I won't try to contact him through our connection, fearing Shaula can tap into it using his own, more tenuous, connection to me. I hate how badly I want the Dracan dead. I don't recognize myself anymore.

We're sitting a distance away from the door, waiting for Shaula's next move, and hoping to hear the Formicians have freed Pax and the other prisoners.

"Jewel," Jaina says, laying her hand on my shoulder. "The door is opening." She hands me her guard's dagger. I want to shove it into Shaula's heart.

The others remain hidden while I move into the clearing to confront our enemy. As expected, Pax is dragged out by the same two goons. Maybe the Ant People can get the others out while we're playing this insane drama.

Shaula's scales are darker than yesterday. He's losing patience.

"Have you reconsidered, woman?" His booming voice hits me in the pit of my stomach. I clutch the dagger in my waistband and draw from the strength Sky is sending.

"Yes," I answer.

"Well? What is your solution to this dilemma? Will you come to me?"

"Yes," I say again. "I will when you release Pax."

Shaula growls and hisses, barely getting out the words, "In that case, I will return him, but your people will have to put him back together."

He whips around and slashes his claws across Pax's face before anyone has a chance to react. He grunts and his legs go limp. The two goons hold him up by the arms. Blood soaks his shirt, pouring through the cuts on his torn cheek.

I scream, and Shaula pulls his fist back, ready for the next blow. It doesn't move. The monster roars in frustration, yanking with all his strength. He whips around to face me, running into his own stationary fist.

I'm no longer alone. Storm and Juliana flank me, both with their hands out. The Dracans holding Pax let him go and fly off to each side, crashing into the cliff wall. While Storm and his sister are dealing with them, Shaula grabs him and runs into the doorway, slamming it shut. I run after them, banging on the door and screaming Pax's name.

Sky tries to calm me down, but I reject her attempts. Gabriella's sweet calm pushes me over the edge, and I collapse and weep. My mother uses the link to say, *We have this. Come here.*

She puts her arm around me and pulls me away from the door, leading me back to the others.

Then Sequoia begins to sing.

"Stop!" I shout. "You could hurt him!"

A picture framed in emotion forms in my mind, Pax encased in a bubble of love, Dracans lying on the ground around him. I understand what Gabriella is saying and pray she and her mother can keep him safe.

Sequoia resumes her song, a chant that grows in power as she repeats the Cherokee words. When my heartbeat matches the rhythm of the tune, and the hair on my arms stands on end, Gabriella laughs. Her sweet laughter transforms, travels along the waves of her mother's song, and blows the door open, continuing its movement through the corridors and into every crevasse in the cliff, traveling through the mountain like the tones of a ringing bell.

Storm and Juliana have their hands out toward the cliff, and I tap the wristband to link with them, finding Sky and Murphy already there. We concentrate on the sound, following it into the mountain in our minds. We find Pax unconscious, and Storm lifts him and builds a protective bubble around him. Juliana floats him along as we follow the sound deeper. We withdraw after we come to the empty cells where the Formicians have broken through, knowing the other prisoners have been released.

There isn't a single Dracan in the mountain. Are they all dead, or did they escape?

The Atlanteans had returned in time to see what we did, and some run into the cliff as soon as the sound stops. I hope they kill Shaula if the sound didn't do it.

Wolf catches Sequoia and the baby when his wife staggers after ending the song. He gently lowers them to the ground and takes Gabri from her arms. He sits, leaning against a tree, and cushions Sequoia's head on his lap while he cradles their baby.

Sky and I rush to where Dylan and Coral are checking their son for injuries. He remains unconscious, thankfully, while they riffle through a Dracan first aid kit for supplies. His cheek has been ripped to shreds, exposing bone, gums, and teeth on the left side of his face. I fight back nausea, and hold his hand, crooning wordlessly, sending love and strength in the tune. Sky kneels next to me, her hand on his foot, pouring her love into him.

Why aren't the Allarans here? They'd know how to fix Pax, wouldn't they? Then I remember they can't come into Dracan territory with their ships.

A Dracan squats next to Coral and hands her a salve for his face. "Pull the skin together and cover it with this. It will help knit the wound and protect it from infection," he instructs her.

"It's shredded," she cries, her face twisted in her effort to hold back tears.

"I am a medic," the Dracan answers. "I will help."

He uses his claws like precision instruments after pouring a disinfecting solution over them. In a few minutes, Pax's face is glistening with the ointment gluing it together, and Coral lays a clean sterile pad over it. The Dracan gently wraps a bandage around the pad and the back of his head, covering his ear while avoiding his jaw.

I point out other places where his injuries show up brown in his aura. Several ribs are cracked, and his right shoulder has been dislocated. My dad helps his father pop the shoulder back into place, waking him up with the sudden jolt.

He regains consciousness fighting, sending weak punches into the air until Sky sends him calm.

"Sky?" he asks, wincing with pain. "Jewel?"

"Don't talk," his sister says. "You're safe with us now. We're taking you home."

An Atlantean soldier waves Dad and Dylan to the side. "We have retrieved the other prisoners," he says. "Our men will report to Thuban when they've been tended to. The two humans are asking for Pax. Jaina is with the Mantoid we found with them."

Relieved Jaina's guard survived and he hadn't betrayed us to Shaula, I watch Juliana pull a bedraggled woman into her arms, while a skinny, bearded man wraps his arms around both. Storm stands nearby but doesn't approach them.

The link opens, and she says, *Storm, come greet our parents.*

Tears flood my eyes as the man, Tom Ryder, turns to his son for the first time in over twenty years, Atlantis time. The woman's voice rises in a wail as she reaches for her son. Trembling, he wraps his arms around his mother.

Wolf and Sequoia approach them, Wolf still holding the sleeping baby.

While a wormhole warped time in Atlantis, twenty years had passed with Tom and Salali believing their son had died in a deadly car accident. Shaula convinced Thuban he'd rescued them, but we know better now. It's been a little over eight years for us since Storm, just ten years old at the time, thought his parents had died.

Sky stays with me, tears pouring down her face. She keenly feels their joy and the agony of having missed so much. I hug her and say, "Shaula will pay for this. If he isn't already dead, we'll make him pay."

"We must go," the Dracan calls to them. "If we have not found all the explosives, and they are on a timer, we do not have long before it blows."

"Did you find Shaula?" my father asks him.

"No," the Dracan answers. "He has fled, or he is in hiding. I am sorry, but we must leave now."

I look around for Jaina, but she and her guard are gone. I hope they've gotten the Formicians out of danger.

Storm floats Pax into the ship, and we crowd in around him. Juliana and Murphy are with her parents, Wolf, and Sequoia in the other ship. I can't wait to get him home to Andros.

STORM

E xhaustion hits as soon as we're dropped off. Juliana and I float our parents up to the house, giving them my room, and then I float Pax into his, settling him on his bed. Sky and Jewel won't leave his side, so I trudge back to our place and crash on the couch. I'm asleep before my head hits the cushion.

I'M STRANGELY LIGHT this morning. We haven't heard whether the giant's dome was destroyed or survived. Shaula is still on the loose, Pax is badly injured, and my parents are like strangers. And still, a load has been lifted off me. Why?

An Allaran ship materializes over the beach and hovers there as Baran, Belena, and Maia descend from the portal. It disappears when they're on the ground and Belena waves as they make their way across the sand. Where were they yesterday?

Baran wisely stays silent while Belena speaks. Her voice doesn't affect me as much as it once did. I guess some of the nectar's effects are permanent.

"We have brought something to help Pax heal," she says. "We are happy you have reunited with your parents."

"Why weren't you there to help us?" I ask.

Maia answers, "We are forbidden to enter the Dracans' domain without express permission. You know this. We did not have it."

I nod. I'll give them the benefit of the doubt. Along with their excuse that Creator wouldn't let them, it's the same reason they gave us for not rescuing Jewel when she was in Atlantis. I open the door and invite them in.

My father, cleaned up, freshly shaven, and with his hair cut short, stands to his feet when they walk in. The Allarans tower over him but bend to take his offered hand to shake it.

When Baran speaks, I watch Dad closely for the reaction we human males have to the Allaran males. He isn't affected at all. Has he been drinking the nectar?

"I am sorry your stay on Allara was unpleasant. Had we known you were there, you would not have suffered, and we would have returned you to your family quickly. We do not tolerate cruelty, nor do we welcome Dracans to our planet."

Wolf struggles to hold his temper, while Sequoia offers the Allarans seats. She's never reacted as strongly as the rest of us, either to the males or the females, whose voices turn our women into raging beasts.

My mother comes out of my room holding Gabriella. The baby reaches for Maia. Maybe children aren't affected like adults. Maia holds her up to get a good look at her and smiles.

"This child is exceptional," she says. "She has greeted me by showing me my face with a bubble over it. I have never experienced such a thing."

"Exceptional may be too mild a word to describe her," Wolf responds, beaming with pride.

My mother is at peace, looking much better than she did yesterday. She comes straight over to me, ignoring the Allarans, and hugs me tightly. The smell of her clean hair overwhelms me with memories, and I kiss the top of her head. Suddenly, she's my mom again, and I'm her ten-year-old. I hold back tears, letting my rage against Shaula rise. He will die painfully.

Wolf turns to Baran and asks, "Did Shaula blow up the dome?"

"He failed," Baran answers. "No explosives were found in Atlantis or Superstition Mountain. He was bluffing. The few the Dracans managed to plant inside the cliff were found and dismantled by Thuban's men."

I'm glad Gienika doesn't have to relocate her tribe of giants.

Belena reaches into a pouch at her side and pulls out a crystal bottle the size of a flask. "We have a gift for you," she says, and I know immediately what it is. I want to warn the others, but the craving isn't there anymore. Has the burden been lifted? Maybe I'm not as addicted as I thought I was.

"The Aracai have gifted us with their nectar as long as we have been on Allara. They are sentient plants who respond to tones sung by their singers. Ours is a symbiotic relationship. The singers care for the Aracai, and they, in turn, produce this nectar."

Maia breaks in, "We need it on Allara to stay warm because our weak red sun keeps our planet cold. The nectar also heals us and gives us strength. Its properties change as the singers' change their tones. We consume food as well, but if we had none, the nectar would sustain us."

Baran says, "When Storm stayed with my sister and her family, the nectar kept him warm and changed his reaction to our voices. We believe he was the first human to drink it undiluted. We watched him carefully to assess his reaction to it. It did not cause him harm. Storm, will you tell us if you have noted anything else?"

The grimace on Wolf's face, and his struggle to stay calm when Baran speaks, let me know it's time to tell them everything.

"My rage subsided," I say, seeing his eyebrows lift in surprise. "I saw the Allarans as people and didn't react to their voices, and the temperature in the cavern became like an early summer day, after I nearly froze to death in arctic clothing. All that was with one sip."

Baran smiles and is about to say something else when I continue.

"The effects began to fade in Heliade. The male voices were more strident and the women more seductive. When the rage returned, I knew it was wearing off. Still, it isn't nearly as bad as it was before. The rage is focused on Shaula and stays there. Your voices mildly affect me.

"What bothers me the most is the way I've been craving more. I've had to fight my need for it, and now that you're here, I didn't want to say anything about its addictive properties because I badly want more of it."

"Why did you tell us?" Baran asks.

"To save my people the pain of addiction. They'd be fine while it's available. But if, like me, they go through days or longer without it, the need for it grows. At least it did until this morning."

My father's voice is gruff when he speaks. I wonder what Shaula did to him.

"Storm is right," he says. "One of the Dracan guards had access to the Aracai nectar. He sometimes put a drop of it in water when he brought us our daily meal. Not every day. Only when we were close to freezing to death. We also craved it, which added to our discomfort. It saved Pax's life, as well."

"Thank you for your honesty," Baran says. "Our council has discussed making the Aracai available to you. We know they will survive in your atmosphere. They are impervious to weather patterns and temperatures, and they do not use photosynthesis like your Terran plants. We have them in our bases here and in your moon, and they thrive."

"The moon?" Sequoia asks.

"When Creator banished us from the surface of Terra to the skies, we settled in Luna. Someday, we will show you our cities there. For now, Pax needs the nectar to recover from his injuries, and you will benefit from it, as well. It will give you four the strength to save Terra and Allara."

"When you have completed your task," he shares, "we will make sure you have a limitless supply."

Sequoia touches my arm and says, "You said you craved it until this morning. What changed?"

"Maybe the effects wore off, or I've gone through withdrawal. I felt light this morning, and it may have been because I don't need it anymore."

"And now?" she asks.

"I want more of it, but I can live without it."

"In that case," Wolf says, "we accept your gift."

"One drop a day will be enough," Belena says. "More will not hurt you, but it would be wasteful."

"I'll administer it," Sequoia says. As our Medicine Woman, no one would dare argue with her.

"You need not serve any to us," Maia says. "We have had ours."

My aunt pours a glass of water for each of us and carefully lets one drop fall from the bottle into each glass. The warmth and sense of well-being flooding me with that first sip is enough.

I WALK with Maia to Sky's house, knowing everyone else is there tending to Pax and comforting each other.

"Do you have enough for all of us?" I ask.

"I have two more bottles," she responds, sounding normal once again. "There is one for each family, enough to last two weeks or more."

"And then?" I ask.

"By then, we hope you will have solved our planets' problems."

42
SKY

Pax's pain is exhausting. I experience every twinge, every sharp stab of it, and send a constant stream of comfort.

I'm here, Sky. Jewel's calm voice in my head reminds me she's lending me every bit of her own strength, pouring her love through me into my brother.

I know, I respond. *I couldn't do this without you and my parents. When Storm gets here, he'll help, too.* Where the heck is he? I send him a jab of annoyance, hoping it'll hit where it hurts. I need him now.

"Ouch," he says as he comes in and holds the door open for an Allaran female. I send him another one.

"Cut it out," he says. I'm about to jab him again when she speaks, and I want to rip her eyes out.

"We are sorry we have kept him from you, Sky. We have brought something to help Pax."

"Hear her out," Storm says to everyone in the room. "This is Maia, and what she's brought will help him heal faster."

She pulls a crystal bottle out of a bag hanging from her belt.

"I will explain what this is, but for now, Coral, please put two drops in some water and give it to him."

"How do we know you aren't poisoning him?" Mom asks, responding as we all do to the Allaran females.

"Do as she says," Dad instructs her. "Maia would never harm Pax or any of us." I can tell he's star-struck by the way his voice softened as he said Maia's name. He's in trouble now.

"Let me," Storm says, taking the bottle to the kitchen. "I've had this, and I can vouch for it and for Maia."

Now he's in trouble too, with me.

We follow him into Pax's room. I can't stand watching my brother writhing in pain, but he can't stay still. I send him as much calm as I can to soothe the stabbing in his face and chest.

Storm takes a straw, dips it in the glass, puts his finger over the top and lets a tiny bit of liquid drip into Pax's mouth. After he does it three times, my brother's breathing stabilizes, and I feel the agony lift.

"More," he croaks. Storm patiently repeats the process until he relaxes into sleep.

"What's in that stuff?" I ask.

Storm hugs me and walks me into the kitchen, while Jewel stays by Pax's side, holding his hand.

"Maia will explain," he says, "but you need to try it now. One drop a day in some water will change your life."

"You sound like a drug dealer. What is wrong with you?"

He laughs and bends to kiss me. "Absolutely nothing. Now you go listen to Maia while I fix your drinks."

It's difficult to listen to her speak in that cheese grater voice, but I take a sip from the cup, and her voice normalizes. She suddenly sounds like any female, smooth and melodic. My animosity drains away, and what she's saying makes perfect sense.

I had wondered about the Aracai in Heliade. I witnessed a singer harvesting nectar but didn't know what it was or why the plant followed her.

When Maia tells us about Storm drinking the nectar on Allara, and how a tiny bit every few days saved Tom, Salali, and Pax, I know the Allarans have brought us a miracle.

"Mom? Dad?" Pax's voice sounds strong from the bedroom. Mom jumps up and runs to him, and the rest of us follow, crowding into his doorway and spreading around the room.

"My face feels strange," he says, "but it doesn't hurt. Did everyone get out?"

43
PAX

The hot sand crunches under my bare feet. I hold my girl close, nestled into my side as we walk toward the aquamarine bay. She glances up, and her smile sends a pleasant jolt of heat through me. If only life could always be this sweet. A sharp twinge in my cheek reminds me we're only here until I'm strong enough to leave. I feel ready now, but I haven't told anyone. The Allaran nectar has done wonders since they dropped it off yesterday.

Once we've saved our planet and Allara, the nectar will revolutionize medicine. Mankind will be at peace, and all the races will get along. Jewel and I will spend our lives together, and it'll be just like this every day–and I'm dreaming. We're a long way from world peace with two massive threats hanging over us: Shaula and our dying world.

"I'm almost sure we can save the world once we figure out how to tune it," she says, "but first we have to deal with Shaula." I'm not surprised she can track my thoughts even without using our connection.

"He wants to wipe out humanity and doesn't care how he does it. I don't think he understands that no one, not even Dracans, will survive Terra's destruction. If he gets wind of our plan, he'll do anything to stop it."

"Tuning a planet is impossible, isn't it?" I ask, turning to face her.

"Murphy's parents are working on something to magnify sound waves along the ley lines. Queen Jaide has mentioned resonance, and her people communicate with vibrations. The Allarans use music to get the nectar from the Aracai and remember what Sequoia and Gabri did to Shaula's ships and your prison with song and laughter. Vega told us we're in tune with the artifacts. It all ties together, somehow."

She gives me a pleading look and starts walking into the waves lapping at the shore. I follow her, wading in ankle-deep water. I know love has its own resonance. Just being near her makes every nerve in me vibrate.

I'm eager to swim out toward the trench. The mineral-rich salt-water will burn my face for a minute, but it'll go a long way toward healing the cuts. Jewel kicks up water as she shuffles in the shallows.

I hate that she refuses to use our connection to communicate, although I understand she's afraid Shaula will listen in. My wristband is useless, and her father needs his lab to make me another one.

"How did Shaula manage to break my wristband? I miss our link," I say, to break the silence.

"You know Dad. He'll figure it out when he opens it up, which will be the first thing he does when we get home." She laughs and explains, "He gets so focused, Mom has to remind him to eat."

"We don't have much time. How will we put all the pieces together into a working plan?"

"We'll need the technology Ashley and Leonis are working on. I also want to know why the Allarans sent us to places where the arti-facts are functioning well. What was that about? Too many things don't add up, and until the questions are answered, and we have full coopera-tion from everyone who sees things as we do, we won't have what we need."

"How do you propose we pull it off?" I ask, bending to splash water on my head, relishing the burn on my cheek.

"We'll ask to meet with the major players, except for Shaula, of course." She watches for my reaction to the monster's name. The nectar affects me the same way it does Storm. Calm has replaced intense rage. How is she responding?

"The last time we did that, it didn't go as we'd hoped," I remind her. "Nothing was resolved, and we're no closer to an answer than we were then."

"Maybe we should talk to Thuban about who should be there. Some of the Allarans, of course, and Jaina, Queen Jaide, Meissa, Gienika, Jayman..." She trails off and grabs my arm.

I lace my fingers with hers. "What about asking Dr. Julian Emery, Izzy, and Gabe to work with us? They know the sea and have seen Triton and the Sea Dwellers."

She nods and adds, "Jack Austin has explored a lot of ancient, mysterious places. He and Al would be helpful in finding a place powerful enough to do what we need."

"Which is?" I persist.

"To find the tone that will bring all the artifacts into balance and hit all of them with it at the same time."

"A tone? I didn't hear one when we fixed the first five artifacts. Did you?" I see where she's going with this, and it would make sense except for that one fact.

"Maybe tone is the wrong word. When we fixed them, what did we do?"

"You know. Why would you ask me?"

"Humor me."

"We sent them love. I can't imagine why it works, but the first artifact showed us how."

"The watchers told us they're failing for lack of minerals the Dracans use to build their cities. How does love fix that? What if they lied or were mistaken? What's the opposite of love?"

"I'd say hatred, but that isn't always true. Apathy, maybe." Storm tried to feign indifference to Sky, but she saw through it, even with his wall up.

She turns and walks deeper into the bay. The water is at our knees, and I'm ready to dive in.

"Consider this, and then we'll swim. Everything has a frequency.

The scents you pick up have unique frequencies, and you told me about the vibrations the Formicians and Mantoids use for communication."

"That's right," I answer. "I think I can learn their language."

Her smile is all the encouragement I need.

She says, "Love has its own frequency, and it's the opposite of whatever is killing the artifacts. Help me find what that is. Then we can change the tone and fix everything at once."

She dives in, and I'm right behind her. When this is over, we'll take as much time as we want to explore these waters together.

Forgetting everything, we dive after each other, racing to touch bottom first in water at least eight feet deep. A shadow suddenly turns the water dark, and I push off and shoot to the surface. She breaks the surface a second before I do, and we stare up at the bottom of a Dracan ship.

"Shaula?" I ask, dreading the answer.

"No, not this time," she says, filling me with relief. If she isn't sensing the snake, then he isn't in there. I wonder who is.

"I'll race you back," I challenge, and start swimming, grinning as she easily passes me.

We stop in the shallows, playfully splashing each other until we spot the entourage on the beach. A shiver races up my spine. It's Meissa, and she doesn't look happy.

44
JEWEL

Pax wraps me in a towel and puts his arm around me. We watch the ship take off and disappear, leaving Meissa and three other Dracans on the beach. The others are already gathered around them, and I hear my mother inviting them up to the house for lunch. Pax's nose twitches at the scent of grilling fish, and my stomach rumbles.

When Meissa spots us, her yellow eyes light up, and she gives me a toothy reptilian grin. If her casual clothing, a colorful batik tunic over loose white pants, is meant to put us at ease, it isn't working for me. I wonder what new challenge she's about to hit us with. Instinctively, I glance up at the five sentinels glinting in the sun, and they calm me. I doubt Meissa knows they're there.

She's in her human form, Pax informs me, knowing I can't see her that way.

"Jewel Adams," she calls. "I am glad you are here."

Smile, Sky reminds me. *Don't antagonize her.*

Thanks, I reply, putting on my best smile for the Dracan queen.

"It's my pleasure to see you again, Queen Meissa," I say, reaching for her clawed hand. It's disorienting to feel a human hand take mine while my eyes see a Dracan one.

"I am pleased you are healing well, Paxton Fletcher," she says. "I am truly happy you are both safe with your families, but I fear it will not be for long."

There it is. This has to do with Shaula, no doubt.

"Come and have a meal with us," Wolf says. "Sequoia is waiting with our baby, who would love to meet you." He gestures toward the veranda, where Sequoia holds Gabriella perched on her hip. The baby is focused on Meissa.

I decide if Gabri accepts the Dracan queen, then I'll bury my suspicions. She's the best judge of character I know.

He offers his arm to the queen and escorts her to the veranda, followed by her three guards and then the rest of us. As soon as they reach the top, Gabri opens her arms and leans toward Meissa.

"It's okay," Sequoia says. "Take her. She's eager to meet you."

I watch Meissa's face soften while Gabri settles on her hip, gazing at her eyes the whole time. The two stare at each other for a moment, until the queen's expression changes to complete incredulity and she exclaims, "This is impossible!"

She quickly hands the baby back to her mother and walks to the other end of the veranda, her back to us. Her scales have darkened, but she isn't angry. Everyone would know if she were. Gabri watches her for a moment and then reaches for Sky.

We leave Meissa alone while we set up for lunch. The boys bring the table and chairs from the dining area to the veranda. Juliana floats the dishes from the cupboard to the table, and Murphy brings out the flatware. It's another perfect Bahamian day, with scattered clouds offering brief splashes of shade from the blazing sun. Dad, Tom, and Dylan finish grilling the fish and place it on a platter while Mom, Salali, and Coral bring out fresh loaves of bread, and bowls of salad and coconut rice. Tom and Salali are already healthier, thanks to the sun and great food, but I can't help but notice the sadness Salali tries to hide every time she looks at her son.

When all is ready, Meissa returns and takes a seat with the women at the table. She watches Gabri play with the food on her highchair tray, nibbling on pieces of fish and smearing rice into her hair while Sequoia coaxes her to eat homemade baby food.

The guards eat in silence, standing by the railing, which is wide enough to hold their dishes. The rest of us sit in scattered chairs, balancing plates on our laps. We attempt to lighten things up by talking about diving the reef.

Meissa watches intently while Storm and Juliana clear the dishes using telekinesis. Her scales begin to brighten, and by the time the cleanup is finished, they're gleaming in the sun.

The queen breaks her silence. "Your child is more extraordinary than I imagined, Sequoia. When I received the prophecy concerning her, I could not imagine how it could be true. A mere human. And yet, here she is, showing me a future bright with promise, more than I would have dared hope for. She also showed me if you fail to complete your mission, Star Children, there is no future for any of us."

The term the Allarans use for us sounds odd coming from a Dracan, but then Jaina also called us Star Children. The name has stuck.

When the realization hits, the blood drains from my face. I tap my wristband and ask, *Since when is Gabriella foretelling the future?*

Juliana asks, *what did she show Meissa about hers?*

Sky sends a blast of annoyance and sadness. *How did I miss this gift in her? She's not only the strongest empath on the planet with a weapon that can take down Dracan ships, but she's also a prophet. What else?*

We turn as Gabri laughs and claps her hands, splattering baby food all over Sequoia's face. In my mind, the faces of my friends are each ringed in brilliant colors, each colored in love. Gabri's gift. Joy rises in me, and I realize we have nothing to fear, no matter how powerful she turns out to be.

JEWEL

The Dracan guards talk quietly with Murphy and Juliana at the far corner of the veranda while Sequoia and Wolf take their baby inside. Storm and Juliana's parents follow while the other adults excuse themselves, as if they know the queen came to speak with us.

She relaxes on a lounge chair between mine and Sky's and the boys lean against the railing. The ocean breeze cools my skin in the sun's heat and I long to dive into the bay.

Meissa breaks the peace. "What do you need to repair the planet, Jewel Adams?"

She's taken me by surprise. All I can think of is to destroy Shaula, but it won't fix the problem. Sky opens the link and suggests, *Cooperation.*

We already have it, but we need specifics, I answer. *What can the Dracans contribute other than what Ashley and Leonis are doing?*

Storm adds, *Tell her your theory about resonance. Maybe she can brainstorm with us.*

I agree, Pax says. He can listen in through our connection but can only speak to me without his wristband. *Meissa could call the meeting we talked about.*

When I turn to face her, Meissa is staring at me with a look bordering on impatience.

"Queen Meissa, we must tune the planet to its normal frequency. Thuban's people are working on an amplifier that would reach all the artifacts at once, but we'll need everyone's cooperation to pull it off if they succeed."

"What, exactly, will this amplifier transmit to the artifacts?"

"Shaula and the Dracan kings laughed when I told them how we repaired the tetrahedra, but I only spoke the truth, Meissa. We each placed one hand on the symbol facing us, and one hand on top of the person's hand next to us until we all touched both the tetrahedron and each other. Then we sent a blast of love into it, amplified by Sky's gift. Each responded with gratitude, then pushed us away and started spinning normally."

I expect laughter or at least a derisive snort, but she sighs, watching a few clouds drift by. "Do you expect your love to transmit to all the artifacts? Is Sky's gift powerful enough, even with the aid of an amplifier? How would it help to tune the planet? What does love have to do with frequency?"

Before I can answer, one of her guards rushes over and says something in their language. She gets to her feet, talking rapidly.

Atlantis is under attack, Murphy translates. *Two Allaran ships have fired on the city, damaging the landing port.*

Everyone but Pax starts talking at once through the link. Pressure builds in my head, but it's nothing compared to the sudden pain in my heart. The Allarans? No. Impossible.

"Queen Meissa," I call, while she hurries down the stairs to the sand. "Please wait! Allow us to contact the Allarans. What if this is another of Shaula's tricks?"

She pauses and glares at me. "There is no time to waste, Jewel Adams. Contact your friends, but if they are indeed attacking our people, then Terra will not survive the war they have begun."

She points a claw at Murphy. "You relay their answer to King Thuban. Quickly. Retaliation will be swift unless Thuban orders otherwise."

Meissa strides to the beach. Her ship appears out of nowhere, but only because of its speed. They don't have the cloaking technology of the Allarans. In a moment, they're gone.

4 6

SKY

My heart pounds so hard it shakes my entire body, sending me into a cold sweat. I break the link, unable to process what the others are saying. War?

"Take it easy," Pax says. He pushes peace toward me, but I can't receive it. I take quick shallow breaths as the panic builds.

Gabri's piercing screams from inside the house send a shock wave through me, and instinctively, I send her love, which brings me back to myself. In return, she sends a picture of my face with a love bubble and stops crying.

"We need a plan of action," Storm says, with so much concern in his eyes, I realize how my emotions have affected everyone. I send out a wave of peace.

He continues. "First we need to let our folks know what's going on. Together, we'll help Sequoia call the Allarans. Murphy, once we've heard from them, you contact your people in Atlantis. I know the Allarans aren't behind this."

I wish I could be sure. I haven't trusted them since they led us to a bunch of dead ends. I still resent them for not letting us know where Storm was when they had him on their planet.

As soon as we've linked to each other and our parents, Sequoia sends out the call to the Allarans. There must be an easier way to contact them.

We hear, Star Children. The voice is Maia's.

We are aware of the conflict with Atlantis, and we are not involved, she assures us before we ask.

Why do they believe you're attacking them? I ask.

They have been tricked, and we suspect those behind this are blocking our attempts to reach Thuban, she replies.

It's Shaula. I hear the growl in Storm's thought, or maybe I simply feel it.

As we also believe. We must stop him before the city launches a counterattack on us. An ensuing war would ensure the destruction of Terra and Allara before the artifacts can be repaired.

Murphy and Juliana leave the link and go down to the beach. I wonder if he's in mental communication with someone in Atlantis, or if he's using a Dracan device. Would the Allarans have a device we could use to reach them? In minutes, they head back and rejoin the link.

Maia sounds calm as she asks, *Murphy, what have you discovered about the conflict in Atlantis? Does Thuban believe we are not involved?*

Her smooth voice comforts me, which is saying a lot for the nectar.

Murphy responds, *Thuban knows you would not have attacked unprovoked, but until now, he believed Shaula's allies goaded you into battle. Two Allaran ships fired upon the dome, damaging the landing docks. At the same time, Dracans sympathetic to Shaula rose up and are now fighting the residents of the city, while the soldiers in the outer ring are preparing to battle Allarans.*

Where did Shaula get two Allaran ships? Jewel asks.

Perhaps he stole them while he was on our planet, Maia responds. *No one expected Dracans to reach our world, and we were unaware of his presence there.*

Murphy reveals what he'd learned. *Thuban has asked Meissa to evacuate my parents. They have finished their project and will take it with them. She'll bring them here.*

What about Max, Marla, and the kids? Marla's mother? I ask.

Murphy nods. I hope it means they're coming, too.

We will transport you to Blue Mountain when they arrive, Maia says.

Home sounds good right now. The way things are going, it may be the last time we see it.

~

WHEN THE DRACAN ship swoops in to hover over the bay, I send assurance to Gabriella, secure in her mother's arms. She giggles, and when she senses my concern she might attack the ships, she sends a picture of Meissa with a love bubble, instantly relaxing me.

You're a super baby, I say, even though she can't hear my thoughts. When she smiles and sends me love, I wonder. Is she naturally telepathic, too?

Meissa floats down the portal beam, every inch the warrior queen dressed in golden armor with a tall red crest adorning her helmet. Avery Snow comes down next, clutching the hands of her twin granddaughters. As soon as they touch the sand, the girls pull away and run toward us.

"Where's Donny?" asks Khatryn. She's dressed in a short yellow tunic over white shorts, while her identical twin Sha'lat is wearing a blue top.

"I want to see the baby," her sister calls out.

Sequoia bends to let Gabri greet the girls. Khatryn's cheerful face deflates when she explains Donny is not here.

While the girls get acquainted with the baby, Max, Marla, Ashley, and Leonis drop down, followed by a half-dozen Dracans unloading equipment from the ship to the sand while Meissa supervises. I watch as five frosted glass domes, each at least as tall as I am, are the last to be unloaded, and I notice how carefully the Dracans set them down. They must be the amplifiers. The scientists check each piece over carefully as Meissa and Thuban's family stride toward us.

Avery's regal bearing and the fierce determination on her face match Meissa's. The two queens, one human and the other Dracan, love their people and will do anything to protect them.

"Jewel Adams," Meissa calls, gesturing for my friend to approach.

Everyone except Sequoia gathers around them.

"What's the situation in Atlantis?" Wolf asks.

"The uprising was a surprise to Thuban and me," Avery answers. "Shaula has more influence among our people than we imagined, and the fighting in the city is still fierce. Many of Shaula's traitors are in the king's own army, and they are well-trained and well-armed."

"I heard him brag about how he's infiltrated both Atlantis and your base in Arizona, Queen Meissa," Tom says. "In fact, while we were held in the cliff prison, a Dracan guard told me his sympathizers were planting bombs in those locations."

"We found no explosives in our base," Meissa assures him. "Thuban had Atlantis swept for explosives and found none there, either. Perhaps Shaula was lying, or he might have been obliquely referring to the Dracans he had planted within the cities."

"In any case," Avery says, "Thuban will end the uprising while you save the world."

"And Shaula?" Pax asks.

Meissa answers, "He is already dead, even though he is not yet aware of it. Do not concern yourselves with that matter, Star Children."

Her words are no comfort. I pray for the people of Atlantis and dread the damage this could cause that beautiful city. I pray they find and destroy Shaula, but he's always one step ahead. We haven't seen the last of that monster.

STORM

Meissa and Avery walk back to the ship while Max and Marla greet us with hugs and back slaps. Murphy and Juliana are in an animated conversation with his parents near domes that could be giant opaque snow globes. I hope they work, even though I still don't understand what they're supposed to do.

Meissa enters her ship, and they're gone in seconds. Two Allaran ships appear as soon as the Dracans clear out. Juliana and I help load them with the Dracan gear, suitcases, and tons of baby paraphernalia. Who knew a baby needs that much stuff?

"What are you thinking?" Sky asks, coming up behind me. I turn and pull her into my arms for a quick embrace, kissing the top of her head. So much power in such a small woman.

"Why not use the link and find out?" I tease. Then the seriousness of the situation hits me. "Do you understand what all that equipment is for?"

"No, but whatever it is, I hope it helps us tune the world."

"It seems impossible," I say, trying not to project my hopelessness. It doesn't work. She picks up every nuance of my emotions.

"Come on, Storm. Everything that's happened to us is unimaginable. We live in that realm. What's one more challenge?" She sends me a nudge of joy, small but effective. I can do the impossible for her.

WHEN WE ARRIVE at the meadow outside Jewel's house, it's fully dark. Juliana and I concentrate on floating the glass domes into the garage, where a freight elevator hidden behind a secret panel in the back wall takes us down to the basement lab. It takes five trips. Meanwhile, everyone else loads their gear into cars or brings it into the house.

Avery and her family are staying with Charles and Analiese, in two of the guest rooms. Juliana and Sky move cots into Jewel's room, where the three girls will stay. Mom and Dad are taking over Juliana's room at our cabin.

It's nearly midnight by the time we're finished, and I'm as beat as everyone else. Pax and Murphy drop me off at our cabin, while my parents ride with Wolf and Sequoia.

They help us unload and head back to Pax's house, while I stagger into bed for the first good sleep in a long time.

WOLF AND DAD have already gone to town for supplies when I pull my dirt bike from the shed. My shirt clings to my back in the humid air, already hot at nine in the morning. The wind should bring relief as soon as I start moving. Wolf's extra gasoline container is still half-full, and I pour it into the tank. I put the container back, secure my backpack to the bike, kick it into gear, and take off for one of my favorite hangouts, the secret Cherokee cave near the ceremonial stomping grounds on Black Bluff. A Dracan ship nearly killed me there, and it's where I met Vega for the first time. It's also where the watchers told us not to touch the quartz in the crystal cavern, which they claimed feeds the artifacts. We thought they were lying, but I'm no longer convinced they were. I want to get another look at the cavern.

I never get tired of riding the back trails in the mountains of North

Carolina. Cool air under the trees and in unexpected pockets intersect the sun-heated clearings, like flying through layered currents. Deeply rutted paths dotted with loose gravel, rocks, broken branches, and tangled brambles require my complete attention, giving my mind a rest from all other concerns.

Arriving at the stomping grounds, I park the bike under the Wolf Clan shelter, one of seven around the center square. Gratitude rises in me. Has the nectar restored my faith in God? I give thanks to Creator for my family, my friends, and especially for Sky. Even if we don't succeed, I've lived more in these last ten months than in my entire life. My parents are alive and living with me, I have a newly discovered sister, I've met aliens, ancient earth dwellers, mermen, and even a dragon, and love has replaced overwhelming rage.

The path is impossible to spot for anyone who doesn't know where it is, but I find it easily and make my way to the cave.

"You didn't really think you could get away from us, did you?"

48
STORM

S ky glares down at me from one of the boulders I tossed at the Dracan ship last year. With her wild red hair and flashing eyes, she's a super woman standing with fists on her hips. I laugh, and she hits me with a bolt of annoyance. Ouch.

"I wasn't trying to run away," I say, and laugh again. "You know you can contact me anytime. Why didn't you?"

We wanted to surprise you, Jewel answers, opening the communal link and climbing up next to her friend. As I round the boulder, the rest of them come into view.

What took you so long? Juliana asks. *We've been here for hours.*

Not hours, Murphy corrects her. *Maybe one hour.*

"There you are," Pax says. I hope Charles can get his wristband working soon.

"Why are you here?" I ask out loud for his sake.

"We thought we should visit the crystal cave again. Jewel has a theory. The crystals might be a piece of the puzzle," he responds.

"We're on the same wavelength," I say. "I came up to check it out, too."

Pax picks up his backpack and heads into the cave, followed by the rest. We drop our packs near the large, broken stalagmite marking the passageway to the crystal cavern and grab our water bottles and headlamps.

"Before we go in," he says, "let's hear her theory."

I find a spot against a smooth rock and pull Sky down next to me. The others form a rough circle, and Jewel says, "You already know most of this."

"Jaina's people gave me my first hint when the artifact in Peru responded to their humming. Since then, everything and everyone is pointing toward sound as being the answer to repairing the artifacts.

"Consider how often we've experienced sound waves being used to affect something else. The Allarans sing to get nectar from their Aracai. The Formicians, Mantoids, and even humans communicate with sound waves. You saw the power of sound when Sequoia and Gabri used their voices against the Dracans. Vega said we're in tune with the artifacts and Queen Jaide said it's about resonance."

She hasn't said anything we didn't already know, but now I see the thread tying it all together.

"Back in Andros, I researched everything I could find about sound frequencies," Jewel says. "What I found opened my eyes to an aspect of the universe I had not been aware of."

She turns to Pax then, and asks, "Did you know scents and colors have unique frequencies?"

He answers, "I knew about scents, but not colors."

Jewel gets up and paces, using her hands to punctuate her words and convey her excitement.

"I asked my father if he's encountered anything about frequencies in astrophysics. He told me planets, stars, and pretty much everything in space has its own unique sound."

Sky says, "You do know sound can't be heard in the vacuum of space, right?"

"That's what I thought," Jewel answers and pauses, taking a swig from her water bottle. "Dad explained plasma waves oscillate at acoustic frequencies between zero and ten kilohertz, and plasma wave antennae have picked up the sounds of planets, quasars, and stars. I listened to the recordings online. Terra sounds like a mixture of whale song and a chorus of voices. It's mysterious and soothing.

"I wish there were time to delve into everything I've learned, but the two things concerning us are the normal frequency of our planet, and the frequency that can heal the artifacts and restore Terra's balance."

"What would those be?" Pax asks.

"Until recent years, Terra hovered at a steady low frequency of seven point eight three hertz, which some call Terra's natural heartbeat rhythm or the "Schumann Resonance." Over the past eighteen years or so, the heartbeat has been speeding up, spiking well into the eighteen-hertz range. Love has its own frequency, which is what we send when we fix the tetrahedra. I'm convinced the ailing artifacts have caused the increase in Terra's vibrations and fixing them will bring the heartbeat back into normal rhythm."

"What does the crystal cavern have to do with it?" I ask.

"I think I might know," Murphy says. "My parents are building crystalline amplifiers. They grow to a certain shape and size, where they remain in stasis. As they grow, my father harvests living crystals to seed new structures."

"Are they contained in those overgrown snow globes?" I ask.

"Yes," Murphy answers. "They also brought dozens of new ones in various stages. My mother has found a way to speed the growth and produce many more structures."

"How do they tie in to the cave?" Sky asks.

"Coral tried to explain it to me in geophysical terms, and this is what I understood," Jewel says. "The amplifiers will cause the quartz to vibrate at a frequency that will spread through crystal deposits along the ley lines. The frequency will be picked up by other amplifiers placed in crystal caves where the ley lines cross. If what the watchers said is true, the artifacts get their nourishment from quartz deposits like this one, then crystal caves must be close to the artifact clusters."

"How can we test your theory?" I ask.

"I'm not sure," she admits. "Maybe we can try sending love to the quartz like we do to the artifacts."

"The artifacts are sentient," Sky reminds her. "The crystals don't have symbols or sides to join hands on."

"It's worth a shot," I say. "If it doesn't work, though, it doesn't mean her theory is wrong. Why else would Ashley and Leonis have invented those amplifiers?"

"If this doesn't work, how can we assume the amplifiers will?" Sky asks.

"We can't assume anything. They'll test the amplifiers the next time we fix an artifact," Pax says. "Let's see if anything happens to the quartz." He stands up and takes Jewel's hand. "Let's go send some love."

I'M as awestruck as the first time I entered the cave. Everyone but Pax turns off their headlamp, and the resulting flashes of light from millions of facets are like twinkling stars buried in the earth. I half-expect the watchers to come out of the far passage, and sadness washes through me as I remember how they gave their lives to get us to the artifact.

We gather close in the formation we've used for every artifact. We tap our wristbands and link hands, and Juliana lifts us in a bubble to float in the center of the cavern. Jewel will communicate with Pax through their connection. No one wants to touch the walls in case something goes wrong. We don't want to have to fix the artifact again, or even try to find it in a cave deep below us.

Love builds among us, and when Sky says, *now*, we send it toward the walls. It's strange to send it in the opposite direction, away from us instead of toward a center. We maintain our hold as we watch the walls, hoping for some sign it worked.

Jewel gasps and pulls her hands away to point. It takes a few more seconds for me to see the light pulsating across the walls, like biolumi-nescent algae on ocean waves. Sky squeals and Pax says, "It looks like those cephalopods in the Tongue of the Ocean when the mermen attacked them."

I wonder if the crystals think we're hostiles.

The drop comes suddenly, shocking me into quick action before we're impaled on pointed crystals lining the floor beneath us. I lift the four of us to the walkway, and shout, "Juliana!"

My sister and Murphy are gone.

49

PAX

Storm grabs Sky's hand and runs out of the cavern. Jewel and I catch up to them as he cautiously pokes his head into the sacred cave. The stalagmite keeping our entrance hidden also prevents us from seeing what's going on. I drop my scent guard and detect the scent of Dracan, but it could be Murphy.

Do you sense Shaula? I ask her.

No, she assures me.

Storm climbs out of the hole and peeks around the rocky stalagmite before striding into the cave, pulling Sky behind him. I'm surprised she hasn't hit him with an annoyance bolt. On the contrary, she looks happy.

"Why did you let us drop?" he shouts. Juliana and Murphy ignore him, staring at something outside the cave entrance. When he catches up to them, he pushes my sister behind him and freezes. Something's wrong.

I pull Jewel behind some rocks close to the entrance. Sky slides in next to her. "A Dracan ship," she whispers. "Not friendly."

A flash of light turns the dark cave to daylight for an instant, and when my vision clears, the three of them are on the ground. I rush out, unarmed and oblivious to consequences, determined to keep the Dracans from taking anyone else.

The clearing is empty. "Our Sentinels are right where they should be," Jewel says, peering up at the cloudless sky. "One of them must have chased whoever it was away."

"You should have stayed inside. Shaula probably sent them for you," I say, rage fueled by fear for her coursing through me in an adrenaline rush. I breathe slowly to calm myself, afraid I'll say or do something that might hurt her. She grabs my hand and pulls me into the cave. Sky is talking to Juliana while Storm and Murphy get to their feet.

"What happened?" Juliana asks. "One minute, I'm holding you off the crystal floor, and the next I'm on the floor here."

"Mind control? Since when do the Dracans have that ability?" Storm asks.

"This is the first time I've experienced it," Murphy says, "and, I hope, the last. It has to be new technology."

"Pax," Sky says, as she grabs my hand. "Could Shaula have figured out how to recreate the tech Charles invented for the wristband?"

"How? No one can remove the bands except our parents."

"Did yours appear broken?" Storm asks.

"No," I answer, "and I have no idea why it stopped working."

"What about the implants we received in Atlantis?" he asks. "I suspected then they could be used against us."

"They're located under the wristband, which Shaula can't remove," Murphy reminds us. Is yours still there?"

I stick my finger under the band and touch the telltale lump in my wrist. "It's there," I say.

"Since Ashley programmed the implants, couldn't one of Shaula's spies have altered the programming to give him access?" Storm asks.

I nod. It's certainly possible. Anything is, at this point.

"Let's go home and ask Dad what he found," Jewel suggests.

My stomach churns. The reason we've kept what our wristbands can do a secret, is to keep our government or anyone else from figuring out how to weaponize them to control minds. If Shaula now has that ability, it's my fault, and she will never be safe. How do we fight that?

No one speaks on the way to the Adams' home. The implications have left us reeling in shock. We're on the porch when Storm pulls up and parks. He's as somber as the rest of us. I'm surprised at all the cars in the driveway. Our folks must be here.

Inside, Marla's twins are on the floor playing with Gabri, who's learned to crawl at two months. I can't help but smile at the kids. Avery is at the wall of windows, gazing out over the summer green mountains, and Sequoia keeps an eye on the baby but doesn't hover. She's a great mom.

Salali and Tom greet their children with hugs, say something to them and lead them downstairs to the lab. We follow, finding our parents talking to Analiese. Sitting on stools next to a long table, Max and Marla watch Ashley carefully hand a pair of tongs holding a piece of crystal to her mate Leonis. Charles is bent over his worktable, intent on the open face of the wristband he's working on.

Leave this to me, Jewel says through our connection. *This is not your fault. Shaula caught you by surprise and you were outnumbered.*

She knows me too well. I nod, not trusting myself to answer her.

"Hi, Dad," she says, bending over to kiss him on the cheek.

"Sweetheart," he answers with a small smile, getting right back to what he was doing.

"Do you know what was wrong with Pax's wristband?" As she asks the question, I remember Max and Marla were never told about our telepathy. Are they about to find out now?

Charles mumbles something, completely absorbed with his task. I go over to the table where Ashley and Leonis are working with the crystals and ask about their work.

Max excuses himself and heads upstairs to check on his daughters. I still can't believe our once high school bully is the father of four-year-old girls. He would have graduated high school last month if he hadn't gone to Atlantis and been caught in a time warp.

Ashley remarks, "The amplifiers are growing rapidly. We'll have twenty-four of them ready by the end of the week."

"Will it be enough?" I ask. "It's a big planet."

"We hope so," Leonis answers. "The Allarans have identified twenty-four quartz caves near loci containing clusters of tetrahedra, some of which are still functional and others which are on the verge of collapse. We will place the amplifiers among the crystals. If all goes well, the resonance will cover Terra and save it."

"You found some of those loci," Ashley adds, "when the Allarans separated you and sent you to places of known power. I am sorry you were attacked and captured, Pax."

"I'm amazed at how much you and our friends have accomplished," Marla says. "I pray this works."

"So do I," I answer, "but we have other problems. Not all Dracans want us to succeed, as you know."

"My father says the uprising is under control. His soldiers are questioning the rebels. He hopes they'll lead him to Shaula."

I wonder if Shaula's mind-control tech works on other Dracans.

Tom places a container with a growing crystal under a light at the next table, while Salali stares at a monitor at the desk in the corner. Her intense frown disturbs me. She's a meteorologist, so I assume the screen shows weather patterns. I drop my scent guard, and the unmistakable odor of fear turns my stomach. What's wrong?

Jewel comes over and hugs Marla, and while they chat about the kids, I move over to Salali.

"What is it?" I ask. She glances up and goes right back to the monitor. I lean over her shoulder and shudder. I've seen weather maps before, but none like this. It's showing the northern hemisphere, where six enormous hurricanes are swirling, two in the Pacific and four in the Atlantic oceans.

"Why didn't we hear about the one about to hit the Bahamas?" I croak through my constricted throat.

"We haven't been watching the news," she reminds me. "We've been a bit preoccupied. Look at North America," she says, pointing out three angry-looking systems, with one stretching from Canada to Mexico, cutting through Montana, Wyoming, Utah, and Arizona.

"We're looking at huge thunderstorms and tons of rain resulting in mudslides in the mountains and flooding in the plains, not to mention the damage done by high winds and tornados."

I'm relieved when Jewel touches my arm and says, "Let's go."

Right now, I don't care where we're going. I need to be anywhere but here.

51

JEWEL

The meadow buzzes with insects. Their life force is too faint to be seen in the early evening light, and the nocturnal animals are still resting in their cool dens and tunnels. The lowering sun casts long shadows from the forest where Pax and I head. I've alerted the others to meet us there, in a clearing near my mother's garden. I'm grateful he doesn't try to use our connection. By now, Shaula might be able to track any one of us through our link.

"What did you find out?" Storm asks when he and Sky arrive, followed by Juliana and Murphy.

I don't waste any time. "Dad says the motherboard had been removed, and the unit was put back together without it. It didn't look tampered with, so Pax didn't know why it wasn't working."

"That stinks," Sky says, spreading her annoyance to the rest of us. "How did they access it? The band can't be removed, and they obviously didn't cut off his hand."

"They must have cut the face off to get to the components," Pax says. "They had plenty of time while I was unconscious after the fight."

Murphy says, "Shaula has his own scientists, as skilled as Charles and my parents. They could easily have altered the circuits to give them mind control. Charles was afraid someone would figure it out."

"Now what?" Juliana asks. "What defense do we have against this new weapon?"

"There's more," Pax says, his face pale. "We haven't been monitoring the news as we should have. In the lab, I saw what frightened Salali on her monitor. We're in for devastating weather, including six hurricanes and back-to-back storm systems across the continent. We're out of time."

"The weather will only get worse until the artifacts are fixed, but Charles may be able to do something to alter the wristbands against mind-control," Murphy says.

"We need to bring everyone into the loop and brainstorm," I suggest. "There's no point in keeping our friends in the dark about our telepathy. We'll need them, and it won't help if they think we don't trust them."

"Let's go then," I say and start walking back to the house. "We tell everyone about the wristbands, and maybe the scientists can help Dad come up with a defense."

DAD IS ALONE in his lab when we converge on him, and I explain our theory.

"If I put a block against mind control in the devices, they would have to be calibrated to each of you," Dad says, "after I figure out how to do it. It will take time we might not have."

"What if we get Ashley and Leonis to work on it with you?" I ask.

He shakes his head. "They don't know about the telepathy. We must keep it secret from everyone who doesn't have one."

"Shaula already knows," I remind him. "So do his scientists. Dad, you could use their help, and you know they're capable."

"That's true," he acknowledges. "Okay. I'll talk to them."

I press the point. "We'll need everyone's cooperation, including Avery, Max, and Marla."

"I won't need them to help with this issue," he says. "Perhaps it's best to share on a need-to-know basis."

"We trust them," Storm says, and Dad gives him a long look.

"I can't believe I heard right. Did you say you trust these Dracans?"

Storm turns toward Murphy and says, "With my life."

Murphy grins and walks over to throw his arm across his shoulders in a side hug.

With a sudden roar, the ground shakes violently, knocking us off our feet. Dad's chair throws him to the ground, and the lights in the basement lab go out.

I curl up in the fetal position, all too familiar with earthquakes, and I pray the ceiling doesn't come down on us.

When it stops, I hear faint voices. The roar wasn't as loud as an artifact's call, but my ears still feel stuffed with cotton.

"Jewel," Pax says. He's probably shouting, or I might not have heard him at all.

"Here!" I shout. "I'm okay."

A light flares and floats across the room. Storm must have had a flashlight on him. It's a unique way of assessing the damage.

Dad is sitting up where he fell, holding his head. Blood drips from between his fingers. Pax pushes some debris aside to get to me. A lantern floats to Juliana, who turns it on and sends it floating to other parts of the room. Murphy makes his way to Dad. Sky projects peace, and it hits me. No one is panicking. We've come a long way since our first earthquake in Blue Mountain last fall.

As my hearing clears, rhythmic pounding from the hallway leading to the kitchen stairs becomes louder. While Juliana lifts debris off us and clears the floor, Storm goes to open the door. He's too late. Max breaks it open and runs down the stairs to help. Marla is right behind him, with flashlights and a first-aid kit.

"How are the kids?" I ask, pressing a bandage to a cut in Dad's scalp.

"They're frightened, but my mother is caring for them outside.

Sequoia and the baby are with them. The rest of the house doesn't appear damaged. We didn't even lose power upstairs."

"It's the Allaran tech," Sky says, as she checks her brother for injuries. "Our homes are off the grid, so power outages don't affect us."

Murphy helps Dad to his feet, and we head upstairs. Even with books, dishes, and furniture in a mess all over the great room, there's no evidence of cracked walls, or even cracked windows.

"We should get everyone outside in case of an aftershock," Wolf says, heading to the front door. "It's safer in the meadow."

"This is going to set us back," Dad says. "Who knows what damage my equipment sustained, and what about the amplifiers?"

"Where are my parents?" Murphy asks. His darkened scales tell me he's worried.

"They're in the lab," Storm answers. "They must be checking on the crystals. Juliana, help me get the amplifiers out of there. We'll need all the help we can get for the smaller crystals."

"The domes won't fit up the stairs," Murphy points out.

"Then we'll need to clear the freight elevator or blast it out of the way."

"Salvage as much of my equipment as you can, too," Dad says. "I'll need it to work on the wristbands."

Thankfully, the elevator works, and Storm and Juliana use their telekinesis to place the domes holding the amplifiers in a line along the front of the garage. The rest of us make short work of bringing up the smaller containers and Dad's equipment. Now what?

One of the sentinels appears in our front yard, and Maia floats down the portal beam. She walks to Sequoia, who is sitting on the porch swing holding Gabri, a pile of infant gear next to her. The baby reaches for Maia and giggles.

"You perfect child," Maia says, picking her up. "You called, and here we are. How can we help you?"

Gabri called the Allarans?

Sequoia tells Maia what's happened, and in seconds, another ship appears over the meadow. Baran exits and strides toward us, followed by ten men dressed in armor.

By now, everyone has come outside, most carrying backpacks.

"Queen Avery," Baran says, bowing slightly to Marla's mother. "We are surprised you are here."

She answers, "I trust your misunderstanding with my husband has been ironed out so we can consider you friends."

"Let us say, we are on high alert but have no intention of fighting the Dracans unprovoked. We are aware Shaula has tricked us all, and that he, not your mate, is our enemy."

"Very well," Avery responds, sounding like the queen she is. "Then we are counting on you to help us."

A roar in the distance alerts the soldiers, who assume a battle-ready stance. They're knocked to the ground seconds later in an aftershock as strong as the original earthquake. What's causing this?

Two more sentinels appear while we pick ourselves up for the second time. One hovers over the garage and, like a giant vacuum cleaner, sucks the domes, equipment, and crystal containers inside. The others hover over us, and within minutes, we're inside the Allaran ships, heading who knows where.

52
SKY

"Welcome to Hyperborea, our city under the North Pole," Maia's voice says over the intercom. The view on the wrap-around screen shows gardens surrounding delicate towers, very much like Heliade, under Antarctica. I hope the Allarans can help us put together the pieces of the puzzle, so we can finally save the world and get on with life. Oh, and someone must kill Shaula. My brain is fried.

Baran leads us from the docking bay to a long car with a glass canopy surrounding a cabin, where we fill rows of bubble seats. The car floats away from the towers in the city, dropping into a valley full of tropical plants growing just inside a dome so large, we can only see its base.

I don't know how long we travel along the dome's edge, because I fall asleep and only wake up when Baran announces, "We have arrived at your quarters."

The squat, flat-roofed buildings nestled among the foliage don't look like much, but I'd be happy with a bunk and a bathroom.

"Our equipment?" Charles asks.

"It has been delivered and set up for you," Maia answers. "The sleeping quarters and dining area are in the building next to the laboratory. Consider this your temporary home and explore the grounds. You will find Aracai and their singers in the gardens. They are eager to meet you."

Storm is excited at the prospect, and I fight a tiny stab of jealousy. I should be grateful at the change the Aracai nectar has made in him. I send him love, and he returns it.

As soon as we step foot on the landing platform, I hear a screech and a female voice yelling, "Storm!"

"Lilyana?" he responds, breaking into a run down the stairs to the waiting Allaran, grabbing her in a hug. "What are you doing here? The children? Hamal?"

His questions clarify who she is. Lilyana is Baran's sister, the one whose family took care of him on Allara. She laughs and points to two girls standing shyly behind her Aracai. He opens his arms and K'amryn and K'ary nearly knock him down in their rush for his hugs.

"Who are they?" Marla asks, stepping up beside me. Max stands next to her with his arms around his sleepy twins' shoulders as they silently watch the Allaran girls greet Storm. I start to explain when K'amryn spots the girls and freezes. K'ary sees them and turns to her mother, who points to the ambulatory plant with the toucan-beak for a head.

K'ary approaches the Aracai and sings softly, holding her cupped hands below the point of the beak. When enough nectar has dropped into her palms, she carefully climbs to the platform and offers it to Khatryn, who catches it in her own cupped hands. Meanwhile, K'amryn sings and collects her own nectar, which she offers to Sha'lat. The twins look to their mother for approval, and when she nods, they lick the nectar.

The transformation is instantaneous. Gone are the shyness and sleepiness. Marla's twins laugh and run with Lilyana's girls down the platform and along the path to the buildings. Max starts after them, but Marla pulls him back.

"They're safe here," she says. "Let them play."

Storm introduces me to Lilyana as we follow the girls.

"You are his mate," she says with a sly grin. "Baran has told us about you and your brother Pax, and about his mate Jewel."

"Not exactly," Storm says.

"Only if we can save Terra," I break in. "Is your mate here with you?"

She answers, "Hamal was called here when war with the Dracans was imminent. I am happy we were wrong, and now our daughters have become friends with the daughters of a Dracan princess. We have you to thank for this."

"What do you mean?" I ask.

"You have proven yourselves to be humans of great courage, with a quest requiring everyone's cooperation to accomplish. I never thought the day would come when we would lay aside our ancient enmity."

I multiply Storm's happiness back to him. If we can pull this off, the races can figure out how to share our planet. I wonder how humans will take to their alien neighbors.

The buildings are larger than they appear from the outside. Each family has a suite of rooms in the sleeping quarters, and each bedroom has a private bathroom. I opt to share a suite with Juliana and Jewel, and the boys share another. There are no windows, but paintings and strategically placed plants almost bring the outdoors in. It has the atmosphere of a luxury hotel.

Before turning in, we enjoy a delicious vegetarian meal prepared by the Allaran staff. The drink tastes like a light lemonade with only a hint of sweetness. I suspect it contains nectar.

I send out a blast of gratitude just before falling asleep.

53
SKY

C hara meets us in the dining room after breakfast.

"Where's Belena?" my brother asks. I shoot him a barb of annoyance for being rude, and he quickly adds, "Of course, we're glad you're here."

"She has other duties, and I asked to spend time with you today," she answers with a smile. "I hope our laboratory meets your expectations."

Dad says, "We're eager to get to the lab, and to brainstorm with your scientists."

Avery, Max, and Marla elect to stay behind with Sequoia to watch the kids. As we leave them, Lilyana offers to teach Wolf and Sequoia more about the Aracai. I can't help but think how Donny would enjoy this place, especially with the girls here. If we succeed in saving the planets, I hope these people will be open to revealing their presence on Terra.

The lab is much larger than the one Charles and Analiese have in their home. Allarans are busy working with various pieces of equipment, and four are checking out the domes holding the amplifiers. Leonis and Murphy, both in human form, join them, along with Ashley. Charles and Dylan greet each scientist we pass, and they nod as we follow Chara to the area assigned to us.

Tom and Salali are impressed with the weather and geological monitors set up in one corner of the massive lab. Coral concentrates on a screen showing weather systems around the globe, and Dylan points to one showing seismic activity. From here, both screens look ominous. They're soon absorbed in their work.

A headband with different eyepieces of various magnifications attached for easy reach, like the one he invented, lies on the worktable assigned to Charles. The Allaran version has each lens nestled into the headband when it isn't being used. He admires it before putting it on and laying the wristband out on the table. He's quickly lost in the mechanics of it.

Chara shows Analiese the genetics lab, where she's eager to study the DNA of the Aracai nectar. She plans to observe how sound waves change the nectar's properties.

That leaves Juliana and the four of us.

"We must test one of the amplifiers before we set them up around the planet," Chara says. "Some of the beings you call watchers have informed us the artifacts under their care are ailing. We will test the amplifier there after we locate the quartz deposit nearby."

"Don't you know where the crystals are?" Jewel asks. "With all this equipment, they should be easy for you to find."

"Yes," Chara answers, "but Terra is a big planet. Since the Formicians and Mantoids have shared their artifact map with us, it should be a simple matter to find the quartz deposits they feed on. Today, we visit a cave north of the Arctic Circle in Alaska."

"When I first tasted the nectar on Allara, I no longer needed the cold-weather clothing I was wearing," Storm says. "Will that be the case here, for all of us?"

"You will not feel the cold. The nectar alters your cellular structure to protect you from extreme temperatures."

We exit the lab from a back door. Baran is waiting with a vehicle the size of a minivan.

"Good morning, Star Children," he says. He sounds like any other guy, and I blush at the memory of my reaction to his voice before the nectar.

"The crystal deposit lies inside a larger cavern your parents once explored, Pax and Sky," Baran continues. "To do our part to fulfill the prophecy, our leaders chose your parents for their superior intellect. We knew where they were and waited for them to arrive at the cave. If not for us, you would not have the abilities you do now. Life comes full-circle."

Our mother had been abducted when they spotted the Allarans outside the cave they'd intended to explore. She was pregnant with us at the time, and her abductors had added their DNA to ours, making us a type of hybrid.

Instead of making me resentful, his admission fills me with peace. Is that another effect of the nectar?

The vehicle is faster than the one we rode yesterday, cutting across the dome to the city in minutes. We board the ship through a ramp, rather than the tractor beam portal. Two men load one of Ashley's domes into the cargo bay. Shouldn't Ashley or Leonis be here? There's no time to ask. Everyone's in a hurry.

We've no sooner settled in than Baran announces we've arrived.

The entrance is nearly large enough for the ship to fly into, but we drop to the ice and head inside with a team of six men and women equipped with lamps and spelunking gear. I don't see the amplifier dome, so it must still be on the ship.

A woman stops, points to a wall and says something to Baran in their language. It's the first time I've heard it. They don't speak like we do. They sing.

One of the men turns on a laser, and the ice wall melts, revealing a stone passageway. Like the Cherokee crystal cavern, this one is near the main entrance, but the crystals themselves are much larger, criss-crossing the space like fallen sharp-edged columns.

"Where are the artifacts?" Juliana asks.

"Deep below us," Chara answers. "We expected the watchers to meet us, but as you can see, they are not here."

"Did something spook them?" Storm asks.

"I am unfamiliar with that term used in that manner," Baran answers. "Is a spook not another word for ghost, or spirit?"

"He meant to ask if something frightened them," I say, jabbing him with what I call a "pay-attention" dart of annoyance.

He taps the wristband, rubs his heart and says, *Ouch. I thought they knew our language.*

"Without the watchers, we cannot get to the artifacts," Chara says.

A sudden boom followed by a series of loud staccato bursts penetrates the cave, and Baran shouts, "Run outside!" just as the crystals begin to shake. Is it an artifact? An earthquake?

Storm lifts me off my feet and flies me through the passage into the bigger cavern, where laser flashes knock stalactites off the ceiling and shatter boulders close to the entrance. I'm stunned, remembering when the Dracans stole the first artifact and abducted Jewel during a battle like this.

Jewel and Pax float to the floor next to me, followed by Juliana, who must have flown them out.

The Allarans run to their ship, dodging fire, and take off, drawing the battle to the sky. We make our way through the debris to the entrance and watch the Allarans battle the Dracan ship. They don't get a direct hit on the vessel, but they manage to chase it off. We won't be testing anything today.

54
SKY

"That's it," Charles says when we return to the lab and tell our folks what happened. "We're removing the wristbands, at least until I can add some protection against mind control. Unless he's directly tracking Jewel through the mark, Shaula or his people might be using them to track all of you."

"How close are you to adding the protection?" Pax asks, deeply anxious. Shaula has been too close for too long.

"I've asked Leonis and Ashley to help. We've drawn some schematics. If we have the materials, we can get them ready in a couple of days."

"All of them? What if you do one first today, and then work on the rest?"

"What's on your mind, Pax?" Charles asks, picking up on his urgency.

"Jewel needs protection more than the rest of us right now," he says. "She's his target."

"You are too," she cries, grabbing his arm. "In fact, everyone I love is his target. Dad, it's all of us or none. I won't take the first one."

I send calm to her, but she fights it off, saying, "No, Sky. I'm serious. He nearly killed Pax trying to get me to surrender. I won't put anyone in that much danger again."

Charles sighs, removes her wristband and turns back to his work. He probably knows he won't win a verbal argument with his daughter, but I sense a great deal of strength and determination in him. He'll finish hers today.

Murphy tears himself away from the crystals to hug Juliana. They come with us to get some lunch.

Sequoia greets us at the entrance to our quarters. Gabriella is inside with Marla and the girls.

Storm holds out his wrist, and she deftly removes the band while his eyes are averted. Then she takes Juliana's and Murphy's off. She and Wolf, and now Tom and Salali, are the only ones who know the code to release the straps for Storm, Murphy and Juliana. Mom removed mine in the lab. I rub my naked wrist.

"Why isn't Gabri crying?" I ask. "She hates when the bands stop working, and I know we'd hear her no matter where she is inside the building."

"I'm not sure," her mother says. "I don't think she senses you through the bands. Hers is a more direct connection. When she lost Storm and Pax, they were off planet. In fact, while the Dracan tech blocked your abilities, she still didn't lose any of you, at least not after the first time Sky met with the giants. She wasn't distressed when Jewel was held in Atlantis, but she was still in the earliest phase of development then."

I find it comforting she can track us anywhere on Terra. I can't wait until she can use words to communicate with us.

Salali and Coral join us for lunch and tell us what's going on in our world. Both look pale.

"I hate to alarm you," Coral says, which gets my heart racing. She's anxious and reluctant to continue, and I try sending her assurance I don't have.

She glances at me and continues. "We've been hearing stories about Yellowstone for years. The alarmists claim an eruption of the super volcano will wipe out the interior of the North American continent, blanketing the rest in a toxic gas and ash cloud. Until now, reputable scientists have believed it to be a myth, worthy only of disaster movies. Earthquake clusters have occurred there for as long as we've been recording them. They've become stronger in recent years, but we didn't think we had reason to be concerned. The caldera has been relatively stable, and if it erupted at all, it would manifest in small volcanoes, destructive but not devastating."

"It has changed," Salali says. Her sadness is contagious. "The alarmists were right, after all. An enormous amount of pressure is building around the ring of fire, relieved in part as more dormant volcanoes come to life. They aren't enough. The pressure now extends into the interior of the continent."

Baran, who has come in unnoticed, interjects, "It is not too late, but we must act quickly. We have found another quartz deposit in Siberia. The watchers have agreed to take us inside, but only the four will be allowed into the artifact chamber."

I wonder why. The entrance to the first artifact chamber, guarded by watchers, had a force field that only allowed us to enter. Triton's cave, on the other hand, did not, and all of us were there when we fixed his "egg." There was no barrier in the caves guarded by the Mantoids in South America, either. It must be a watcher thing.

When we get up to leave, Gabri starts crying and reaches for me. I take her from Marla, and she holds my face in her tiny hands and stares into my eyes.

She shows me a crystalline tree with an artifact spinning next to it, and she and Sequoia are in the chamber with us.

"No. It's too dangerous for you, and the watchers might not let you in," I say aloud. She cries and shows me Jewel's and Pax's face covered by black blobs.

I try to send her comfort, but she screams louder when I hand her to Sequoia. She's only projecting her fear, I tell myself. She can't predict the future. Can she?

∼

THIS TIME, Storm floats the amplifier dome into the crystal chamber under the critical eyes of three watchers. The little aliens resemble the ones depicted all over the town of Roswell, New Mexico, where a craft crash-landed in 1947. Many people have reported seeing them through the years since, with their huge domed heads and onyx oval eyes. Their noses and mouths are little more than slits, but they speak with their minds and don't need to verbalize. I still don't know how or if they eat. I do know they come in fours, and the fourth is with the artifact.

One of Baran's men runs in and sings what sounds like a warning.

"We are again under attack," he says to us. "Storm, you and the others follow the watchers and do not stop. We will take care of the Dracan problem." He and his people run out through the larger cavern to their ship.

In the crystal cave, much like the one in Alaska, Storm and Juliana position the dome as close to the center as they can. They lower it into a hole made by three crossed giant crystals.

"Lift the dome off the amplifier," Murphy directs.

I gasp at the beauty of the thing when it's revealed, a crystalline tree about as tall as I am, with several thick, stubby branches quivering with pent-up energy. It's covered in leaf-like shards, sparkling in the dim light of Murphy's headlamp.

"It's so delicate," Jewel says. "I wish you could see the colors in it. Imagine a tree made of millions of rainbows, only the way I see rainbows. I can hardly breathe."

A slow clap startles us, and I turn toward the entrance while the most hated voice in the universe says, "Bravo."

55

STORM

As soon as I hear his voice, my body freezes in place. Since no sound comes from the others, I assume they're frozen, too. Shaula has taken us by surprise.

I can only see what's directly in front of my eyes, which is the amplifier and a small area of the path we're standing on. I'd been turning toward Shaula's voice when he froze us.

Three massive Dracans jump to the crystals holding the amplifier in place. I try to throw them to the ground, but my telekinesis is as incapacitated as I am. They wrestle it out of the hole, knocking a good number of small crystals off the branches. Once it's up, one of the Dracans carries it out. The other two grunt and mumble complaints, but I can't tell what they're doing. When they brush past me, heading back to Shaula, they have Pax and Jewel, both stiff as cardboard cutouts. There is nothing I can do.

When they leave the chamber, I concentrate on moving my hands, and to my surprise, my muscles suddenly relax.

"Sky, are you alright?" I pick her up and set her on her feet, wishing I could hold her while she sobs. Juliana wraps her arms around her friend, and I run after Shaula, with Murphy right behind me. Since he has the only light, I hope the girls are following him.

Just as I get to the large cavern and can see outside, I watch an Allaran ship rise slowly. Is that snake taunting us? By the time I get to the entrance, it's gone. Rage burns like a living thing in my chest, tearing at my insides in its frenzy to be released. The nectar has its limits, and only Shaula's death will calm it this time.

A ship materializes in the clearing, and I shove out my hands, ready to smash it against the ice.

"Stop!" Sky shouts. "It could be Baran. Shaula isn't coming back."

I'M STILL SHAKING when we get back to Hyperborea. Everyone has been alerted to what's happened, and they're on the way to the landing dock. Baran and Chara wait with us while Vega and Belena transport the others here.

The last thing I want to do is face Jewel's parents and Pax's family. They've already been through so much. Sky sobs quietly and still sends me comfort, which reminds me how much I love her. Her brother's missing again, and she's sending comfort and love to me. It should be the other way around. I draw her close, handing her the corner of my shirt to wipe her nose and eyes.

"Now, that's love," Juliana says, wiping her own eyes. Murphy pulls her to his side, and we wait.

When the others arrive, Sequoia and Gabri are here, but Avery and Marla have stayed behind with the twins. Max's thunderous face matches my rage. He'll make a good ally.

Baran invites them into his ship. Even with enough bubble chairs for everyone, the observation room is crowded. He says something into a communicator on the wall and the view screen changes to the view of the reef we saw the first time we entered Vega's ship.

"My crew has located the stolen craft, and we are tracking it," he announces. "In the meantime, we must figure out how to defeat Shaula."

Before I can say anything, Dylan says, "Describe what happened while you were under Shaula's control. Was it the same as the first time?"

I think about it, and Murphy answers, "No. The first time we didn't remember what had happened. We blacked out. My mind was perfectly clear this time. Only my body was unable to move."

I nod and add, "Same here. What's changed?"

"We didn't have our wristbands on," Sky says. "The first time, we did. Also, Pax, Jewel and I weren't affected then, so line of sight must be important. Only the ones who witnessed the Dracan ship were affected."

"We didn't actually see Shaula," I remind her. "We only heard his voice."

"But he saw us," Murphy says.

"Murphy," Analiese chimes in, "if Shaula can control her body and not her mind, can he force her to submit to him?"

"I doubt it," Murphy responds. "The Dracan male can only function if the female is willing."

"Please explain, Murphy," Vega says. "We are unfamiliar with this aspect of Dracan physiology."

Murphy explains how Shaula essentially raped Jewel while she was in captivity. Using recessive fangs designed for that purpose, he injected her with biochemicals. When fused with her nervous system, they cannot be erased or counteracted.

"The mark is a unique and life-long bond between mated pairs. It is willingly given and willingly received when a couple commits to each other. She was unconscious when Shaula bit her."

Belena stands to her feet and I recognize the rage in her. Vega stands next to her and puts his arm around her shoulder.

"Are they not a bonded pair now he has marked her?" Vega asks.

"She has not given herself to him, which is the deciding factor. The act will cement the bond. In addition, my mother and Analiese found a way to bind her to Pax through her marked blood. She is the first female in history to be marked by two males, and the second to share the mark with a human male."

"She loves Pax," Belena says. "Does it not override the first mark?"

"No. However, a Dracan male cannot mate without the female's full consent. Our physiology prevents it. Even if Shaula can control her body, unless he can control her will, certain enzymes will prevent him from physically mating with her, and thus the bond cannot be cemented."

Analiese speaks up, her voice shaking with emotion, "There is one way the monster can bend her to his will. Jewel will do anything to protect the ones she loves. If she gives in, the first thing Shaula will do is kill Pax."

"It will be the one thing that prevents her from submitting," Charles says. "She knows what Shaula is capable of."

A voice comes over the com, saying, "Rendezvous in five."

"Who are we meeting up with?" Wolf asks.

PAX

The Dracans must think it's a joke to stuff us in the narrow storage closet, but I'm fine with it. They close the door, and my muscles go limp. Jewel falls against me, and I lower us both to the floor. Thank God the paralysis is temporary.

"Are you okay?" I whisper. I expect tears, not the growl emerging from her, taking me by surprise. I'm sure my laughter does the same to her. After a minute of muffling laughs in our shirts, I realize we're reacting to the shock.

"I can't believe he got us again," she whispers. "He's a virus that never dies."

"Not yet," I say, "but his time is getting short. We'll figure a way out of this."

"When he opens the door, he'll zap us again. What if he separates us?"

"Did you notice he only controlled our bodies?" I ask. "My mind stayed clear. What about yours?"

"You're right," she answers. "We might be able to connect when we're under his control, but what if he's listening?"

"Are you sure he can hear us through our connection?"

"No, but if you and I can mind-speak, he should be able to. He shares a mark with me, too."

"How can we test it?" I ask. Then it comes to me, and I say, "I know. When I connect with you, play along. Whatever you do, no matter what he threatens, do not give in to him. Do you understand? It would kill me."

As she squeezes my hand, a Dracan flings the door open, momentarily blinding us. He hauls me to my feet, and Jewel stands up behind me. I could take this guy by surprise, using my karate training, but it would leave her vulnerable. Besides, we don't know where we are.

The second guard falls in behind us, and we're led down a ramp and into a gray docking bay. We continue into a corridor where everything is gray and seamless. I can't tell where the floor ends and the walls or ceiling start. It's disorienting.

"I've been here," she says. "If I'm right, this is where he held me prisoner."

"Silence!" The lead Dracan hisses.

Why didn't Shaula paralyze us? If he can control us, why didn't he simply compel us to obey his guards and follow them? He did it to Jewel the morning in the meadow when I had to help break her away from his influence. Something doesn't add up.

The guards halt and the one in front opens a door. We enter a room, empty except for an ornate golden throne set on a dais at the far end. Dragons engaged in battle decorate the back and sides, and a red velvet cushion sits on the seat.

Shaula enters through a door on the right, and the guards snap to attention. He snarls as he climbs the steps and takes a seat on the cushion. His claws curl around the ends of the armrests, their rhythmic clacking the only sound breaking the silence.

We stand straight and stare him in the eyes.

"You are looking well, Paxton," he says. "It pleases me I can break you little by little now your health has been restored."

My hands curl into fists, and I glance at Jewel and notice her face has gone pale. I want to reassure her through our connection, but now isn't the time to test it.

"By now you know I can control you. Jewel, I can command you to surrender to me, and you will."

"Why don't you then?" she asks, lifting her chin in defiance. "When you do, you can let Pax go."

He roars in laughter, sending chills down my spine. "What would be the fun in that?"

He gestures, and the guards grab us and shove us toward the wall, where another door slides open. They march us down a maze of corridors, all the same uniform gray. If our feet didn't hit the ground with each step, it would be like we're floating in a sensory deprivation tank. We finally stop, and the lead guard opens another hidden door and shoves Jewel inside, closing it behind her.

"What are you doing? What's in there?" I ask, suddenly frantic with worry for her.

"Silence!" he roars, resuming the trek into nothingness. I count my steps, and we stop when I reach forty-five. A door opens on the opposite side of the corridor, and I'm shoved into a nightmare.

There is nothing in the room, and like the hallways, not a seam shows where any part of it connects to any other part. I close my eyes, but it doesn't help the growing vertigo much. I drop my scent guard and take a deep breath. A slightly metallic scent indicates an air-conditioning vent is to my right.

With my eyes closed and my hands out, I find the vent. When I open them, my hand is sinking into nothingness. It's an illusion.

Jewel! She might not be aware of it. Shaula will know she's using her gift as soon as he sees her reactions. I assume there are cameras.

I pull my hand back and sit with my head between my knees, hoping he didn't see what I did.

I open our connection. *Show me what you see.* I concentrate on looking through her eyes, and there it is. A square room with an air vent near the floor and cameras in each corner of the ceiling.

Now look through mine, I say. Hoping she doesn't try to tell me anything.

Oh, she says. *You're in a void, too.*

Good girl.

It helps if you keep your eyes closed, she says.

Hopefully, we can keep Shaula in the dark about our gifts. Unless he followed what Jewel and I did through the connection.

5 7

STORM

W e land in a familiar snow-filled valley. The peaks surrounding us are the same, but it was summer the last time we were here. Ice and snow smooth the contours of the boulders, and the decent-sized, bubbling pool is now a steaming hole in the ice. This is where we regrouped after the Ant People and Jaina's Mantoids rescued us from the tunnel before it became an active volcano.

One of the crew members hands me an arctic jacket before I step into the portal.

"I'm not cold," I tell him.

"It is not for you, Star Child. It is for them. They do not know about the nectar," he reminds me.

I thank him and put it on before I touch down and look around. It doesn't surprise me Queen Meissa and King Thuban are here with six Dracan ships. I am surprised to see the others.

Jack Austin, Al Loren, and Jaina Chen, in her human shape, wave as we descend from Vega's ship. They're dressed in furs and mukluks, like Arctic explorers, and it hits me how great it is not to be shivering with cold anymore. I understand why the Allarans would want Al and Jaina to tag along, but Dr. Austin? What good would a publicity-seeking archaeologist be on a rescue mission like ours?

While the Allarans confer with the Dracans and Jaina, I admire the view. Allaran disc-shaped, silver craft float among the dark pitted triangular craft of the Dracans. If we manage to save the world, cooperation like this will be necessary to keep it going. Add humans and our considerable firepower to the mix, and we might achieve world-peace unless a power struggle wipes out all our efforts. I shrug and turn to find Sky. Our first responsibility is to rescue her brother and Jewel.

I grab her hand, and we head down to greet our friends. Al slaps me on the back, nearly knocking me down. He's a big man with a jagged scar running down his face, stark white against the ruddy complexion brought on by the cold. If I didn't know about his gentle nature, I might have retaliated. Jaina stands back while he and Jack hug Sky and then me. Al and Jaina work for Jack when they aren't helping to rescue us.

"Queen Jaide sends her regards," Jaina says once we've settled down. "She has located Jewel and Pax under the Perito Moreno Glacier."

"Isn't that the base where Shaula had her the last time?" Sky asks. "Why would he take them back there?"

"He probably thought it'd be the last place you'd look," Al says. "Only he underestimated my Jaina and her queen." He draws her close to his side, and she pushes him away. His grin reminds me of my own when Sky jabs me with her emotional darts. It's what happens when you love strong women, I guess.

Jack speaks up, "Jaina told Meissa and Thuban where they are before you got here. They must have told the Allarans. They're waving at us. Let's go. I guess we're riding with you."

THE ICE IS THICKER than it was, and the glacier has moved. There's no sign of the battle that took the Dracan ship down when we rescued Jewel in the late South American summer. I hope the Allarans have the coordinates for the base. Even if they do, how will they get in?

The view screen is set to our actual surroundings, and two Dracan ships take the lead. At least I think they're leading. I can't see the Allaran ships now they're cloaked again.

They separate and dart across the glacier and back again, as if they don't know where the base is. I wonder if anyone is watching from the ground. It's unlikely tourists would be around in the dead of winter, but some people are crazy enough.

Sequoia is playing peek-a-boo with Gabri when the baby suddenly stiffens and screams. I watch her mother pull her close and rock her, but nothing helps.

"Let me take her for a while," I offer, reaching for my cousin. She quiets as soon as I lift her. When I sit back down next to Sky, Gabri reaches for her. I hand the baby to her and put my arm around her. When Gabri touches her face, the sudden images she sends to her startle me.

Shaula is sitting on the only piece of furniture in a large square room. The door opposite him opens, and Jewel stumbles in, followed by Pax. The Dracans who pushed them retreat to a hallway, leaving them in the room alone with the monster.

"Where are they, Gabri?" I ask, and in my mind, she shows me a spot on the ice marked by a deep blue circle, and then there it is, on the view screen.

Sky points to the view screen and shouts, "There! Vega, take us there!"

We hover near the spot and watch Thuban's ship vaporize the ice, exposing a metallic roof. He moves away, and Baran's crew positions our ship over the exposed metal.

5 8
JEWEL

T hank God, Pax showed me the void he sees, and I came in here and just sat in the middle of the floor. He and I never talked about hiding our ability from Shaula. I needed the reminder.

Now what? How long will we be here? Will the others find us? Pax used our connection through the mark to find me the last time. Without the wristbands, we can't call the others or let them know where we are.

I stretch out on the hard floor, thankful I don't feel the cold. I'm too tired to care if Shaula notices I'm not shivering. I might as well get some sleep.

The familiar buzzing wakes me from a nightmare, in which Shaula leaves me in a hole in the ground, dragging Pax away with him.

Queen Jaide? I ask.

She answers with a jolt, *Yes.*

Shaula mustn't know I'm communicating with the Mantoid queen. Until we know for certain he can't enter our connection, I don't dare share this with Pax. Not this time.

When Pax barely survived the process of assimilating the mark through my blood, he saw everything Queen Jaide showed me. We didn't know better, and I only suspected Shaula might be able to connect with me after I was rescued. I'm more careful now.

The queen immediately switches to images of Allaran ships gathered in the mountains.

Our rescue parties? I ask.

Jaina, Al, and Jack are talking with Meissa and Thuban. Then half a dozen Allaran ships appear among the others, and Sky and Storm come out of one.

Do they know where we are? I ask.

This time she uses words, and my teeth buzz. *I told them. They are coming for you.*

Thank you, I say. *I owe you so much.*

She sends a picture of our planet, and I know my debt will be paid when we save it.

She leaves the link and I try to go back to sleep, but my grumbling stomach won't let me. I hope we're rescued before we're too weak from hunger to move.

I sit in the lotus position, pull my arms across my stomach, fold over to put pressure on the hollow ache, and let my mind wander.

When Shaula's ship appeared at the Cherokee cave and Storm, Juliana, and Murphy were hit with his mind control, they fell and didn't remember anything. This time, we didn't fall, and we were conscious the whole time. The first time, we had our wristbands on. Was Dad right? If Shaula is using the technology from Pax's wristband, maybe our own bands amplified it. Without them, the tech is limited in what it can do.

Then there's the compulsion I felt in the meadow. I wasn't paralyzed, but my body obeyed Shaula's pull, even as my mind reached out to Pax. Could he compel me to surrender to him? My entire body shudders.

Jewel? Pax's mind-speech is like a warm shower in my brain, until his next words nearly stop my heart.

I can't take this anymore. It's time to bite down on the poison capsule. When I'm gone, you're free to surrender to Shaula, and no one else will suffer.

A shard of ice penetrates my chest, and I jump to my feet, about to scream, when I remember what we'd talked about in the closet. Play along. There is no poison capsule. This is Romeo and Juliet.

If you do, Pax, I'll bite my own. I'd rather die with you than give in to that monster.

He responds, *On the count of three then, my love. We'll meet on the other side.*

I hear the pounding feet before the door flings open, and I struggle with every ounce of strength left in me when the Dracan grabs me and carries me into the hall.

He knows! He heard us!

The goon pulls me to my feet and prods me along the corridor with his claws. We wind up in the throne room again, where he pushes me to the floor in front of Shaula. I lie there, unmoving until the door opens, and Pax is shoved in.

"Stand up," Shaula says, his voice harsh. Pax helps me to my feet. Shaula doesn't know what's coming.

"So, you think to rob me of my mate, Paxton. She is mine, and you will die."

"If you kill him," I say, "then I will also die. My connection to him is stronger than your claim on me. You know that."

He gets up and paces back and forth along the dais. When he stops, my feet begin to move toward him.

"You cannot resist me, Jewel Adams. You see how your body responds. You will do everything I ask without question."

Jewel, stop! Pax commands, and I do.

With a roar, Shaula leaps off the dais and swipes his claws at him.

He ducks and kicks at the Dracan's legs, and I hear a sickening pop. The monster drops to the floor, groaning, and Pax rains blows on his head and body more swiftly than I can follow.

Shaula catches his leg in the middle of a kick, tosses him like a ragdoll, and pushes himself up to stand on one leg. Pax flips to his feet and circles the Dracan, watching for an opening. He's highly trained in karate, and this time he isn't in pitch darkness. Shaula's goons are outside the door, not in here to gang up on him. I can stall them if they decide to join the fight. At least for a few seconds.

The lizard lunges, claws extended, faster than I've ever seen a Dracan move. He catches Pax around the middle with his claw and pulls him to his chest as he drops, unable to put weight on his broken leg. Pax struggles, trying to spin away, but the claw penetrates his skin and pins him while Shaula tightens his crushing hold.

Pax! I scream his name in my head and out loud, watching his life force fade and the red and black streaks in his aura turn to gray and magenta.

"Shaula, if you kill him, I will die!" I scream, running to him and pounding on his scales with my fists. I pull his claws away from Pax's flesh, and he lets me.

I pull Pax away from him. Blood squirts out of the hole in his chest. Shaula must have hit an artery. Without help, he'll bleed out in minutes. I press as hard as I can, trying to keep my love's lifeblood from pouring out of his wounds. Oh my God!

Pax, don't die. Come back to me. I need you! I gather every ounce of love for him and try to push it into him like Sky does. I'm not an empath, but maybe it will give him strength through our connection.

You will not die, Shaula says, shredding my nerve endings like they've been whipped with razor wire. *I marked you first. You belong to me, and I will not allow you to die.*

You can't stop me, I answer, growling like a demented tiger.

A tickle in my brain startles me. For a second, Pax's face appears with a bubble of love over it. What the heck? It must be Gabri, but how?

A rumble followed by crashing debris is all I notice as a beam of light obliterates the ornate throne. I throw my body across Pax's and wait for tons of ice to crush us. Instead of closing my eyes, I watch as a hole grows in the ceiling. Storm and Juliana drop into the room. He aims a Dracan weapon at Shaula's head and pulls the trigger.

Shaula twists away from the lethal beam and pulls his body toward the door in a military crawl, his broken leg useless. Juliana concentrates on a large piece of the dais and throws it in front of him, blocking his way. He twists, pulling a weapon from his belt and aims at Storm. Big mistake. Storm's aim is true, and Shaula has nowhere to dodge this time. The laser hits him below the sternum, but Storm stops the beam before slicing him in half. Two Dracan soldiers pick him up and carry him, screaming in pain, to the portal beam.

"Where are you taking him?" Dylan asks sharply, his teeth clenched with the need to end the creature right now.

"He will stand justice, human. We take him to Meissa."

If Shaula were anybody else, I'd feel sorry for him, but this monster deserves every bit of pain coming to him.

The room quickly fills with people from two ships. Dracans march into the hall to capture the rest of Shaula's forces. Sky runs to her brother, while Baran packs something into his wound and binds it. Belena injects him with something and answers, "Nectar" to Sky's silent query.

"Will he live?" I ask, frantic to know. His life force is a dim shadow of its normal brightness but holding steady for now.

"I believe so," Baran replies, carrying him into the beam. The look on his face is somber. I want to believe him.

59

SKY

Storm holds me close to his side, his love and strength loaning me a bit of comfort, but Pax is fading. Jewel's pacing is making everyone nervous, but no one tries to stop her. Her connection to my brother is at least as strong as mine. Maybe stronger. Why haven't we heard anything yet?

"Jewel, as long as you're walking anyway, would you mind carrying Gabri?" Sequoia asks. The baby has been irritable since we rescued them. It's becoming evident to me our little girl may be prescient, at least to some degree. Foreseeing the future is not a gift I'd want to have.

She takes the baby without a word, and Gabri settles, soon falling asleep on her shoulder. I hope it's a sign the surgery has gone well.

I jump to my feet when the door opens, and Belena comes in. "The surgeon was able to repair the artery, and Pax's body is rapidly replacing the blood he'd lost. Had Jewel not acted quickly, he would have bled out. The puncture was sizable."

"Is he in a coma?" I ask.

"Yes," she replies. "The doctors decided, given the amount of nectar they gave him, they can better assess molecular changes while he's in a deep sleep."

"What molecular changes?" Jewel asks, her alarm evident in her raised voice.

Wolf takes his sleeping baby while Charles gently sits her down. A bubble chair rushes to cushion her. I wonder if we'll forget we don't have these at home and sit on the floor a few times before we remember to physically move to the chairs first. A giggle escapes me, and Storm shoots me an odd look. I send him reassurance. Stress does funny things to people.

"Time will tell," Belena says. "We do not know what to expect when a human receives as much nectar as he has. I am sorry."

She grows a shade paler, and I suddenly understand this may affect her connection to Pax. What if the nectar erases the mark in him? Would it make her more vulnerable to Shaula?

"Do we have time?" she asks. "I thought we were on the verge of an earth-shattering event."

"You're right," Coral answers.

She turns to Belena and asks, "How quickly can he be brought out of the coma, and when can he join the others to save our two planets?"

"I will remind the doctors of the urgency," Belena says. "They may be able to monitor him remotely, even if there is no time to run their tests. Are you willing to take the chance he may exhibit changes you aren't prepared to handle?"

"If he's alive and out of danger, he'll work with us," Storm says. "His love for Jewel isn't based on the mark."

I send him love and gratitude, thankful for the reminder. No matter what happens, he will always love Jewel.

WHILE PAX RECOVERS, we return to our quarters with all but Jewel and our parents. I can monitor my brother from anywhere. Meanwhile, I need to keep busy, and I make myself useful in the lab. At least I'm watching everyone else work.

Leonis, Charles, and Baran have their heads close together over the table where they're working on the wristbands. With Shaula out of the picture, there's little chance anyone else will use the bands for mind-control. Still, no one is willing to chance it, and they've found a way to defend against incoming mind-control waves.

With Max, Marla, and Avery now in the loop, along with our Allaran friends, the three scientists are working on a way to include them. Leonis has figured out a way to make the network expandable as needed.

"We will use a mesh like the one forming Terra," he says. Charles appears to know what he's talking about, but our blank looks must have alerted Chara.

She explains, "We have shown you Terra is a tetrasphere, as are all the suns, planets and their moons. Each sphere is formed by a mesh, or web of interconnected tetrahedra, leaving a hollow center. The web expands and contracts with variables in pressure, atmosphere, and climate. It emits sound frequencies which change when things are out of balance. This movement, with the resulting tonal fluctuations, causes electromagnetic energy to flow along the ley lines between the tetrahedra. The energy gives us gravity."

"Is the hollow interior why suns eventually become smaller, and some collapse into black holes?" Storm asks.

"Yes," Chara answers. "It also explains why they maintain their density no matter how small they become. The density of each tetrahedron remains constant. When a sun collapses, it is like one of your balloons losing air, or one of those toy balls that expands to many times its size when stretched out and is easily pushed back into the original small size."

"What role do the artifacts play in all this?" Salali asks.

"They keep the planet in balance. The sound waves they emit equalize the pressure inside the mesh with the atmosphere on the outside. Jewel had it right when she understood you four must tune the planet by first tuning the tetrahedra."

"If the artifacts have been keeping the earth together since it was first created," Tom interjects, "what happened to knock them out of sync?"

Tom and Salali weren't there when Vega explained a lot of this to us. It's all new to them.

Chara's voice takes on a sad tone when she answers. "The great war between the Allarans and Dracans started the decline of the artifacts. We knew then Terra's demise would come about unless Creator intervened. He spoke the solution to our wise ones, who passed it to the humans who believed our watchers were their ancestors. It became what you know as the Cherokee prophecy."

"Why doesn't the prophecy come right out and say we'll save our planet?" I ask. Prophecies have always been vague, but when they concern me, they're especially frustrating.

"Creator has always left the choice to his creation. Complications occur when many choices are made by many beings."

"Why now?" Tom asks.

"The decline of the artifacts escalated with the use of atomic weapons," Chara explains.

The weapons that sterilized the Dracan women also set in motion the ends of Terra and Allara.

"If you don't mind," Charles says, peering through an eyepiece that makes his eye look as big as the moon, "we're in a race against time with these wristbands."

JULIANA and I get ready for bed without talking, each lost in our own thoughts. If the wristbands were ready, we'd share our concerns, but we don't have the energy to speak using our voices.

I lie in bed staring into the dark and pray for my brother and for the world. What if Yellowstone blows before we can do anything? What if those hurricanes and tornado-producing storms kill millions of people in their paths while we're waiting? What if we fail, even after Pax recovers?

60

PAX

Jewel's face swims into view when I open my eyes. Her aquamarine eyes sparkle with tears even as she tries to smile. She's beautiful.

What's wrong? I ask her through our connection. When she doesn't answer, I try to say the words, but my mouth feels like it's been sandblasted.

She holds a spoon of ice chips to my lips, and I suck a few in. The cool liquid relieves the dryness enough for me to croak, "Why are you crying?"

"It's nothing," she says, trying to sound cheerful. "I'm happy you're awake."

I take another spoonful of ice. The soreness eases, and I answer, "Do you normally cry when you're glad I'm awake?"

The sight of her perfect lips curving into a smile does more for me than the ice chips. Energy returns to my arms and hands and I reach for her.

She takes my hand, and her next words bring everything flooding back.

"Do you remember what happened?"

I struggle to sit up, but she easily pushes me back. "Don't get up, Pax. Wait for the doctor to check you out."

"Shaula. Is he dead? How did we get out of there?" The questions flood my brain, clamoring for answers.

"The Dracans and Allarans rescued us together. You'd broken Shaula's leg, which made it impossible for him to escape. Storm shot him but didn't kill him. He was taken into Meissa's custody with a gut shot. He may not survive it, but if he does, he won't survive Meissa."

Why am I here? I try the connection again, and again she doesn't answer.

"Jewel, are you ignoring me?"

Her sudden sobs take me by surprise. She turns away and walks out of the room. Why?

An Allaran in scrubs and with his white hair in a braid down his back comes in and, without a word, holds a humming instrument over me, moving it from my head to my feet.

"It appears you are healed, Paxton," he says, sounding satisfied. "We closed the hole in your artery, and the nectar has finished the healing process. We will release you when your parents come for you."

"Hole in my artery? Please explain what happened to me."

"I am sorry," he says, taking a seat next to the bed. "I thought you knew the details. Your artery was punctured by one of Shaula's claws during your battle. Jewel prevented you from bleeding out until your rescuers arrived. We performed surgery, injected you with healing nectar, and here you are. Now we must monitor you for changes the nectar might cause in your physiology, but we can do it remotely."

Could that be her problem? Is it why she can't hear me through the connection?

"What kinds of changes are you anticipating?" I ask, afraid of the answer.

"We do not know," he says. "You are the first human to receive intravenous nectar. It was needed to save your life. The Dracan biochemical marker also complicates matters, but your Allaran DNA should mitigate some of the possible negative effects."

That explains it. I'm a weird universal hybrid, and I've lost my connection with the love of my life.

She doesn't return, and I don't see her when my parents take me back to our quarters. I hope she's getting some sleep.

I EAT breakfast with my parents in the big dining room. Mom keeps patting my hand and doesn't say anything. Dad asks me repeatedly how I feel, and I keep calling Jewel through our now-defunct connection. I wasn't this low when I was Shaula's prisoner.

Sky sends a blast of joy as she runs into the hall, followed by Storm. She grabs me in a hug and then quickly pushes back with a look of shock on her face.

"I'm sorry, Pax. Did I hurt you?"

I stand up and hug her back. "Not at all," I assure her. "Doc says I'm healed and ready to tackle anything."

"Great," Storm says with a big grin. "We can spar anytime you want. It was obvious you could use some training when you tangled with Shaula."

I throw a punch he easily blocks, and Dad laughs and says, "Enough. You both need training, but you have something important to do first."

That sobers all of us. We have a world to save.

I SPOT Jewel with Salali and Juliana, who's lowering a dome over a fully-grown crystal tree. I wave, but she turns her back on me. What's going on with her?

I stride over to her, but when I slide my arm around her shoulders, she stiffens.

"Are you angry with me?" I whisper in her ear. Whatever this is, it's between us.

"Why are you ignoring me?" she asks.

"I'm not, and I asked you the same question. Remember? Let's go where we can talk."

I take her hand and lead her outside to the gardens. I let my scent guard down and smell the blend of fragrances. When I detect the scent of her fear, I'm both relieved and concerned. The nectar hasn't affected my gift, but it broke our connection.

Her eyes fill with tears. "I'm afraid. We don't hear each other's thoughts anymore. Have we lost the mark?"

She turns to me and wraps her arms around my waist. I hold her and try to reassure her. "It's impossible. You have the biochemical in every cell in your body. I do too. Only death can break it, remember?"

"Then why is our connection broken?" she asks. Good question.

"Maybe it's temporary," I reason. "We don't know how the nectar is affecting me. This could be a side-effect that goes away with time."

"Pax? Jewel?" I welcome Sky's interruption. We can't do anything about our connection now, but we do have a monumental task ahead of us.

"It's time," she says when she finds us. "We're going to test the amplifier, and this time no Dracan will dare interrupt us."

61
SKY

Oh, criminy. I hate the tension between Jewel and my brother right now. It isn't anger, which I could understand and even sympathize with. They're both terrified. I send them calm, but it isn't helping. Our amplifier test should get their minds off their troubles, especially if it works. If it doesn't, we may be back to square one.

"We have found a large deposit of quartz crystals under Devil's Tower in Wyoming," Baran informs us once we've settled into the ship. Vega is carrying the crystals and equipment in his ship, along with Juliana, Murphy, and the Ryders.

"It is also a place of power, where multiple artifacts are located. Queen Jaide has told us many of the artifacts there are critical. They have been emitting cries heard for miles, drawing the attention of surrounding tribes. Some of the local Sioux leaders have led an expedition deep into the mountain, discovering the crystal cave. It is only a matter of time before they encounter the watchers."

"Are we going to run into them?" Wolf asks.

"Perhaps," Baran answers. "The mountain is sacred to them and many other tribes. We believe they will keep our presence secret."

"Not all men in the tribes are honorable," Wolf reminds him.

"Perhaps Creator is opening the door for us to rejoin our human brethren," Baran says with a smile. Wolf is concerned, and I hope there's no one in or near the cave when we arrive.

The area appears deserted when we land outside a cave barely visible inside one of the many grooves running down the mountain. According to legend, seven sisters were chased by a bear, and just when it was about to get them, they prayed and the clearing they were in began to rise. It grew into this mountain, with the bear clawing deep grooves all around it in its effort to get the girls. Instead, they were launched into space and became the seven stars of the Pleiades. I'd read about it when I saw a movie about alien encounters on this mountain.

Storm and Juliana float the equipment along a steep curving tunnel. Baran and his crew lead the way, and Vega's crew takes up the rear. When we enter the crystal cave, I'm astounded at the size of the crystals. Each is at least as large as a girder, and some are as wide as a two-lane bridge. I hope we're alone, but there are plenty of places to hide in here. Storm and his sister set the dome up between two of the smaller structures, and he removes the dome, leaving the crystalline tree in place.

I don't have time to admire it, because just then three watchers appear. I grimace at the buzzing in my head when one of them says, *Come, Star Children. You are needed.*

Storm answers, *we come willingly, but my sister must be allowed to accompany us.*

If not for Juliana discovering her gift in Triton's cave, none of us would be here today. She saved us from burning up on fire-heated sands. We might need her again.

The buzzing resumes. *Agreed.*

"Hold on," Charles says. He approaches his daughter and clamps a wristband on her. "This is one of the two we've completed," he says apologetically. "Yours and mine. Let me know when you've repaired the artifact. If the amplifier works, we'll know it, but if not, we'll need to come up with plan B. Tap it twice. We've done away with Morse Code."

Jewel nods, and we follow the watchers into another tunnel.

⁓

THERE'S no telling how much time has elapsed since we left the crystal cave. We passed several openings where we heard the humming of working artifacts. A few sounded discordant, but the watchers kept us moving.

Finally, they stop, and I understand why when I spot the distressed artifact wobbling in the air, no more than six inches off the ground.

"Hurry," I call out, rushing to get close.

"Wait," Jewel says. "The force-field is still in place. Don't touch it!"

Too late. When I hit the invisible wall, it throws me into Storm, knocking us both to the ground.

Now what?

A different sound fills the cavern.

Go closer, the watcher instructs us.

I hear the excitement in Pax's voice when he says, "Formicians! They've come to help."

Confident they'll sing away the force field like they did in Peru, I follow him to the artifact, ready to touch the face that stops in front of me. Jewel and Storm line up and we form a circle around it.

"I'll catch it when it slows," Juliana says. We're ready.

Like the ones before it, the artifact slows enough for us to make out the symbols carved on each of its triangular faces. When it stops, Juliana raises it higher, giving us access to all four sides, and, like before, it stops with the same face in front of each of us. The side with the four stick figures surrounded by earth, with the sign for love above and below it, stops in front of me. I place my left hand on it and reach to the right to cover Pax's hand with my own. His hand is on the symbol of the moon and serpent, and Jewel's, whose left hand he covers, is on the side with the coyote, star, and butterfly. She reaches down to touch Storm's hand on his symbol of the sun of hope. When his hand covers mine, we focus into the center of the artifact, and the love builds between us. Sensing the right time, I push the love into the artifact and feel its gratitude as it pushes us away.

Jewel says, "It's building the force-field again. I wish you could see the colors."

"Tell your dad it's done," Pax reminds her.

She taps on the wristband, and her expression changes from joy to frustration.

"It didn't work, did it?" I ask. Then I remember the picture Gabri had shown me the first time I suspected she might know the future. The amplifier was in the chamber with the artifact.

"Tell your dad I know what we need to do." I explain what Gabri showed me. "The amplifier will work if we bring it in here."

"He's calling us back," Jewel says. "Baran is on his way to pick up Sequoia and Gabriella, and he's dropping off Max and our parents. Vega will be ready to go when we get back to the entrance."

"What's going on?" Storm asks.

She tells him, "Jaina contacted Vega and told him it's imperative we return to South America. She said something about a key."

62

STORM

When we get to the ship, Vega explains there is no time to test the amplifiers. His world and ours are on the verge of breaking apart.

"Amplifiers are being delivered to the areas you visited and to others you did not get to, each a locus of power where multiple artifacts are clustered," he explains.

"Dr. Julian Emery and his team are in the Indian Ocean, and Doctors Gabriel and Isabella are covering the Pacific Ocean with their new research vessel. We have put them in touch with Sea Dwellers in those oceans. Triton and the Sea Dwellers you have met are dispersing them to points in the Atlantic. We have the Arctic Ocean covered. Ashley and Leonis have grown enough amplifiers to spread evenly around the globe."

"What did Jaina say about a key?" Sky asks.

"She merely said it is important. She also insisted Wolf and Sequoia bring the baby," Vega answers.

I'm glad they're coming along. She grows quiet, and I pull her close. She isn't projecting, which means she knows more than we do. I'm nervous, and I suspect everyone else is, too. Why not Sky?

Jewel plays with her new wristband and throws glances at Pax but doesn't say anything. He's as worried as I am. Murphy has his arm around Juliana, and they're deep in silent conversation. They don't need wristbands to communicate, but Pax and Jewel might.

We land in the empty desert in front of the Stargate. The setting sun casts long shadows from the oddly shaped cliffs making up the City of the Gods surrounding the Puerta de Hayu Marca. Vega is already there, his crew unloading one of the amplifier domes as Wolf supervises. My aunt stands under the hovering disc, staring at the Puerta, which we call the Stargate.

When I approach her, she says, "The boulders along the top are shaped like a woman reclining, gazing at the stars."

I hug her, take my sleeping cousin, and respond, "And the door itself is nothing more than an indentation, small enough to stand in and touch the sides. It doesn't look like much until it's activated. I wonder if the key Jaina referred to is the sun disk which fits in the round hollow in the middle. I believe her friend Jayman has it."

Sequoia doesn't respond, focusing instead on the Stargate. She points to the cliff. "Is the blue light the portal to the giants' dome?"

The last time we were there, the Dracans had taken us in their ships. Since the Allarans can't enter, they had brought us to this door.

The light grows, and Jayman steps out, followed by Gienika and her daughter Autumn. They wave as the blue glow fades away. Apparently, we aren't going in this time.

"Greetings, my friends." Jayman's booming voice echoes among the cliffs.

Vega says something to his crew members, and several of them dash back to the ship and return carrying bubble chairs. I hope they're big enough for the giants.

Gienika is a bit out of breath when Jayman gently helps her to sit on one of the bubbles. It easily forms to fit her body, and she sighs. Autumn sits next to her, and Jayman remains standing behind her.

Sequoia takes Gabri from me and walks over to Gienika, the truth-sayer, handing her the baby. She's like a tiny doll in the giant's arms, but the tenderness in Gienika's eyes leaves no doubt she's perfectly safe. My aunt gratefully sinks into the bubble seat a crew member offers her.

Jayman points to something behind us, and as I turn, the ship above us disappears, leaving the Allarans on the ground with us. Did it leave, or cloak itself?

From the headlights bouncing over the rough terrain, I make out four Hummers heading toward us in the fading sunlight. Jack and his crew must be joining us. I'd assumed they'd returned home after we found Pax and Jewel.

Jaina gets out of the lead vehicle and comes to greet the giants. Al is right behind her. If it were up to him, he'd never leave her side. It's how I feel about Sky, and it's obvious the man is in love with the Mantoid shapeshifter. Jack walks over to stand next to Wolf.

"Before you go to Dr. Austin's compound, there is something you must know," Gienika says, getting our attention.

"Sky Fire Hair, come here." As she steps forward, I grab her hand and go with her. She sends me an annoyed barb, making me smile. She won't be facing anything alone again if I can help it.

"I am happy your Storm has come to his senses," the giant says, nodding at me. "You will need each other."

A trickle of love pushes aside the annoyance. Even without the wristbands, I'm learning to read her.

"Do you remember the prophecy, Sky?" Gienika asks.

"Jaina told me it essentially says a mighty red-haired woman will unite the races during the time our planet is dying. Then she'll save the planet, and everyone will get along. You said I'd be a bridge, and I assumed it meant a bridge between the races."

"It is close, but far from an exact translation," Gienika says with a smile. "Fire Hair will unite the races, but it does not say she will save Terra, nor that the races will get along. It says the planet will be saved and the races will thrive. Do you understand the difference?"

"I do," I interrupt. "It means she won't be alone. She isn't responsible for what happens after the races unite to save the planet."

"That is true," Gienika says. "However, there is more to the prophecy. When Meissa heard ours, she came to me and told me of another given to her about this little one, who will cross the bridge made by another to bring hope to the nations."

The giant touches the top of Gabri's head with her finger, and the baby smiles in her sleep. "This child's hair is also red and will become more like yours as she grows, Sky. We believed you to be the bridge, and then we heard about what she and Sequoia did to free Pax from the Dracans. She has changed everything."

"Are you telling me I'm not the Fire Hair you thought I was?" Sky asks, sounding relieved. "I told you that from the beginning."

Gienika pauses before she answers. "Because of you, the Dracans and Allarans are now working together, as are the earth dwellers, who had long gone their separate ways. But it has not been by your efforts alone. The four of you have done this. If you are not the one our prophecy speaks of, then you have paved the way for the true Fire Hair to emerge."

She begins to rock backward and forward, careful to protect the baby. It takes a few seconds for Jayman to realize she's trying to get out of the bubble chair. When he helps her stand, she pulls herself to her full height, scoops the still sleeping baby into her large hands, and holds her toward the sky.

"Gabriella O'Connell, who has yet to be given her true name, is the Fire Hair of the prophecy, and her mother, Sequoia, is the bridge."

Love mixed with relief pulsates from Sky. Stunned by the announcement, Sequoia's face pales, and I'm glad Wolf has his arm around her. Pax glances down at Jewel with confusion, while she's staring at Gienika, who hands the baby to her mother.

"It became evident to us when we heard how your song carried your child's laughter, forming a weapon against those intending harm to Gabriella's loved ones," Gienika explains.

"Your song is the bridge, Sequoia. Music is the basis for the existence of all things. Your song provided the resonance your daughter needed to rescue her people. Her laughter was the tone that saved them."

Autumn gets up and takes her mother's arm, but Gienika isn't finished.

"Sequoia, you and Gabriella are the key to saving our planet."

As the giants return to the Stargate, where the blue glow has reappeared, everyone talks at once, sharing their shock at what the truthsayer revealed.

"This didn't surprise you, did it, Sky?" I ask as she calmly walks to one of the waiting vehicles.

"I figured it out when Gabri laughed the Dracan ships out of our lagoon," she says in a matter-of-fact tone of voice.

"Why didn't you tell anyone?" Resentment is a far cry from the rage I once had trouble controlling, but I'm hurt she didn't tell me.

"I believed you still had your wall up, and Jewel was grieving over Pax, as I was. I suspected, but I wanted to be sure before I dropped the bombshell."

"Later, when she did it again at the cliff, were you sure then?"

"I didn't think about it then," she answers. "Pax was dying, which drove everything else out of my mind. It wasn't important."

"When Jaina called us here today, you didn't seem concerned. Why not?"

"I had a feeling Gienika would meet us here and share what she did. I already knew I wasn't the person in their prophecy. It was a relief to hear her say it."

Juliana and I transport the amplifier globe to one of the vehicles with a canvas top pulled back, and she rides in the bed with it, holding it on a cushion of air, Murphy sitting across from her. The Allarans gather their bubble seats from the desert and take off silently. I can't see them, but Jewel has told us they stay close no matter where we are. I hope they're ready for anything tomorrow. How will we handle it if we fail this time?

63

JEWEL

Sky, Juliana, and I share the same basement room we had when we were here before. Sky keeps sending me peace, but it doesn't help. I can't stop worrying about my connection to Pax. I wish Dad had finished his wristband at the same time he gave me mine. I guess I should be glad I don't feel Shaula's pull anymore. I wonder if he's dead already. Of course, none of it will matter if we fail tomorrow.

"Move over," Sky says, pushing me to the wall. "You're keeping me awake with all your worrying, so talk."

Juliana crawls under the blanket at the foot of the bed and rests her back against the wall. I sit up between her and Sky, who pulls the blanket across her lap.

"We're going to save the planet tomorrow, so let's talk about afterward," Sky says. Brown streaks smear through her otherwise flaming aura and I know her words are sheer bravado. She's as afraid as I am, and as Juliana is, judging by her aura. I choose to play along.

"After tomorrow, Pax and I are going to figure this out. Dad will finish all the wristbands, and we'll have our telepathy back. Now it's your turn, Juliana."

She's quiet for a moment. Magenta overtakes the brown in her aura. "After tomorrow, I'm going to marry Murphy. He's afraid I'm too young, but our mark is forever, and I'm ready. We'll go back to Atlantis and raise a bunch of kids."

"Why in Atlantis? You have family here," I say.

"Murphy's family is there, and we can travel back and forth like Max and Marla. What about you, Sky?"

Magenta replaces her brown streaks, too. "Since Storm has acknowledged he loves me, we'll figure out what we want to do with the rest of our lives. I'm not Fire Hair anymore. My life will be my own, and I choose to spend it with him."

"It's settled then," I say. "The world is safe, and we have beautiful futures. We should get some sleep."

The girls go back to their beds and Sky turns out the lights. I wish we could be sure of tomorrow's outcome. What if the amplifiers don't work? What if they're not enough?

DESPITE MY OVERACTIVE BRAIN, I must have conked out at some point because Jaina is waking me up.

She holds out a pill and a glass of water and commands me to take it.

"What is it?" I examine the capsule in my hand.

"It will help with altitude sickness," Jaina says, handing one to each of us. "We're going to Machu Picchu."

"How high is it?" Juliana asks.

"The central point of the city is over seven thousand, nine hundred feet above sea level, but we're going into the mountain about a hundred feet higher. The artifact cluster is approximately four hundred feet below that, inside the mountain."

Jaina gestures toward the door. "Vega is picking us up in half an hour. We just have time for breakfast. We should arrive at the cave entrance ten minutes after we leave here, and it will take about an hour to reach the artifacts once we're in the cave."

Ten minutes from Lake Titicaca to Machu Picchu. I'll never get used to the speed of our sentinels, especially since we can't tell they're moving from inside the crafts. We embark in one place, and minutes later we disembark somewhere else in the world. Amazing.

I take the pill, although we probably don't need it after our daily dose of nectar. Jaina doesn't know anything about that.

WHEN THIS IS OVER, Pax and I are coming back here to explore. We catch a glimpse of the magnificent ruins in the viewport, but Vega drops us off at the mouth of a cavern on the opposite side of one of the peaks, hiding the city from view. Storm and Juliana guide the amplifier's dome along as we descend into the mountain.

The wide tunnels, with smooth walls and a curved ceiling, have obviously been engineered. I'm not complaining. I'm glad they found a place with easy access, especially since Sequoia and the baby have come along.

Gabri hums and laughs as her voice echoes back to her. She isn't experiencing any discomfort. I wonder if anyone tried to give her medication, knowing Sequoia would have rejected it outright. Wolf walks behind his family, keeping guard.

We come to a crystal cavern and Sequoia gasps. She didn't get to see the road-sized crystals in Devil's Tower, so we pause a few minutes to let her enjoy the sight. This time, we keep the amplifier with us as we head deeper to the artifacts.

Three Mantoids dressed in armor block the entrance to a chamber holding a distressed artifact. Jaina transforms, and they move aside for us. Juliana and her brother set the dome on a flat rock, stabilize it, and remove the glass covering.

"It's beautiful," Jaina remarks, her voice sounding strange in her Mantoid form. The gleaming crystalline tree reflected in her enormous eyes makes them sparkle. The others gather around it until she disperses them around the walls.

"The force field is weakening," I tell the others. "Juliana, get ready to catch it."

We approach the wobbling tetrahedron, and I watch the colors around it dissolve when the Mantoids begin their humming.

"I have it," Juliana says, and we approach in the same order as before. The pyramid slows and stops, with the same symbols facing us as usual.

Once our hands are linked on its faces, the love builds faster than it has in the past. Pax's hand sends a current of warmth flowing into and through my hand on top of Storm's. Sky sends our love into the center of the pyramid, but this time it pulsates several times before sending gratitude. This time, it sends pure joy to us before it pushes us away.

The room spins with sparkles and what I see when I glance back at the crystal tree nearly knocks me to the floor. The tips of the branches are on fire, popping with colors I know don't exist. They pierce my soul with a yearning so sharp and deep I want to dissolve into light and be one with them. I ache when they begin to fade. And then Sequoia sings.

64
JEWEL

Her song, with words in the Cherokee language, pierces my heart with love and desire I don't understand. I fold over and weep. Pax covers me with his body, wraps his arms around me, and I hear his heartbeat in my mind, keeping time with my own.

Instead of laughter, Gabri sings, too, weaving her baby voice into her mother's song, like golden threads branching out and stretching through the crystal tree and into the quartz pathways. Time ends and time stretches forever until the song ends and forever becomes now again.

No one moves. No one breathes until Gabri laughs, clapping her hands, breaking the spell.

Sequoia is the first to speak. "When will we know if it worked?"

Jaina, back in her human form, coughs a few times before answering, "If the song comes back to us within the hour, we will know it has traveled Terra's circumference. Echoes will then occur every few minutes if it successfully branched to the other amplifiers covering the grid."

"And the artifacts?" Wolf asks.

"Your daughter's song, carried by Sequoia's melody, will have created the resonance resetting the artifacts to their original tone. In turn, they will bring Terra back to her original heartbeat."

"Now what?" Pax asks.

"We wait."

We find a spot out of sight of the others. He leans against the rock wall and pulls me close, cushioning me.

Can you hear me? I ask, hoping our combined heartbeats indicated the connection is working again. He doesn't answer, and my heart grows heavy.

"You didn't hear me, did you?" he asks.

"No more than you heard me just now," I answer. "I thought we had it back. I heard your heartbeat and felt it in my body. Pax, it can't be gone forever." Tears burn, but I hold them back.

"The nectar is changing me, but my love for you is deeper than I dreamed it could be," he assures me. "Let's say it can negate the effects of the mark. How would it affect us? Once Shaula is dead, his mark will be broken forever, and you'll be free to be with me. If my mark is also broken, then what would change? We'll still be together."

I relax, and he kisses my head. His voice soothes me. "The mark isn't meant for a human couple. Besides, once your father finishes the wristbands, we'll be able to communicate mind-to-mind again. We're not losing anything important."

His arms tighten around me, and I feel his love, returning it with everything in me. He's right. We'll never lose this.

Exhaustion overtakes me. I close my eyes, only to open them when a wall of sound suddenly shakes the floor, causing the walls to vibrate. Joy reverberates through the cavern. An anthem of pure love and praise to Creator brings us to our feet, shouting and laughing with indescribable bliss.

The sound fades, leaving our hearts light with the assurance every race on earth who knew the danger our planet was in is rejoicing with us. Especially the Allarans. Their planet is also safe.

65
PAX

W e return to a triumphal celebration in the city of Hyperborea. Crowds of people meet us at the landing dock, throwing flower garlands around our necks and cheering while they open a way for us to walk to our transport. I had no idea there were this many Allarans here. I hold tight to Jewel's hand.

"Many have come through the stable wormholes to thank you," Belena shouts. "You will forever be hailed as heroes."

"I hope not," I shout back. "The heroes are Sequoia and Gabriella. We did the only thing we knew to do."

We reach the transport and slide into the relative quiet. I pull her in next to me, and the bubble chairs rush to accommodate us.

"Exactly," Belena says. "Each played his or her part, but your willingness to take the challenge set everything in motion. Had you four not begun the journey, the ending would have been disastrous for everyone."

It will still be disastrous for Shaula and his gang. I push the thought aside and enjoy the spectacle of the celebrating city as our slow-moving vehicle glides along the inside of the dome. Fireworks explode in the shapes of flowers, in colors we humans haven't invented yet in that medium. I recognize an Aracai in a blaze of green and white.

"You must see so many more colors than I can, Jewel," I say, but when she doesn't answer, I realize she's asleep. I draw her close and lean her head against my shoulder. Our quarters should be quiet enough for us to get a good night's sleep.

SKY RADIATES infectious joy at breakfast, making us giddy with it. Jewel laughs at Storm and me as we joke around. Max and Marla's twins race each other among the tables, and no one stops them. Everyone is euphoric, including our often-serious parents. Even Charles and Leonis stay awhile rather than rushing off to the lab, but eventually, they excuse themselves.

"The wristbands won't build themselves," Charles says, patting me on the back on his way out. Avery rounds up the girls and leads them outside, where a crowd of Allaran children greet them and draw them off to play. The rest of us move outside to sit on the stairs before heading into the laboratory, while Juliana and Murphy wander off into the gardens, holding hands.

Baran marches toward us from the lab building, his face deadly serious.

"Good morning, Star Children," he says, bowing a little from the waist. "I have news."

For some reason, dread turns my insides cold. Maybe it's the look in his eyes. Maybe it's the scent of anger emanating from him.

He doesn't leave us in suspense. "Meissa requests your presence at the trial of Shaula and the traitors."

Storm glances at me and I smell the rage seething just under his surface. I probably smell my own too.

"When?" Jewel asks. She looks sad. I hope she isn't feeling sorry for that monster after what he did to her.

"Today. Chara is notifying your families, but only Tom, Salali, and Juliana may accompany you."

"She won't go without Murphy, Baran," Jewel says. "Meissa should understand."

"Then he must also come. Her presence is required, along with her parents."

It makes sense. Shaula directly impacted each of our lives by his evil acts. The others suffered, too, but we will have to testify.

"Let's get on with it," Sky says, her voice cold with anger. "Where's the trial being held?"

"In Superstition Mountain, where Meissa reigns. Her mate is standing trial as well."

66

PAX

B aran drops us off in the desert near the hidden entrance to Meissa's underground base. Eight Dracan soldiers escort us inside, while Baran and Chara go back to Hyperborea. They aren't permitted inside the base.

We're taken to a room set up like one of our courtrooms, only with three tiers of thrones rising to the right of the judge's bench. Tables and benches, also in tiers, rise on our side of a sunken oval arena, probably fifty feet in length. Steps, placed at the end of four aisles on this side, provide access to the arena floor.

Thuban sits on a throne in the front row, and Meissa sits one row behind and above him. A number of Dracan kings occupy other thrones, but many are left vacant.

Two of Thuban's guards stand in the arena directly in front of him, dressed like Mongol warriors, wearing green crisscrossed sashes across their breastplates with long curved swords in jeweled scabbards at their waists. Meissa's guards, wearing bandoliers across their chests and sporting leather holsters holding laser weapons, flank Thuban's men.

Our escorts lead us to a table next to the arena. As we take our seats, a metal cage, about four feet square and maybe ten feet tall, is wheeled into the arena and parked in front of us.

Shaula, broken, slumps against the bars, a bandage circling his middle, and something resembling a hinged splint along his right leg.

The judge comes in and, like in a human court, everyone stands. She stares at the prisoner for a moment before taking her seat. Like Meissa, she's fierce and may be a full-blooded Dracan.

We sit when she does, and the proceedings begin. She calls on Thuban to testify. Shaula had once been his trusted advisor. The king takes a long time listing his crimes in their language, and I reach for Jewel's hand under the table. I'm surprised she's trembling.

What's wrong? I ask without thinking. She doesn't hear me.

I'm shocked when a rough voice invades my mind. *She is mine. Your hold is broken.*

She stands and moves around the table, stepping down into the arena and circling to the opposite side of the cage. When she turns to face me, her eyes are blank, as if she's in a trance. There is no expression on her face. By now, Thuban has figured out what is happening and freezes in place.

I stand and shout, "Stop!" At the same time, I shout it in my mind. *Stop! Jewel, stop!*

She slowly moves toward the cage, no longer obeying my voice. Our mark is truly broken, but Shaula's isn't.

Storm and I charge to the floor at the same time. I grab her and pull her away from the cage. The judge's shout rings out, and everything stops.

"You must not interfere, human. By our law, if she willingly gives herself to this Dracan, she is his."

"What about his other crimes?" Juliana yells.

"His fate is yet to be determined for whatever crimes he has committed."

Murphy stands and in an unusually loud voice declares, "He marked an unwilling female in an act of rape. Even now, it is obvious she is under compulsion. That alone is a crime punishable by death. Paxton has also marked her with her full consent. She has already chosen her mate."

At this, the kings, other than Meissa and Thuban, roar and pound their fists on the arms of their thrones.

"Silence!" the judge shouts and calls Jewel to the bench, breaking Shaula's hold. She shudders and reaches for my hand, and we face the judge together.

"How can this be? Two humans cannot share the mark. It is physiologically impossible."

"It was done by injecting my blood into Pax after Shaula raped me," Jewel says, her voice growing strong. "I reject Shaula. He compelled me to come to him just now. I am not willing, nor have I ever been willing."

The trial is cut short when the kings shout "Death!" and resume pounding their armrests. When Meissa gets to her feet, the others grow quiet. She is the only queen among them, and they deeply respect her.

"Most honorable judge," she addresses the court. "My mate Algol is one who stands accused with this traitor for crimes against the Dracan people. He and all those who plotted with Shaula to overthrow the will of the people and harm those who were willing to risk their lives to save Terra for all of us, must die."

"Continue, Queen Meissa," the judge says.

I put my arms around Jewel, who's still trembling.

"Despite everything the traitors did, they failed to stop these humans. These four, with help from Sequoia and her baby, found a way to save our world, and all of us. We owe them everything."

She turns to address us directly. "When you restored balance to Terra, our monitors showed the artifacts dispelled every trace of radiation left by the atomic bombs. There is hope again for Dracan purebred females. We may one day be able to bear our own young."

"Is that possible?" the judge asks, turning to us. "And these Dracan males, led by the accused, tried to stop you?"

Without waiting for an answer, she slams her fist on the bench and declares, "Death to the traitors."

She is still mine, Shaula snarls, invading my brain again.

I turn to Thuban who, noticing my face and fisted hands, nods to one of his guards. The Dracan marches over and hands me his sword.

The sword belonging to the second guard flies out of its scabbard into Storm's hand.

The kings stand, and the room goes silent.

"Release him," I say.

"Would you grant him an honorable death?" Meissa asks.

"No, Queen Meissa," I answer. "But we will not allow him to rob us of the honor of killing him ourselves."

Shaula roars, "There is no honor in killing one who is unarmed while you wield swords."

Storm growls and shouts back, "Your talons are your weapons. You have used them often enough against Pax. Use them now, Monster."

As wounded as he is, Shaula charges out of the open cage like the raging beast he is. His claws flash, just missing my face and I bring the sword down across his hand. It glances off his scales, and he charges again, swiping at Storm.

Juliana shouts a warning and tosses Shaula toward the ceiling. Storm positions his sword so when she drops him, the sword will pierce his heart. The Dracan twists at the last moment, landing on top of Storm while the sword only grazes his side.

I seize my chance. With the monster on the ground, I lift my sword over my head and bring it down on his neck, rage fueling my strength. The hated head rolls away, and Storm lifts the body off himself and dumps it in the cage. The head rises in the air, and I see satisfaction written on Juliana's face as she concentrates on throwing it on top of the body.

Once again, the kings roar, but now they're slapping Thuban on the back and shouting with approval.

Jewel runs to me and throws her arms around me, kissing me, ignoring the spatters of blood all over me.

"He's gone, Pax!" she shouts. "We're free!"

Meissa catches my eye and points to an open door behind the now empty judge's bench. I call to Storm and Murphy, and they make their way to the door, bringing Tom, Salali, and the girls. Meissa and the judge meet us in her well-appointed chamber.

The judge wastes no time. "If what Meissa said is true, that when you saved Terra, the nuclear radiation disappeared, and I have no reason to doubt her word, then you will be known as heroes. If, in fact, we can once again bear children, your names will never be forgotten. If ever you need anything, you must call on us."

"I will be the first to congratulate you," Jewel responds. "And we are truly happy for your people. Right now, we need showers and food."

"Meissa will attend to your comfort. Thuban was right in choosing you to be our first Ambassador to humans, Jewel. I hope you will consider it."

She smiles, and we follow Meissa to her chambers, where we find hot showers, fresh clothing, and a banquet fit for heroes.

6 7
JEWEL

I love the smell of autumn in North Carolina. The annual color show comes later than in New England, and people migrating south for the winter pass through, extending their pleasure at the reds, oranges, and yellows of the dying leaves.

Two months have passed since Shaula's death. All the traitors have been executed, and balance is being restored to our planet.

Scientists are still trying to understand why the pressure under Yellowstone suddenly decreased. According to national news, they believed the reports of a coming catastrophe were greatly exaggerated publicity stunts by Hollywood and survivalist groups. I imagine they're wondering how their own instruments could have been so wrong.

Cleanup is still underway after earthquakes and storms took a steep toll around the world, but everything has settled now. Newly active volcanoes are no longer erupting, and there have been no new earthquakes since the day the entire population of Earth heard the world hum. No one is talking about it anymore.

Where are you? Pax's voice in my head makes my heart sing.

In the meadow, I answer. *Thuban should appear any minute. Are the others ready?*

Marla replies, *We're on our way. The girls don't want to leave, and Max is play wrestling with them. He has one under each arm.*

I can hear the laughter in her thoughts. Dad and Leonis had expanded the network of people using wristbands. Max, Marla, Avery, Ashley, and Leonis each have one now. Avery has the one prepared for Thuban. Opening links is a bit more complicated but doable.

We're ready, Juliana says, and my heart drops. She and Murphy have decided to move to Atlantis. We're going to miss them.

We make quite a crowd in the meadow, but no one wants to miss saying farewell to our friends and family.

Gabri runs toward us, Sequoia right behind her, watching her every move. No four-and-a-half-month-old baby should be running, but Gabri's development has been remarkable, even from the time before her birth. Her squeals of delight when she spots her cousin cause him to turn and scoop her up.

"My 'Towam,'" she says, patting his face.

"My 'Ty?'" she twists around and holds her arms out when she spots Sky, her next favorite person in the world. I admit to a twinge of jealousy now and then, but Gabri loves us all. In fact, the only creature she did not love was Shaula, and only because he hurt her "Pak" and threatened me, her "Dewy."

The Dracan ship drops down to hover near the line of trees where the forest starts. Thuban descends, and Avery runs to him. I'm surprised to see Meissa float down the portal beam behind him, followed by a large Dracan male I don't recognize.

She comes to me and envelops me in a surprisingly gentle hug. She greets the others the same way, picking up the baby and bowing to Sequoia. Gabri pats her reptilian face, oblivious to how different from us she appears. Only then does she introduce us to the Dracan male.

"This is Eltanin, my mate."

He graciously bows his head to each of us, and we return the bow.

Meissa's voice softens. "As my marked mate, Eltanin has taken leadership of the North American continent."

"Congratulations," Storm says, holding out his hand to shake Eltanin's. His aura has changed to bright red shot with blue. Blobs of magenta float around him like a lava lamp. Gone are the black streaks and angry reds.

"It is my honor to meet you," Eltanin says, his gruff Dracan voice sounding smoother than most. "Meissa has told me of your exploits. You have brought honor to your people, yet Meissa informs me they are unaware of what you have accomplished."

"We like it that way," Sky says.

Sequoia explains, "Until humanity is fully aware of your presence here, and of the Allarans and earth dwellers, they will never know how close we all came to extinction."

"We don't want accolades," Pax says. "We simply want to live the rest of our lives in peace."

"We have a surprise for you," Meissa says, and Eltanin drapes his arm over her shoulders. "Our surprise is the result of a gift you gave us, one we will never be able to repay. Thanks to all of you, Eltanin and I are expecting a baby, the first full-blooded Dracan since the atomic war."

Sky and I squeal and run to hug her. The commotion draws everyone close, and the clearing is soon filled with shouts and laughter as we congratulate the pair. Human auras are bursting with color, and Dracan scales shine brightly with joy.

Then it's time, and Storm helps Juliana and the Dracans load up luggage. When they're ready to leave, we exchange hugs with Ashley and Leonis, Murphy and Juliana, Meissa and Eltanin, Max, Marla, and their twins, and Avery and Thuban. After last-minute words and thanks, they're gone. We're left with the assurance we'll soon meet up with them again.

Storm heads back to the cabin with Wolf, Tom, and Salali, to help gather their things and close the house for the winter. Coral and Dylan go home to make sure they have everything. Mom and Dad finish packing their lab equipment for our extended stay in Andros, and Pax's suitcase and backpack are ready and waiting in our hallway, next to mine and Sky's.

The three of us sit on the porch swing, waiting for the Allarans to show up.

"This is where it all started," I say, remembering the first time Sky came to visit, frightening me with her flaming aura as she bicycled through the woods.

"I'll never forget hearing Terra's call for help when the artifact sounded its cry," Pax says, pulling me close. "I think I have a permanent ringing in my ears from that noise."

"If we knew then what we know now, would we have chosen to meet the challenge of the prophecy?" Sky asks.

"Of course," I answer, "At least now we know it worked."

TONY AND MEG MICHAELS meet us at the beach when Vega and Baran drop us off. They've become accustomed to alien ships coming and going.

"Here are the deeds to the houses," Tony says, handing them to Wolf and shaking his hand. "They now belong to the Cherokee nation, lock, stock, and barrel."

"What will you do now?" Sequoia asks.

"Our home by the docks will be here when we get back," Meg replies. "For now, we plan to take our boat to Costa Rica, and from there–who knows?"

Meg takes Gabri from her mother and engages in a sweet conversation with her, while Tony takes the four of us aside.

"I don't care to hear about the details, but I know you did something to stop those hurricanes. Dozens of them were flying off the coast of Africa, growing into superstorms and headed our way. We were goners. Then this sound happened. Indescribable. Like music deep in our bones. Never heard anything like it. Then the storms dissipated all at the same time. Something tells me you were at the center of it."

Storm throws an arm across his back and says, "Keep believing that, Tony, but if you tell anyone…well, you know."

Tony's eyes grow wide, and his tanned face pales. "Seriously?"

"He's messing with you," Pax says, and we all laugh. Tony's laughter sounds a bit forced until Storm reassures him.

"You and Meg are great friends. When you get back, we have some diving to do."

We head to our homes to unpack and get some rest. We have a ceremony to attend tonight, under the full moon.

NO ONE SPEAKS as we make our way to the fire the boys built on the beach. Salali and Sequoia wear soft doeskin dresses, their shining black hair in braids woven with flowers. Bells on the hems jingle as they walk. Gabriella wears bells, too, on the toes of her tiny fringed moccasins. Her dress matches her mother's, but without the bells on the hem.

Pax, Storm, Wolf, and Tom are magnificent, bare-chested in the moonlight, wearing strings of beads around their necks. Pax's hair isn't long enough to wear in a braid, but the Cherokee men do, leather straps woven in their hair.

The rest of us, in summer dresses or batik shirts and jeans, are privileged to witness Gabri's naming.

After Salali and Sequoia sing a song in the Cherokee language with a haunting melody, followed by a song of praise and thanksgiving in English, Sequoia hands Gabri to her sister, saying, "Our mother would be proud you stand in for her. The name you give our child will belong to her, and our family gathered here, never to be spoken to any but the most trusted brothers and sisters. You have sought Creator for her name. What name has he revealed to you?"

Wolf stands beside Sequoia as Salali lifts Gabri up to the heavens four times, once in each direction. The baby is awake, but makes no sound, as if she knows the solemn importance of this moment.

Then Salali turns to Wolf and her sister and, with the tears on her cheeks reflecting the flames, says something in the Cherokee language. Both parents bow their heads while Salali turns to us and translates. "Creator has given this child the name meaning She Sings Laughter. Her song and laughter have brought healing to our planet, drawing light from the Great Spirit. So shall it be throughout her life."

When Gabri laughs, we all join her, happy with the name that fits her so well.

Storm and Pax begin to douse the flames when Sequoia stops them.

"Before we return to our house to celebrate with the feast we've prepared together, I wish to fulfill a promise I made to Sky, who will someday become Tom and Salali's daughter. Wolf and I have come to love and trust each of you. You know our daughter's name, and now you shall know mine.

She says her name in her language and then repeats it in English.

"I am Beloved Mother."

As she speaks it, my body tingles with power. Apparently, Triton, who must have been watching through Sky's eyes, feels it, too. His bugling call fills the air with the sound of joy.

∽

"Sing to God a brand-new song. He's made a world of wonders!"
Psalm 98:1 (The Message)

∽

Thank you, dear Reader, for traveling this journey with Jewel, Pax, Sky and Storm and their friends and family. I sincerely hope their story moved you as it did me while I wrote it. If it did, please be so kind as to leave a review where you purchased the book (books if you've read the series). Every review sends good vibes into our planet, making you one whose resonance keeps everything in balance. Thank you.

Whatever happened to the baby, Gabriella O'Connell? How would you like a peek into the future? Almost sixteen years in the future, Gabri is about to embark on a thrilling adventure. This is how it all begins, in chapter one of **SANCTUM: Dragon Guild Book 1.**

SANCTUM

DRAGON GUILD BOOK 1

The Vision

"Gabri!" Donny's voice echoed through the forest, disturbing Gabriella O'Connell's peace in her favorite hiding place. She didn't respond.

On the bank of a stream swollen with snow runoff, her bolder hid her in a smooth hollow on the river side, away from the trail in the woods. Clusters of trees on the slopes across the water puffed out vapor, painting the land foggy blue. They resembled a gathering of long-haired tribal elders smoking pipes. Her people, the Cherokee, named these highlands the place of blue smoke for good reason. On many mornings, Gabri woke up to fog shrouding her home in Blue Mountain valley, a Cherokee reservation in the Great Smoky Mountains.

Sun sparked off fast-flowing water, tumbling over rocks as it carried tree debris dropped during a recent storm, while fragile fleeting rainbows formed in the mist. An aggressive wave splashed over the bank, soaking her bare feet.

Gabri had shared the location of her secret place with only three other people: her parents, Wolf and Sequoia O'Connell, and her friend,

Donny. Right then, she wished she hadn't told anyone. Donny didn't call out again, but he'd show up at any moment.

She rested her chin on her fists, elbows propped on her knees, resenting the intrusion while she waited. After the nightmares she'd been having, she needed some alone time.

"There you are, little wolf." Donny climbed up and settled next to her, taking deep breaths of the warming air.

Gabri glanced sideways at him, noting his frown and admiring his unconscious grace. Donny's frown melted into a heart-stopping grin when he looked at her. It wouldn't win him any points, though. Not now.

Gabri had known Donny since before she was born. Nine years older, his perfect smile contrasted beautifully with his smooth, dark skin, the color of milk chocolate. Thick, wavy hair framed warm, brown eyes and a straight nose. He wore it neatly trimmed. After Donny had completed his post-graduate engineering degree at M.I.T., he'd settled nearby. He fancied himself her personal bodyguard. She didn't need one.

Born with a unique ability, Gabri had been manipulating frequencies since before she could talk. As a baby, she'd protected her family and saved the world with her gift. Since then, she'd learned she could make sound do anything she dreamed up, including create invisible objects.

Gabri reached for the subtle tones of water bubbling over a rock and leaves swishing in the breeze and wove them into a net. She added the bite of nettles disturbed by a nibbling creature and tossed it over Donny's arms, all without moving a muscle.

Donny squirmed and jumped to his feet. "Stop, Gabri. That stings."

"Sorry." She smirked and lowered her forehead to her crossed arms, not at all sorry. Maybe a little. It wasn't his fault he had to come find her. She'd left the cabin without telling her mother.

"Come on." He gave her shoulder a gentle shove. "Your mom's getting lunch ready."

Her stomach growled. Sighing, for show more than from annoyance, she got up and dusted off her shorts. Do almost-sixteen-year-old girls have growth spurts? She was always hungry.

They followed a deer trail toward the cabin Gabri's dad had built when he was Donny's age. Their alien friends had insisted on enhancing it with advanced technology after her cousins, with Gabri's help, had kept the world from imploding. Dad had agreed, so long as they didn't change its rustic appearance. Weathered logs and a wrap-around covered porch looked authentic, but it was far from a simple log cabin.

Gabri quickened her steps at the familiar thwack of an axe chopping wood. She and Donny soon reached their clearing where her dad, bare chested and glistening, raised his axe for another hit. Sequoia watched from the porch swing, gently patting her belly swollen with Gabri's brother, due in six weeks. The baby sent out contented waves when he wasn't sleeping. Empathic ability ran in the family. Gabri hoped he'd be this happy once he was born.

Warmth filled Gabri's heart. She took a step toward her mom when everything changed.

~

Join Gabri on her thrilling journey through the **Dragon Guild** series, as she bonds with her dragon, Makani, and her Aracai, Ting. Discover the power of friendship, courage, and love when she joins Elio and the Guild to fight against the destruction of everyone she loves — all without the powers she once had.

Order your copy of **SANCTUM: Dragon Guild Book 1** today!

Visit my website www.ptlperrin.org for this and other books by P.T.L. Perrin.

I love hearing from you! Please connect with me!
  Amazon: www.amazon.com/author/ptlperrin
  Facebook author page: www.facebook.com/PTLPerrin
  Facebook page: www.facebook.com/AuthorPattyPerrin
  Facebook Group: Patty's Book Pals
  Email: ptlperrin8@gmail.com

~

ABOUT THE AUTHOR

Patty Perrin, (P.T.L. Perrin), grew up in Europe as a military brat, with no television and a huge imagination. Books were her entertainment and augmented her education in German, Italian and American schools overseas. She speaks several languages and enjoys the diversity of people and cultures.

She wrote the Teen/YA Scifi *TETRASPHERE* series as pure entertainment and to answer some of the unanswerable questions about our amazing universe. Why would the Creator of this vast universe limit intelligent life to one tiny speck of a planet? What if other inhabited planets are interacting with Earth?

Terra's Call, the first book of the tetralogy, was a finalist in the Royal Palm Literary Awards. *Triton's Call*, the second book, won third place.

Patty's *Literary Titan Award*-winning *DRAGON GUILD* series combines a few characters from *TETRASPHERE* with new characters and magnificent dragons in an epic quest to save two worlds.

Patty and her tennis-pro husband Bill are parents and grandparents of a fluid, constantly growing family. Happily married, they live in south Florida where they exercise bragging rights in the winter, and enjoy the long summers, and where Patty is writing books she would have enjoyed reading back when she didn't have television.

ALSO BY P.T.L. PERRIN

∽

TETRASPHERE Series

Terra's Call - Book 1

Triton's Call - Book 2

Voice of Viracocha - Book 3

∽

DRAGON GUILD Series

Sanctum - Book 1

Aerie - Book 2

Dominion - Book 3

∽

Reflections of a Misfit

∽

www.ingramcontent.com/pod-product-compliance
Lightning Source LLC
Chambersburg PA
CBHW060621260626
47161CB00008B/2766